DEA   ∪

EVE BONHAM has an MA in English from Trinity College Dublin and worked as an English teacher in Asia. She has been a fine art auctioneer, a journalist, a retailer, a lecturer, and has worked as campaign organiser for a charity and in the property business. She has sailed across the oceans, competing in yacht races across the Atlantic and Round the World, and has travelled far and wide overland.

For fourteen years she lived with her family in a Breton village in France. Eve now lives in Dorset with her husband, writes most days, works for the family business and is involved in community projects. She also paints watercolours, collects art and plants trees. Eve is a Christian.

She has been writing fiction for over fifteen years and is the author of three books: a collection of short stories, *Madness Lies and Other Stories* (2008) and two novels, *To the End of the Day* (2011) and *The Lost Journey Homeward* (2015). She gives talks with readings at literary events and festivals, libraries, book clubs and other societies. She writes a blog and has a website: www.evebonham.co.uk

ALSO BY EVE BONHAM

Madness Lies and Other Stories
To the End of the Day
The Lost Journey Homeward

Best wishes,

Eve Bonham

x

Dear Magpies

Eve Bonham

SilverWood

Published in 2019 by SilverWood Books

SilverWood Books Ltd
14 Small Street, Bristol, BS1 1DE, United Kingdom
www.silverwoodbooks.co.uk

ISBN 978-1-78132-932-0 (paperback)
ISBN 978-1-78132-933-7 (ebook)

British Library Cataloguing in Publication Data
A CIP catalogue record for this book is
available from the British Library

Page design and typesetting by SilverWood Books
Printed on responsibly sourced paper

For my granddaughter Mary and my grandsons Michael and Alistair – and for any future grandchildren

ACKNOWLEDGEMENTS

For their help, advice and encouragement I am very grateful to:
Carlos Altuzarra, Helen Baggott, Madeleine Caro, Matthew Caro,
Sarah Caro, Alan Chun, Mary Falk, Sue Joiner, Ed Handyside,
Christopher Little, Hazel Perkes and, as always, to my daughter
Julie, my son Jack and his wife Claire, and my patient husband,
Michael.

PART I

IN THE MIND

5th April 2012

Dear Magpies,

I still love you so much that I ache for you.

But I haven't seen you for years and I've no idea where you are.

After searching for ten years, I've failed to find you – my only grandchildren. I'm numb with despair. You are living out there somewhere, probably in ignorance of my existence.

The chances are that you'll never read this.

Tom, you will now be fifteen and Lottie, you must be twelve. The last time I saw you both was when you were four and one. I hope you don't mind if I address you as 'Magpies'. You will now be too old for such nicknames, but it's what I called you when you were little.

Why? You both adored water – just like your daddy and your Colombian grandpapa – and you splashed around like ducklings in a pond. One day, when I was staying with you, your father brought you both some big black and white fluffy towels for bath-time. When I wrapped you in these towels, I said you looked like magpies – and your father agreed and took to calling you his 'Magpies'. Soon I adopted this endearing term for you, though I don't think your mother ever used it – she didn't like nicknames. Parents and grandparents often use loving but ridiculous endearments for little ones. These can be a bit embarrassing later on, so let me assure you that no one will read this, so no awkwardness will result.

How did this sad situation happen?

The last time we met was in 2000. The millennium should have been a milestone in my life but it turned out to be a millstone – because that was the year when Julian died. He was my son and your father. This sudden tragedy devastated the family and it was also the year when I last saw you, though I was unaware of this at the time. You were living in Australia, where no doubt you still live with your mother, Melissa. She was as heartbroken as I was, but for some strange reason, that I have never been able to understand, she decided to move away and not keep in touch. I lost not only my son but my grandchildren too. Over the intervening years I've tried to trace you and get back in touch. I've done everything I can and if my last effort brings no results – and I should hear about this soon – I shall have to accept the barren prospect that I may never track you down.

So, I'm writing this letter to you, though unable to send it, to give me the illusion that I am in touch with my beloved Magpies – my 'long lost' grandchildren. This might help me to reconnect with you in my head since I can't do it physically.

I'm gutted that there's so much I don't know about you and what kind of life you lead. I don't even know what you look like any more. I have a few photographs but these date from when you were tiny. You were both dark-haired, like your father, although your mother has fair hair. I seem to recall that your eyes were blue like Melissa's and not brown like Julian's. I expect you are quite tall, Tom. At fifteen you are only a few years away from being a full-grown man. And Lottie, I'm sure you are very pretty and growing up fast. I wonder what your favourite colours are and what you like doing and whether you laugh a lot, as I do – to keep despair at bay. In the absence of any news, I have convinced myself that you are both alive and healthy.

It is just possible that you are aware you have a grandmother who lives on the other side of the world. No doubt you still see your Australian grandparents – your mother's mum and dad – though I've lost touch with them too. It might be more accurate to say that they moved and chose not to keep in touch with me. This puzzles me because I remember them as a friendly couple who were courteous and kind. I would like to give your mother the benefit of the doubt and assume that she tried to keep in contact but was unable to find me. I've been worried that you might mistakenly believe that I don't want to see you. Nothing could be further from the truth! I have missed you, Tom and Lottie, so much and I still do.

Enough of these dispiriting thoughts! Let me tell you a little bit about myself and where I am. My father, Miles Hansford, your great-grandfather, was born in Dorset where his family had lived for hundreds of years. I am half-French because my mother, who was called Marguerite, was French. We never lived in France and, although I spent some of my childhood in London and Dorset, my father's job meant that we lived overseas much of the time. I've lived in Colombia and briefly in the USA but now, after many years and two marriages, I have come back to live in a Dorset village, a place I imagined would be peaceful and without problems, though now I'm not so sure. I seem to have lost most of my family along the way, but life is not always an easy journey.

I decided to make my home in this green and graceful county in the south-west of England, where I spent some magical childhood holidays. I am, after all, half-English. You both have a more unusual divided nationality, being half Australian and half a mixture of Colombian, English and French.

I live in a rural village and rent a little cottage with a front door in a pastel green colour, though the paint is peeling. I have some unusual neighbours. On one side, in an identical cottage in rather better repair than mine, live William and Louise Stickley. We are friends and I call them Bill and Lou. He is a professional gardener and has huge hands and a gravelly cough. He smokes a pipe. If you met him you might think him a bit dour because he doesn't say much and, when he does, he speaks very slowly. But he's the 'salt of the earth', always helpful and reliable. Lou is diminutive

17

and neat in appearance – someone who talks a lot but rarely listens. She is active in the village, the church and the community, darting about like a bird looking for twigs to make a nest. When she tries to boss her husband, he just pretends he hasn't heard and silently continues what he is doing. They have two children who are adult and live elsewhere. Bill works for the man who owns both our cottages, James Trevett, who lives in a large house with quite a bit of land around it at the top of the village. He is a younger man, unmarried, unfortunate in appearance and awkward in manner. But he was lucky enough to inherit the property from his uncle, an accountant who died without children, some years back. Bill and Lou's house comes with their job and is known as a tied house, because their occupancy is tied to his job. My cottage used to be a tied cottage but now the owner rents it out and I am his tenant.

On the other side is a rather dilapidated cottage, owned by a man called Matthew Tapper. Matt lost his lovely wife, Ann, a couple of years ago. She died of cancer and his life has gone to pieces since this tragic event. He doesn't bother much about his appearance and, when I'm downwind of him, I realise he doesn't wash much either. I always try to be friendly and neighbourly, though I do respect people's privacy. We all feel sorry for him but he repels all sympathy. He goes out to work but doesn't want to talk much to anyone, and so we don't really know what he does.

My cottage is called 'The Haven', which is very appropriate because I think of this home as a port of refuge from hostile seas. I'm told that it was built as a farmworker's dwelling about a hundred years ago. It's not large but it suits me well. It has a sitting room at the front with two windows: one looking out over the street and the other at the side with a view of Matt's cottage. At the rear there is the kitchen where I usually eat. I have a large old wooden table and occasionally I give it a good scrub and invite someone in for a meal. There is a back door leading out into a long thin garden, where I have two rickety garden chairs. I love sitting out there in the summer sun, pretending to relax. Relaxing is something that often eludes me. I don't seem to have the knack! But I sleep alright – most of the time. My bedroom is upstairs overlooking the street and at the rear there is a small bathroom which has pipes that make a funny thudding noise when I turn the tap on. Next to it is another small room with a bed, which I can use for guests, although I rarely have any. Most of the people I know these days live in the village. My friendships have diminished along with my horizons.

I am not alone, however, since I share my home with a feline friend called Folly. I did consider calling her Alli – short for 'alliteration' (if you don't know what this means – look it up in your dictionary). She was a stray cat and, because I have been stranded without a home at times in my life, I feel we have something in common. In truth, it was Folly who adopted me. I woke up one morning and found her asleep at the bottom of my bed. I must have left a window open downstairs and she crept in to explore my cottage. Having padded her way upstairs, she decided that my bed was the most comfortable place to sleep. You can imagine how surprised I was when I woke up with a purring weight on my feet. She has tortoiseshell colouring with elegant markings and I have the impression that she sees herself as an aristocrat who has come down in the world. She's certainly slumming it, living with me! That's why I couldn't call her Alli, as her spelling isn't too good and she might think I took her for an alley cat, which would offend her. I feed her well and chat to her, and in return she has condescended to make her home here. It suits us both.

Whilst writing this, I had the illusion that you were going to read it – and then reality clouted me over the head. I have no idea where to send it! But I shall create a folder in my documents called 'Dear Magpies', in which my letters to you will go, pending sending. Perhaps one day…

It is now getting late and Folly is nuzzling my ankles telling me that I've forgotten to feed her. I have also forgotten to feed myself so I shall put down some cat food for her and make myself an omelette. There may be a few mushrooms to put in it.

That's all for now. I'm blowing imaginary kisses to you. Goodnight, my beloved Magpies, and sleep well wherever you are and whatever roof you have over your heads. My roof is made of thatch – though it's a bit dilapidated and lets in the odd drip. Each spring amazing birds called house martins fly back from Africa and build their conical mud nests under the eaves below the thatch. There are many other birds in my garden, including your namesake, a magpie or two that visit me during the summer. I wish you were here instead of them!

How should I sign off? I was born with the name Josephine, which as it happens is the same in English and French. My first husband used to call me Josette but my second husband (I'll tell you about them another time) always called me Josie, and that is what I now call myself: Josie Cuff. I don't feel that old – I'm nearly sixty – although that might seem ancient to you. I've decided that I'll end by showing how proud I am of my status as a grandparent, even though I'm far away. And even though you don't know me.

With masses of love from your,
Grandmama

The woman looks up from where she has been writing at a table in the window. This is where Josie sits when reading, writing or using her laptop. She stares out at the village street, first looking up the slight incline towards the church and then turning her head to look down the street, towards the pub and the duck pond. Doris Bugler is walking along the road and Josie gives her a little wave, but there is no response. Doris, who would never be caught peering in at anyone's window, stares straight ahead as she passes. She never intrudes on people's privacy and deplores gossip. Josie drops her hand, which has been frozen in the gesture of a wave, and looks down at what she has written. Her lips move as she reads silently, even though she is alone in the house. After a few minutes, she gets up, stretches her arms to ease her shoulders and goes through to the kitchen at the back of the cottage, moving out of the view of the person outside who is discreetly watching her.

8th May 2012

Dear Magpies,

A month has skittered by since my first letter to you. I can't really call it an email, because it hasn't been sent. But I thought I would write to you again because it's my birthday today.

May 8th is a special date for another reason and I hope you know why. In history lessons you should have learned that this was the day in 1945 that the Second World War ended in Europe, though it took a bit longer to finish in Asia. I was born six years exactly after this momentous day. By a strange coincidence my mother died many years later on 8th May. So today I celebrate my own birthday and remember my mother.

(You are also in my mind. But I've no context for you. No connection with you. Yet.)

My mother was brought up in the Normandy region of France. Though she claimed to have done little at school, she had a talent for learning languages, spoke Spanish well and had some English, although she never lost her alluring French accent. In her mid-twenties she lived for two years in Madrid, where she worked in the French Embassy. My father, Miles Hansford, worked for the Foreign Office, and was often posted overseas. In his mid-thirties he was working at the British Embassy in Madrid.

My father once told me the romantic story of how they fell in love and you might like to hear it. He met my mother at a grand embassy dinner party. My mother, who was often absent-minded at home, became animated at parties. She had the reputation for being a bit flighty or perhaps 'flirty' might be more accurate, though Daddy never accused her of this. My father was a serious man, reliable and self-assured; he had a straight back, blue eyes and was British to the core. When he met Marguerite, he lost his sangfroid and his heart. She was a tall, elegant Frenchwoman with aristocratic high cheekbones and arched eyebrows. Her daunting manner was softened by a cascade of dark hair and luminous brown eyes. When I was in my teens and blighted with spots, I remember being so envious of her creamy unblemished skin.

Miles proposed to Marguerite within three months of meeting her. They got married in France in a town called Coutances, from where her family came, and afterwards they lived in whichever country his career took him. My father adored his pretty wife, whose Gallic charm at social events made her popular with his friends and colleagues. At home, however, she was disorganised and disinclined to deal with domestic matters and staff, so the running of our various overseas residences was left to my father. He had little time to spare because of his responsible position in the embassy, so home life was often chaotic. I'm a bit untidy too and reluctant to waste good reading time cleaning the house, so I may have inherited my shambolic approach to housekeeping from my parents.

My mother enjoyed the graceful social life which her husband's job entailed. Soon they were posted to Peru in South America. Whilst living in the capital, Lima, she discovered she was pregnant. The city was hot, the surrounding country parched and the dust bothered her, so she insisted on returning to France for the birth of their son, my older brother. She named him Henri and, after a few months' recuperation in her beloved France, she travelled back with her baby son to my father, who had already returned to the embassy in Peru. Henri was a small, sturdy child with dark hair, big round eyes and a serious expression. As a young child, he said little and was much admired. People often complimented 'Maman' on her fine- looking well-behaved son, but it was his silence that pleased them.

(Now, six decades later, his 'silence' means I've no idea whether he's alive or not! He disappeared years ago and no one knows the end of his story. Yet.)

My story started two years later. Expecting their second child, my parents were back in Europe and I was born in Paris on 8th May 1952, which makes me sixty years old today. I was pale, thin baby with frizzy blonde hair but my father was delighted that I looked English and always loved me unreservedly. I cried a lot and woke often, so I gave my poor parents disturbed nights. Maman, who needed her beauty sleep to enable her to dazzle her admirers the next day, became bothered by my erratic sleeping habits, though Daddy was more patient. I was a noisy naughty child, always running around and knocking things over. My father

23

was very tolerant of his clumsy daughter and I loved him so much when he put aside more pressing matters to play games with me. My boisterous behaviour irritated my mother who sighed and said that my peacock shrieks gave her headaches. When I tried to hug Maman, her body become stiff and unresponsive, and I felt awkward and rejected.

I have just had a cup of tea and, whilst drinking it, I decided to check my email inbox.

I am stunned with disappointment! I have just opened an email from a contact in Australia, whom I employed to try and trace you through any means possible including social media. About a month ago, he said he had found a trail that led him to believe that you had all moved from the west coast of Australia to Sydney in the east. After so many setbacks, I was excited because it seemed that he was making real progress with his investigations. But he now tells me that his search has come to a dead end and he cannot locate where you are. He has concluded that you must have changed all your names or left the country. He can do nothing more.

I cannot believe that the little flame of hope I was nursing along has now been extinguished.

I have just spent an hour in the garden trying to come to terms with the bleak fact that I have no family left in my life. Wherever you are, Tom and Lottie, I hope that you have each other. Sibling ties are strong. I had a brother once but I lost him too.

Writing has always calmed me, so I'll turn back to the time in my past when I did have a family and tell tales of my childhood.

My mother adored Henri. And I think she loved me too. But less. Why was that? Probably because he was docile and she could control what he did. My brother was much more obedient than me and kept himself tidy. The other boys I knew were always grubby and dishevelled – like me. The girls looked neat and clean and demurely pretty. But I was different – you might say I was a bit of a tomboy. Henri liked music and reading whilst I much preferred racing around the garden and playing games. At school I often got into trouble – I was always late for lessons or found I'd forgotten the right books or the correct shoes. Henri liked learning and was able to concentrate on his schoolwork, whereas I was always staring out of the window where everything seemed more fun and exciting under the open sky than in the stuffy classroom. During the break between lessons I would dash around playing with my friends whilst my brother stood leaning against the wall watching all of us, as if we were crazy and he was the wise one. Actually, he was quite clever – his favourite subject at school was history. Mine was English and about the only time I was ever quiet was when I had my head in a book. We both spoke French because our parents had brought us up to be bilingual.

I wonder what school subjects you both like and whether you are boisterous or calm, studious or sporty or both! And will I ever find out?

As children of a diplomat my brother and I became used to moving with our parents and attending international schools in various capital cities. After a couple of years back in London at the Foreign Office, during which my mother often visited relatives in France, my father was again posted to South America, this time as first secretary to the British Embassy in Colombia. I had spent two years in an English day school, where I became besotted with Romantic poetry and managed to pass a couple of A levels. Maman suggested that her daughter should spend some time in Paris to try and absorb some style and French chic, but I preferred to be with my parents and so I returned with them to live in Bogota.

Colombia, as you will know from geography at school, is a country at the north-western tip of South America just below the Panama Canal, with coasts on the Caribbean Sea and the Pacific

Ocean. It is a country of glorious rainforests, towering mountains and coffee plantations. The high-altitude capital Bogota is the country's largest city and although there are many wealthy inhabitants and an old cobblestoned centre with beautiful period buildings, there are also huge poverty-stricken suburbs and slums.

This was where in 1971, as an impressionable nineteen-year-old, I met the magnetic Raul Moreno. I think I'd better leave that story for another letter, because I've just remembered that I've arranged to have coffee with Flora Elford, who lives and works in the local pub, 'The Anchor', which is at the far end of Long Lane, opposite the village pond. Her husband, George Elford, is the pub landlord and, though he is a competent cook and produces pub meals, we all know he's a secret cider drinker. He's a bit antisocial and likes to stay in his kitchen most of the time, whilst Flora, who never drinks alcohol, runs the bar efficiently and is friendly with customers. But she's worried about George, who has another bad habit – which is his addiction to buying junk in local auctions. He started doing this a few years back to acquire odds and ends for the bar. Pubs in England are often decorated with curios, pictures and quirky objects to give the place atmosphere. However, George has cluttered the Anchor with so much stuff that it's like walking into an antique shop. His backyard is full of rusting farmyard tools and his shed is crammed with clobber but still he goes on buying.

The bar opens in an hour and Flora is expecting me. Bye for now, unreachable ones!

With loving thoughts from your,
Grandmama

It is May and the hawthorn is spilling white froth along the hedgerows, but the wind is cool, blowing Josie's tangled halo of hair around her head, as she strides down the street. She has forgotten her coat again and wraps her arms around her chest to keep warm. A few minutes later, she is sitting in the kitchen of the pub. George has let her in, called his wife, and has gone down to the cellar to "sort things out". Flora hurries in from the bar where she has been wiping down the surfaces and putting glasses on shelves. She makes coffee and wishes her friend a happy birthday. They are meeting to discuss a small birthday celebration which is to be held that evening at the Anchor, when some of Josie's friends in the village are invited for a simple meal.

"I don't think there are going to be more than ten of us and we'll be quite happy eating in the main bar with the other customers," says Josie.

"As it's a Tuesday, there probably won't be many coming in. More's the pity."

Flora looks worried and Josie asks her gently, "Are you alright? You seem a bit down."

Flora sighs. "We don't have enough customers. This village is a backwater not on the way to anywhere, so passing trade is non-existent. Even though we do good food, it's hard to make enough to pay the rent to the brewers who own the pub. Money is tight." She glances anxiously at the cellar door, which is ajar, but George does not reappear for a minute. When he emerges, he is accompanied by a sweet smell - and both Josie and Flora know he has been at the draught cider again.

There is an awkward silence and then Josie says brightly, "Flora tells me you are cooking for my guests this evening. Just to let you know that I'll settle the food bill, but we'll each pay for our own drinks." They know that money is tight for her too. George nods and goes out into the yard. The two women drink their coffee and Flora shows Josie the cake she has made for her.

Josie leans forward. "Why don't you consider doing proper lunches in addition to bar snacks during the middle of the day? Retired people often eat at lunchtime and you might attract business people. There's money to be made from Sunday roast lunches too."

Flora sighs, saying, "We could do that, but it would mean taking on someone else to do the waitressing. It'd be too much for me to serve at the tables and run the bar. George would spend more time cooking and we certainly can't afford any more bar staff. Not to mention the costs of all the junk that George keeps buying, which we don't need and can't afford. I try to keep an eye on his activities, but I can't watch him all the time."

As she walks home, Josie instinctively looks over her shoulder from an intuition that someone is watching her. She exhales slowly to rid herself of the uneasiness this causes her and thinks about what Flora has told her. Her friend should try to keep her husband occupied in the pub kitchen on Thursday mornings, which is when the auctioneers in the local town hold their sales. Josie feels sorry for George, a compulsive bidder with an addiction to cider-drinking, because not all the villagers are tolerant of eccentrics. She wonders if others think her strange with her unruly hair and dreadfully untidy house.

She rarely glances in a mirror - the time when certain people thought her beautiful has passed. These days she prefers to be useful and to help friends in need.

24th June 2012

Dear Magpies,

Midsummer's Day has come and gone, and I feel the urge to write to you, my dearest grandchildren, wherever you are. I'm longing to tell you about an extraordinary thing that happened yesterday when the village held its annual celebration around the duck pond.

The pond is near the pub, and it has grass and reeds at one end. Some years the algae grows so thickly that the pond looks like pea soup. Most summers the water level drops drastically, but the ducks, who fly in and out, don't seem to mind. The mallard drakes look decorative as they swim with their dowdy brown wives, and though children are asked not to feed them, they cannot resist, and ducks love to be given food. Some people say we should clip their wings so they cannot fly away but we don't do this, because we don't want too many of them waddling around our paths and messing up village gardens. Anyway, they stay for the food.

The name of our village is Winterborne Slepe. You may think this rather an odd name, but there are other villages in the county whose names are prefixed with Winterborne. So, what does it mean? A 'bourne' is an old English word for a stream, and a 'winter bourne' flows only in winter and often dries out in summer. This is what happens with our stream – but not every year. It rather depends on how much rain we've had. Today there is only a trickle and it might dry up in August, but it always surprises me how much water hurtles down our little stream in the winter. The duck pond has some shade from overhanging trees and rarely dries out. Just as well as it would annoy the ducks! They don't have an easy time of it, because there are foxes which roam outside the village and often devour the ducklings. But most of the ducks and drakes seem to survive this heartbreak and they return every year to try again.

I wonder if you have any pets, or whether you live in the country or the town. Perhaps you keep chickens or live on a farm with pigs or sheep and a few rats in the barn. A mile down the road here, there's a farmer who has lots of sheep but doesn't have enough grazing himself, so he rents fields from people who do. The land behind my cottage is steep and wooded, but on the other side of the road, it slopes down into a small valley, through which the winter 'bourne' flows. It's good pasture for animals, though not much good for agriculture. From my front window I have a view of the sheep as they munch the grass, unaware of the impending departure of the lambs to the market and the abattoirs. As you live in Australia, I expect you eat a lot of lamb. I don't eat as much meat as I used to – it's rather expensive. I try to grow a few vegetables in my back garden, although many of them get gobbled up by slugs or rabbits or caterpillars. Pigeons are a bit of a menace too, but I suppose the birds, insects and animals have needs and I feel morally obliged to share my produce with them. My cat, on the other hand, far prefers a tasty mouse or, if she hasn't got one, some tinned cat food. Last week I discovered some mouse droppings in one of my cupboards and noticed tiny claws and sharp teeth had nibbled their way into a bag of my favourite muesli, so I told Folly that if she didn't spruce up, she'd be off the payroll!

I've become diverted and must go back to what happened yesterday which caused an uproar during our village fete. Lots of people were milling round the pond, with families eating picnics, men drinking beer at the bar tent, women chatting and buying from stalls, and children running about. A local folk band was playing music and people were sitting on hay bales listening. Everyone – villagers and those from nearby hamlets – seemed to be enjoying themselves. Except for one person.

I don't know his name, but I was told afterwards that he lives in the area and works for a farmer. I think he's a 'cow man' – which means he gets up very early and does the milking. He was with his girlfriend who might soon be his fiancée. I was told this by Alice Diffey, who lives in the village and always knows who anybody is and what everybody does. She has an irresistible urge to pass on titbits of gossip to others, even if they don't want to hear it. Anyhow, she noticed this fellow drinking heavily with some mates at the bar. His girlfriend, wearing a short skirt and a pink blouse, had been playing skittles with two teenagers and was then chatting with a man called John Damon.

This gentleman happens to live opposite me in a trim little house and I was surprised to see him at the fete, as he keeps quite a low profile in the village. He and his wife, Maggie, moved to the village about a year before I did. Last year she moved out and he's now living on his own. He leaves for work each morning, smartly dressed. I don't know where he works, though I expect Alice does! She couldn't resist informing me that John and Maggie are getting divorced because she left him for another man. People think him good looking, but I don't find him attractive. He's too reticent, though he tries to be polite and friendly when we meet in the street.

Anyhow he was standing beside the pond, talking with this pretty young woman who was laughing and flirting with him. Suddenly there was a roar. Everyone turned to watch as her red-faced boyfriend, beery and belligerent, strode down to seize her arm and pull her away. She gave a feminine shriek of protest, whereupon John remonstrated with him. This was unwise, because the stocky lad swung round, lunged at the middle-aged man and pushed him backwards into the pond. Then, having repossessed his girl, he grabbed her hand and swaggered back to the bar. She was upset and so were the ducks who had skittered off to the end of the pond in a flurry of wings and indignation. The pond is shallow and ducks don't care where they do their business, so it is slippery with duck poo and mud. The victim took a while to pick himself up out of the weedy water and wade to the edge, swearing under his breath, soaked to the skin, his face dark with mud and fury. Half of those watching were horrified and the rest, including me, found it marvellously entertaining.

John didn't deserve such humiliation. But he is aloof, suave and lacks a sense of humour, so it was fun to see him lose his dignity. He must have seen me giggling because, when I offered to get him a towel, he shook his head savagely and stalked back to his house, leaving a trail of muddy footprints and ignoring all bystanders. He wasn't hurt at all and if he had grinned and made a joke of it, we would all have thought him a good fellow to laugh it off. I should have been more sympathetic, but it isn't every day that one sees a neighbour get a ducking.

This incident yesterday reminds me of the embarrassing time many years ago on the day Raul Moreno drove me down to the coast in Colombia to show me his boat. So how did I meet this wonderful man – my destiny? I had been in the country a few months, living with my parents. My father went to work every day at the embassy and, to keep myself occupied, I gave English lessons to children. Maman did not work and flitted in and out of our home as her full social life demanded. My father knew a lawyer called Juan Carlos Moreno, whose wife, Paola, was a politician. I met their son, Raul, purely by chance at a party in the French Embassy. He had gone along to accompany his mother because his father was unable to attend. I was there in the wake of my mother, but she had sailed off to the more important end of the elegant drawing room, and I was tossed to the side by her bow-wave. Adrift, I was left pretending to be enthralled by the paintings on the walls. It was not the first time I'd been abandoned. If Daddy had been there, he would have rescued me and introduced me to yet another grey-haired diplomat, who would have been utterly courteous, attempted a stilted conversation with an ingénue schoolgirl, and soon found an excuse to slip away. My French and my Spanish were quite good, but the English are rarely credited with any language skills and local people often made no effort to understand me.

A few minutes later, I had moved on to examine the porcelain ornaments, and as I stared hard at an ornate floral bowl, I was offered a glass of wine. Initially I thought the extended hand belonged to a waiter but looking up I realised someone had taken pity on my solitariness. To my amazement, a beautiful young man was smiling at me. We began to talk in French and he explained that he was escorting his mother, who clearly didn't need him and preferred the company of a group of politicians. I told him I was English and that my mother was at the far end of the room, armed with a glass of champagne and witty chatter. We commiserated with each other. It was refreshing to find out that his French was as flawed as mine, but he soon discovered that I spoke Spanish and so we reverted to his own language.

A week later, he asked me out to dinner. I accepted, without mentioning it to my mother until I had to tell her that I would not be eating at home that evening. She had raised her eyebrows and asked what I might be doing. I told her that Mr Raul Moreno would be calling for me in half an hour and that I would try not to be back too late. She blinked but said nothing.

It was a magical evening. But not at all romantic! His car was battered, his suit crumpled. The restaurant was unimpressive and the meal unexceptional. But Raul was so funny, so attentive, and so very different from anyone I had ever met before. He pulled silly faces to make me laugh and he charmed the waiters too. Afterwards we went for a walk, during which he chatted to strangers, bestowing a radiant smile on them and pretending to be tipsy, though I knew he had drunk little. He drove me home and kissed my hand. Dazzled, I drifted upstairs to my bedroom and fell asleep thinking of him.

On our third date he turned up at our residence, standing on the front steps almost hidden behind a gigantic bouquet of exotic crimson heliconia, also known as 'red fire birds'. In the midst of the flowers he had concealed some paper butterflies on springs, which he released as he gave them to me. I was delighted with the flowers and Raul laughed at the startled expression on my face when the butterflies shot up and bounced around. He had brought his camera and took a photograph of me with the flowers and the mad butterflies. Waving cheerfully at my mother, who was watching from the window, he swept me off and we drove to the Embalse del Neusa, which is a lake with a dam. This was a popular place just over an hour away and Raul explained to me that it was possible to hire dinghies and go sailing. The wind was blustery and I was wearing a new dress, which was white, frothy and unsuitable for sailing, so we decided not to go out on the water. We wandered around the small marina, looking at boats, and then walked along a jetty to look at the view across the lake. He asked me to stop and pose for a photograph, which I did, and he then held up his hand encouraging me to step back so he could get a better shot. This I did and with a small cry I disappeared over the edge into the water. Dropping his camera onto the dock, Raul promptly jumped in to rescue me. This was unnecessary as I am a competent swimmer, but I let him help me to the ladder and we climbed out of the water. I was trembling with embarrassment and shock but he was shaking with laughter. As we stood dripping on the dock, he enfolded me in his arms and told me that he had fallen in love with me as I hit the water. I never did discover if he had set me up. But I didn't care. I was in love too.

I soon got used to Raul's love of jokes and his *joie de vivre*. (If you don't know what this means, look it up in your French dictionary – or perhaps you don't learn French at school?) He told me that I made him laugh. I told him he made me feel beautiful and he said that I was. Three months later he asked me to marry him.

Our parents were apprehensive and asked us to wait for a year before marrying. My parents wanted a delay because I was much younger than him (Raul was twenty-seven, some eight years older than me) and we needed time to be sure. Maman called me 'impressionable'. His parents wanted time to persuade him to reconsider his wish to marry a foreigner who was not a Catholic. As we waited our love grew stronger. Eventually, when I had convinced her that I would not change my mind, Maman pointed out to Raul's family that she was Catholic and therefore, her daughter was also. Raul and I were married in 1973.

I think the story of our marriage should wait for another time, as I need to go out and get some fresh air, and perhaps knock on John's door opposite and apologise for my lapse in good manners yesterday. I hope he'll be in a better mood. He's a bit unpredictable: some days he's charming but sometimes he's rather sour and secretive. And sometimes he's almost creepy.

With lakes of love,

Grandmama

Josie Cuff has returned home in a taxi. She has been away for two weeks visiting Scotland, though she did not take her car, which is small, old and not reliable enough for such a long journey. She went by train. Before her departure in mid-July, she made the mistake of answering Alice Diffey's enquiries about her mode of travel and her destination, and soon everyone in the village knew she was in Dundee, even though her car was parked outside the cottage. Her neighbours, the Stickleys, have fed her cat and kept an eye on her home, but it is common knowledge that Josie owns nothing much and whatever she has is shared with anyone who has less. There are some who think her open-handedness irresponsible.

One of the villagers, who covertly observes her movements, knows that Josie gives time to others and has seen her walking round to visit residents or inviting friends into her home for a coffee. She is careless and rarely locks her kitchen door, often leaving it wide open on summer days. She is not remotely embarrassed by the fact that her home is not just untidy but in a state of permanent disorder. Nor does it worry her that anybody who calls by or looks in through her window can see this. Her laptop sits on her sitting room table amidst a tottering pile of papers or books; her mugs and plates are stacked randomly on an old pine dresser in the kitchen, alongside buttons, paper clips, coins, cards and envelopes. Josie does not seem to value privacy and her possessions are of little worth. And yet she has a secret.

3rd September 2012

Dear Magpies,

I hope, if you were to read this, you might wonder why I haven't written for a while. This would encourage me to feel that you liked my letters, though you might not admit this. Teenagers can be short on enthusiasm when communicating with adults, whilst unreserved about their emotions when interacting with their peer group. Your father was a bit like this – strong and silent, but your mother used to be very open about her feelings. I wonder what character traits you have inherited from them.

Anyhow, I have been away. This doesn't happen very often as most of my friends in England live in Dorset or in my village. However, I do have a stepdaughter who lives in Scotland. Her name is Emily Robertson and she is married. She is the only child of my second husband, Oliver Cuff. It gets a bit complicated here. I was married twice and now I'm on my own. I have more to tell you about my first husband, Raul, and what happened to him – but first a word about Oliver. I was his second wife. He had been married before and his first wife was Scottish. After about fifteen years, when their daughter, Emily, was about thirteen, this marriage ended because Oliver's wife ran off with an oil-rig man from Aberdeen, who had been a 'sweetheart' of hers at school. After divorcing Oliver, she married him and Emily went to live with them until she too grew up and moved to Dundee for her work, where she met and married a placid man called Angus Robertson.

Emily and I have not always seen eye to eye, because, for some reason, she resented her father remarrying, even though this happened some years after she and her mother left him and moved to Scotland. She kept in touch with him during the years when Oliver lived alone, before he and I got together. She used to come south to stay with her father, but these visits were rare as they lived far away and train fares were expensive. After I married her father, she and I were friendly enough with each other at first, but later our relationship deteriorated. Nevertheless, during the years I have been on my own, I have kept in touch with Emily by sending a card or letter when the mood takes me. Last year she reciprocated by sending me a Christmas card. I imagine she feels a bit guilty about what happened five years ago (I might tell you about this unpleasantness another time), and this may have prompted her to invite me to come and stay with her and Angus in Dundee. I decided to forget about our past disagreements and accepted.

I stayed with her for a week in July and then spent a few days in Edinburgh, the glorious capital city of Scotland, before taking the train back south. I have to say that I far prefer Dorset to Dundee, mainly because it's a lot warmer. If you look at a map of the United Kingdom, you'll see Dundee on the eastern side of Scotland, in the central lowlands. It lies on the north bank of the Firth of Tay which opens out into the North Sea. A 'firth' is a narrow inlet from the sea, often the estuary of a river; and in Norway, they call it a 'fjord'. Emily's husband told me that an ancestor of his, Captain Thomas Robertson, on a Dundee whaling expedition in the 1890s discovered a firth whilst in Antarctica, and named it the 'Firth of Tay', after the one in Scotland.

The weather during my visit was dire, with much rain and a chill wind. Do people in Australia talk as much about the weather as we do here in the UK? This is a rhetorical question which requires no answer, but then I expect no answer to any of my questions addressed to you.

Back to my stay in Dundee, before I start feeling mournful.

There is a huge bridge across the firth and I was reminded by Angus that on 28th December 1879, the first Tay rail bridge collapsed into the wild seas during a violent storm, killing everybody aboard a train that was travelling across it at the time. The Tay Bridge Disaster was the subject of a poem by William McGonagall, and strangely enough this work, in spite of its sombre subject, is renowned for being one of the worst (and inadvertently one of the funniest) poems in the English language. If you wanted to read it – a good yarn told in rhyming doggerel – you will be able to find it on the internet. If you don't know what 'doggerel' means, look that up too.

I spent a blustery day tramping round a sturdy fifteenth-century fortress called Broughty Castle, where I had to shelter from the driving wind in a doorway. I took a walk around the city centre and visited St Paul's – a fine cathedral with a soaring spire. I imagine this is how the word 'inspiring' arose. I was surprised to see that there was a tall house built right alongside the tower and I felt a bit sorry for the people living in it when the bells toll out on a Sunday morning. The people living near the church in our village bellyache, though the sound of bells doesn't upset me at all. I have often thought I'd like to try being a bell-ringer, but it's one of those things that I never get round to – like learning the ukulele, joining a choir, or going on expeditions to remote places to find rare wild flowers. That's the problem with being disorganised!

Another thing I discovered about Dundee is that in 2014 the city was recognised by the United Nations as the UK's first UNESCO City of Design. The inhabitants have contributed much in fields as diverse as medical research, comics and video games. Not that I know anything about any of these – though I expect you might play various video games. And it seems that it's not just children who like them – I have a neighbour who is addicted to them. What a solitary form of entertainment!

I'm all for communicating with others and having shared experiences – so much more worthwhile! I wonder what you both do for fun, when you are not having bracing walks, refusing wholesome food at mealtimes, or yawning over lessons at school. I should love to know something about your life. I assume your mother is still keen on fitness and health foods. Are you?

It's so frustrating that I know nothing about you! You were born to blush unseen – by me. Though God knows I've tried to find you.

To cheer myself up and to banish my wistful mood, I shall revert to a time when my world view was unclouded, when I was Josette Moreno living in Colombia. The twenty years of my marriage to Raul Moreno were a rollercoaster ride. For six months after our wedding, we rented a small flat in the capital, Bogota, but we soon moved to Barranquilla, a busy seaport on the Caribbean coast. This was where Raul had been at university and it was a lively city where he felt unfettered and carefree. Although his father had wanted him to train as a lawyer, he had studied business management and had been working in Bogota for a large firm involved in shipping and exports. With his usual charm, he had managed to wangle a transfer to their office in

Barranquilla. I didn't mind where I lived, so long as I was with my husband.

Raul was passionate about the sea and boats and had learned how to navigate. His favourite weekend activity was sailing and diving. Our weekends were spent aboard his small sailing boat, dancing over the waves, wet with spray as we tacked back and forth across the bay. Sometimes we anchored the boat in a small cove and leapt over the side into the crystal-clear water. I liked snorkelling on the surface, but Paul preferred to go deeper with an oxygen tank on his back to get a closer view of the tropical fish, corals and sea fans.

Do you live near the sea? Have you ever snorkelled? Perhaps you now live in Queensland and have been to the Great Barrier Reef. Or you might live inland. Who knows? I don't!

Back to my life in South America. My Spanish was fluent and, though I had no college qualifications, I thought I'd easily find work. In fact, it proved quite hard to get a job doing something other than waitressing work or looking after people's children, neither of which Raul thought suitable for his wife, especially now that she was pregnant. I had not been bothering with contraception, as we both wanted children sometime, but I was surprised at how quickly it happened. How easy it is to make a child! Morning sickness discouraged me from seeking work and, when I started to get larger, I gave up bothering. Without a job I found that I met few people and, with Raul at work during the day, I was lonely. Raul discouraged too many visits to the capital where my parents were still living, and although I had never been that close to my mother, I found I really wanted her company. We took to chatting on the telephone when Maman was at home and not prancing around on the social treadmill.

But weekends were fun. This was when we met up with

Raul's university friends or work colleagues, many of whom were still unmarried. I was barred from sailing, as it exacerbated my tendency to be sick, and though I was often treated as a fragile foreign wife, his friends were courteous to me and I was captivated by their enthusiasm for life. Sometimes Raul decided to speak to me in French in front of his friends – as if this were a special love language – and he told everyone how much he adored his 'Josette'. His vivacious personality and sunny sense of humour meant he was well-liked and, like many Latin men, saw nothing wrong with casually flirting with beautiful women with whom we came into contact at various dinners and parties. As I began to swell and grow bigger, these slender damsels flitted in and out of our house when we were entertaining, showing exaggerated concern for my welfare ('Was I tired?' 'Would I like to lie down and rest?' 'Alcohol no good for baby – have orange juice.') whilst they batted their eyelids at my handsome husband. I was not unduly bothered as I felt secure in Raul's love, and though he was a risk taker, I knew he was faithful. I trusted him.

Over the years I have learnt that there are some inherently untrustworthy people. I look at some of the inhabitants in my Dorset village and see that unfaithfulness can really damage people's lives. Take my neighbour, John, whom you met in my last letter, rather wetter and worse-tempered than usual. One of my friends in the village, an older woman called Doris Bugler, told me recently that I shouldn't pay too much attention to all the gossip that Alice Diffey drips into our ears about the faithless Maggie. Doris, a single woman who is retired but used to work as a nurse, guards her tongue and keeps her opinions to herself. Though she seems brusque when you first meet her, underneath that iron grey hair and upright posture is a caring woman with a kind heart. We all knew the Damons' marriage had been rocky for a few years, but

Doris hinted that John was not blameless. The break-up of their marriage was acrimonious, and we have not seen Maggie since she left. Which is a shame because I rather liked her. She and I used to go for walks together with their black Labrador, Bailey. He was one of those trusting but brainless dogs who bounce around with bright eyes and lolling tongue, exhausting themselves by dashing everywhere and sniffing at everything. Maggie was much the same and she loved to chatter in between darting here and there, looking at insects and wild flowers. Such a different character from her husband, John, with his good looks, black scowls and serious conversation. And his roving eyes.

I've just remembered that I must dash off to a meeting of the PCC – the parochial church council. I'm late already and have to get a move on. I cannot imagine why I have let myself become embroiled in matters such as dogs fouling the churchyard and whether we need to ask old Joe to stop bell-ringing now he is tone deaf.

More about my life and the arrival of your father, Julian Carlos Moreno, in my next letter. Perhaps by telling you about my past – even though you can't hear – I might be able to make some sense of it! I'm still trying to fathom out why we are estranged and if I did something to alienate your mother.

With claims of love,

Grandmama

The weeds are stubborn. Even with a small fork in her hand, Josie finds it hard to clear her overgrown herbaceous border. She has been attacking bindweed and buttercups for a couple of hours. In October the late afternoon light is beginning to wane and she decides to call it a day. As she straightens up, rubbing her back, she hears a voice.

"It be right difficult to get the fellas out – you should pull en out when they're little." Her neighbour, Bill Stickley, is leaning on the garden fence which separates his garden from hers. The rickety structure seems to wilt beneath the weight of his huge elbows.

"I'm not a very efficient gardener," says Josie, wiping her hand across her forehead, leaving a muddy smear which Bill doesn't notice. He spends his days working in James Trevett's garden and estate, so mud means nothing to him. "I'm trying to clear this bed so I can put in some spring bulbs. The weeds seem to have taken over and I'm launching an offensive. It's the brambles I don't like – they're fiendishly difficult to pull out."

"I can come over at the weekend and dig en out if you want. That be the only way to be rid of en. And I got some daff bulbs left over I can let you 'ave." Bill lights a cigarette and the smoke wafts across to Josie and reminds her of Oliver. She doesn't smoke herself but does not condemn it in others. Bill's wife, Louise, is less tolerant, and Josie sees her come out of the kitchen rear door in a lilac-coloured housecoat and hurry down the garden path towards them.

"Evenin', Josie," she chirrups. "Nice to see you out in your garden – it's a bit of a jungle, if you don't mind my sayin' so. And you've got dirt on your face." She turns to her husband. "Bill, you gave me your word that you wouldn't smoke no more, and here I am catchin' you at it in the garden. It'll wreck your lungs. It's a smelly

44

disgustin' habit and cigarettes cost more than we can afford." She looks across at her neighbour. "I don't know what I'm goin' to do wi' him, Josie. I spent all afternoon cleanin' the house and washin' the floor, and when he gets back from work, what does he do? He walks all over my clean floor wi' muddy boots. Now I find him down here in the garden, when he promised me he were goin' to mend that leak in the pipe under the sink." She turns back to her man, hands on hips. "And when are you goin' to replace the bulb in the 'anging light in our bedroom, tell me that?"

Bill does not reply but turns his shaggy head and gazes down the garden. His wife's words spray around him like water from a sprinkler. They bounce off his gigantic chest as he exhales and blows smoke up into the air. His powerful lungs don't seem at all damaged.

"I'm goin' to look out some bulbs," Bill says tossing the cigarette butt to the ground, and crushing it with his huge boot, before slowly ambling off to the shed at the end of the garden, leaving Josie and Lou unsure as to whether he is going to get some spring bulbs for his neighbour or find an electric bulb for his wife.

Lou lets out a dramatic sigh. "There's always so much to do and he gives me so little 'elp. Tryin' to have a conversation with Bill is like talkin' to a brick wall."

"He's done a hard day's work and I'm sure that over the weekend he'll get all the little jobs done inside and out. He may be a man of few words but Bill's reliable," Josie says, thinking that Lou has plenty enough words for the two of them. "Must go inside - it's getting chilly."

"The nights are drawin' in and they say it'll rain

tomorrow," Lou continues. "I hope the bonfire which the kids are building for Guy Fawkes Night won't get soaked. You 'eard the news about Matt? I was amazed – though not much in this village surprises me."

"Yes, Alice dropped in earlier and insisted on giving me all the gory details." Josie turns, determined not to put up with any more poisonous gossip this afternoon. She walks to her back door. "Bye, Lou. I need to wash this earth off my hands."

"And off your face." Lou throws this parting remark over her shoulder as she trots back up to her house. The door bangs behind her and Josie lingers on her threshold. Soon she can smell smoke wafting up from the shadows of Bill's shed. A pigeon coos as the dusk drifts over the still garden. Folly emerges from under a bush and like a grey shadow slinks into the house before Josie closes the door.

31st October 2012

Dear Magpies,

In my last letter, I said I'd tell you about the birth of your father, Julian, and although you never received my email for the very good reason that I have no address for you and was unable to send it, I will keep my promise. Don't bother to respond.

In 1974 Raul and I were living in Barranquilla and I was pregnant. The city had a good hospital but my parents-in-law, who lived in Bogota, were keen that I should return to stay with them for the birth of their first grandchild which they wished to arrange at an expensive private hospital. I would have none of it as I wanted Raul to be with me and the thought of him being many hours away was unacceptable. At first, he sided with his parents in the matter but soon he realised I was adamant and so we arranged to have the baby in a private local clinic. My parents-in-law kindly offered to pay for this. My mother, who was in Bogota with my father, did not suggest that she come down for the birth and I was relieved. To have her fluttering around whilst I was in labour would have been a nightmare.

As it happened, Julian's arrival was dramatic, taking place during a tropical storm. Raul nearly missed the birth, but he made it just in time and was ecstatic to have a son. Soon afterwards he was on the telephone, telling our parents about the arrival of their first grandchild.

Within a couple of days, both sets of parents descended on our small home in Barranquilla. I was exhausted from the ordeal and from lack of sleep, but blissfully happy. Even my mother could do no wrong. Raul's mother was pleased but not keen on having anything to do with small babies, nappies or feeding. Soon we sent them all back to Bogota and settled down to being parents. For the first month or two I felt cocooned in the warm afterglow of giving birth and having a tiny son. Raul was hugely proud and spent much time celebrating with friends and then rushing back home to ensure that his family was safe. Julian, a strong baby with dark eyes and a fuzz of black hair, took up all my time and deprived me of sleep. I loved him so much. I look back on it now and remember the start of motherhood as a golden time of glorious exhaustion.

That's enough sentimental memories for this letter. Perhaps what I'm writing is a diary to remind myself of the euphoric happiness I once experienced. Back then in Barranquilla, the world was like a box of delights – toys – sweets – jewels – spread open in front of me and I could choose any to enjoy. Blessings overflowed. Now, bereft of family and with few resources to live on, my choice is more limited. But I do have some good friends in the village – Flora, Bill, Doris – and I can retain my optimism and persuade myself that contentment is a steadier substitute for elation and prosperity. And there is still a slither of hope that one day I might see you both again. That would be joyful.

So, what's happening in my village? There was a baby born here last week to a couple who live in a small house beyond the pub. A couple of hours ago Alice knocked on my door to sell me some raffle tickets, and she told me that the couple were keen on natural childbirth and had a baby girl at home with a midwife delivering it. She told me that they were going to call their daughter Isla, adding that the mother was only twenty-one and the father had recently lost his job. I didn't need to know, I murmured. She didn't hear and scurried off, saying she still had half the village to call on with her raffle tickets. And her gratuitous gossip.

It's Halloween tonight. I expect you know that Halloween stands for 'All Hallows evening', and it comes the day before All Saints' Day which falls on 1st November. During the month of October in England many shops sell masks and trinkets associated with witches, ghosts and ghouls. The event has become another excuse to market all this trash and I don't approve of it any more than I do the commercialisation of Christmas. I'm not averse to children having fun and love to see children enjoying themselves, but sometimes the reason for the celebration is lost amid all the razzamatazz.

During a period when I was a child and we were living in England, I was told about Halloween at school, and decided to dress up as a ghost and haunt my brother during the night. I borrowed a white sheet from the laundry cupboard and spent a bit of my pocket money on a ghost mask. After he was asleep, I sidled into his room and stood over his bed. As I moaned and flapped my arms, my brother woke with a start and shrieked. Behind the mask I smirked – delighted I had terrified him. My mother dashed in, calmed down Henri and was furious with me. I thought it was a great joke and told all my friends at school, which only reinforced his reputation as a bit of a wimp.

Do you celebrate Halloween in Australia? In the springtime it cannot be as atmospheric as a chilly autumn day with dead leaves blowing around and the mist rising up off the stream. I try to ignore Halloween and prefer having fun on Guy Fawkes Day which is a few days later on 5th November, and commemorates a foiled plot to blow up the Houses of Parliament with gunpowder. In Dorset, a village nearby has a huge bonfire in a field and holds a firework display. Everyone arrives in warm clothes and there are hot drinks and hot dogs to eat. Perhaps you have bonfire nights in Australia? I wonder if you like fireworks?

I ache with sadness that I won't be getting any answers to these questions. My words to you will stay on the page and your answers are blowing in the wind. It's so cruel to have contact with my grandchildren wrenched from me. I wonder if you are good friends with each other. There are three years between the two of you and I'm aware that siblings don't always get on. My brother Henri and I didn't have a lot in common when we were young, but I was always fond of my brother, who was very clever but rather vague. He became an archaeologist and when he mysteriously disappeared, it was as if I'd lost a precious part of me that I'd never truly appreciated. Here's the story:

For some years, Henri had travelled overseas on archaeo-logical trips. He had done teaching work at the university whilst working on his PhD, and he stayed on in this post afterwards. He became involved with helping to organise student archaeological digs and projects which sometimes included spending weeks at ancient sites in remote areas of far-off countries. He had spent much time in South America during his childhood, and he developed a passionate interest in the Moche civilisation and culture from about 2000 years ago. I seem to remember he did his PhD thesis on the subject and later on produced an erudite book, which sold few copies but helped to establish his reputation in his chosen field.

He didn't come to Colombia for our wedding so, when my son was born, I pleaded with him to come out and meet his nephew. A few months after Julian's birth, to my surprise Henri came to visit us for a few days in Colombia whilst on his way to Peru. He appeared to like his nephew, though babies were infinitely more foreign to him than ancient pots. He seemed bewildered that his wayward sister had settled down and become a mother, and he found his brother-in-law's extrovert personality difficult to cope with, not having been blessed with a sense of humour which was in any way compatible. Raul was puzzled by Henri, who seemed to exist in a different millennium from the rest of us.

My poor brother was academic but impractical and unwise. Shortly afterwards he was working in some remote place in Peru searching for a lost city, but it was Henri who got lost. He went off for a day on his own, away from the rest of the archaeological team, and was never seen again. A huge search was conducted but they found no trace of him and after a year he was presumed dead. Our parents were devastated and when they finally gave up all hope, my father asked for a posting elsewhere. Colombia was painfully close to Peru and the tragic loss of their son. They returned to Europe and never came back to South America.

The loss of my only sibling was immensely sad, but my brother and I had been far apart for a long time, both physically and emotionally, so his absence affected me less than it might have done had I seen him more often and known him better. To compensate, my sister-in-law, Natalia, two years younger than Raul, became much closer. Deeply religious and unmarried, and with little prospect of having her own children, she took a real interest in her little nephew and often came to stay. She was a gentle person and her calm unflustered manner was appreciated by us all, especially by little Julian who developed a real bond with her. I got to know her better and we became close friends. She adored her brother and her nephew, and I think she was fond of her madcap disorganised sister-in-law. Although I lost one sibling, I gained another.

It is getting dark, and I have decided to draw my curtains to try and deter small bands of roving children pounding on my door and demanding 'trick or treat'. But they know that if they persevere, I will relent. I have bought in a large tin of biscuits and some sweets, as I prefer giving out treats than having to perform tricks. Last year on Halloween, when my bell rang for the third time, I went to answer it, but stepped behind the door as I pulled it wide open, so they did not see who was there. I wailed like a banshee and the three boys standing on my doorstep were scared witless. I don't think they appreciated my 'trick'.

I think of you both, dearest Magpies, somewhere in the pale blue yonder, and realise that with you today is probably already tomorrow. You will be sleeping somewhere, with peaceful faces and soft eyelashes. I fantasize about a day when I might see you again, but until then, sweet dreams.

With windfalls of love,

Grandmama

The pub, this early in the evening, is almost empty as most people are still at home having a meal after finishing work. It is dark outside and the landlady, Flora, finishes pulling a pint and puts the glass of ale on a beer mat in front of her customer, who is looking out of the window. As she wipes the bar she glances up and they both see a small car stop outside. The driver opens the door to get out and can be identified from the interior light. It is Josie Cuff. Flora has already spotted her and, putting down the cloth, she fetches a full carrier bag and goes outside to give it to her friend. Seen through the pub window, Josie, with an orange scarf wound round her neck and a cheerful grin on her face, appears to be very grateful and takes the bag. She climbs back into her car and drives off up the road towards her cottage. It is a Wednesday in December and one of the three days a week, when Josie drives to a village about fifteen miles away where she works as a part-time carer to an elderly couple, who both have mobility problems and ill-health. She shares this job with another carer who works on the other days. Flora comes inside and, as she goes back behind the counter, remarks to the person drinking at the bar that the bag is something which her friend left behind by mistake in the pub over the weekend. The customer takes a swig of beer and smiles, aware that Flora is being tactful. Everyone in the village knows that Josie is chaotic and is always mislaying things. The bag probably contains leftover food – it is common knowledge that Josie can hardly make ends meet. She is known for her generosity but often leaves herself short. He has little sympathy for such recklessness.

24th December 2012

Dear Magpies,

It is morning on Christmas Eve and I know that, somewhere in the warmer hemisphere, you are both going to bed full of excitement about Christmas Day tomorrow. I expect you still hang up your stockings. You, Tom, are now sixteen and Lottie will be thirteen in January – so you have long been aware who stands in for Santa. I hope you are equally knowledgeable about the real reason for Christmas and that it is a time when we remember and celebrate the first Christmas over 2000 years ago and the birth of Jesus Christ, the Son of God. The reason behind the giving of presents is because three wise and wealthy men travelled from the East to bring the baby Jesus gifts to celebrate his birth.

Your father was, of course, a Catholic by upbringing though he was not particularly devout. I am unsure if your mother was a Christian, as she always avoided discussing her beliefs, but she might have been, or she might have become one in the intervening years since we last met. Parents naturally influence their children and fervour can be passed on as easily as apathy. But you are both now of an age when you can make your own minds up, and I'd like you to know that I don't think there's ever any justification in being apathetic about anything. Always be enthusiastic, and never say, "I don't care". Listen to advice, read about the subject in question, learn from others but decide for yourself.

Anyhow, I hope you both have a wonderful Christmas. Try to think about others in the world who might not be having such a happy time, but enjoy yourselves. I do ache to know where you are and whether you live in the country or the town and what you will be doing today. Be good if you can, but you don't have to be perfect – and a bit of naughtiness now and then is allowed. But be kind and considerate to your mother and anyone else with whom you might be spending Christmas. On the subject of mischief, I should mention to you that I have a penchant for collective nouns. 'Penchant' is a French word for 'inclination' which in this sense doesn't mean the slope of a hill but a liking for something. So I collect unusual examples of collective nouns. The usual ones are common – such as a herd of cows or a flock of sheep. But there are some wonderful exotic words for animal group names. Back in the Middle Ages the hunting fraternity invented these with much wit and ingenuity. There was a book on hunting, hawking and heraldry which was very popular in the sixteenth century so there are lots of collective nouns for animals and even more for birds. We have a murder of crows, a charm of goldfinches, an exultation of skylarks and a murmuration of starlings. But the one that will amuse you most is: a mischief of magpies. I should like to think that my two grandchildren and their friends qualify.

Your father Julian was mischievous. I think he inherited this from his father, my beloved Raul, who was an entertaining combination of joker and clown. When Julian reached the 'terrible twos' – I expect you know how troublesome two-year-olds can be – he wanted to explore everything. My parents were no longer in South America, and Raul's parents lived in Bogota, and we didn't see them too often. I had no grandparents to help with a lively son, but I managed fine until I became pregnant again. For much of this second pregnancy in 1976 I was very sick. Raul tried to help but he was very busy at work, and I'm not sure how I would have coped without the help of my kind-hearted sister-in-law, Natalia.

Though I was fluent in Spanish, Raul and I decided that our son should be bilingual, and so I spoke English to Julian, whilst his father always addressed him in Spanish. His aunt, Natalia, spoke no English and always conversed with her nephew in Spanish, so the little boy grew up speaking both languages, but I recollect that he could never spell in either of them which is often the case with children who are bilingual. I hope you are both good at spelling – I always used to win the spelling competitions at school, which amazed my teachers as I wasn't much good at anything else.

Natalia and Raul were responsible for bringing up Julian as a Catholic. There are few Protestant churches in South America, and the four of us used to go together to Mass. Julian was never naughty in church – I think he was overawed by the huge building, the dim light, the beautiful singing and the mysterious incense. Or perhaps he was just a bit scared of his strict aunt, who was firm with him even though she loved him very much. She was an excellent teacher and adored children but knew that discipline was important. I too think that children need boundaries and sensible rules – those without any are often badly behaved.

Julian was very excited about the prospect of a baby brother or sister due to be born just after Christmas, but I went into labour early in mid-December and there were complications. Our little baby daughter was stillborn. We were all devastated by this tragedy – and without Raul's love and Natalia's caring support I would have fallen apart. I didn't know then that I would be unable to have any more children.

Julian was very upset to not have a baby sister, who would have been your aunt. Your mother had no siblings so you two don't have any uncles or aunts. This is a pity, as they can be rather good fun and often spoil nephews and nieces by taking them out for deliciously unhealthy meals and to watch delightfully unsuitable films. Grandparents can be fun too – if they are permitted to keep in touch! I'm sure you are still in contact with your mother's parents whom I envy because they see you and I don't. Though I live very far away in Europe, that's no reason to lose touch completely. As you must be aware, your mother has chosen to keep me in the dark as to where you live. This is cruel and has made me very unhappy, and one day I hope to find out why.

Other misfortunes in my life have meant that I've lost all my family. But you are still alive. Out there. Somewhere.

I last saw you both a month after Lottie's birth, when I came out to Australia to visit you early in the year 2000. It was a wonderfully happy visit – all of us unaware that we were together for the last time. In December your father Julian died whilst on a visit to Colombia. One day, if you want to know, I will tell you all about this catastrophe, even though it still causes me distress. It was, of course, appalling for your mother to lose her husband so suddenly and to become a young widow with two very small children.

Let me make this quite clear. Whatever she may say to the contrary, I have always wanted to keep in touch, to know about your lives and have the opportunity to love you and relate to you as a grandmother. It was Melissa's decision to sever our relationship and to move away without letting me have your new address. I was stunned when my letters were returned and the telephone number was disconnected. I thought it was a mistake and expected for many months that she would contact me, apologise and give me your new address. Naturally I contacted your Australian grandparents, who refused to let me have your contact details. I was horrified and pleaded with them, but they were adamant that your mother wanted nothing more to do with me. I tried to trace you in all parts of Australia but the name Moreno elicited only a few people who were not you. I tried your mother's maiden name, Jones, of which there are many thousands, but was unable to track you down.

I saved money for the fare to Australia and in mid-2002 I arrived in Perth and set off on my search to find you. I first went to where you had been living two years before when I last visited you, but the people living there had no forwarding address for your family.

I asked neighbours and the nursery school where Tom had been, but no one knew where you had gone. I travelled to Melbourne to pay a call on Mr and Mrs Jones, your grandparents, but discovered that they too had recently moved away. It was apparent from neighbours that they knew where the family was but were not going to tell me. Everywhere I met a brick wall. After a few weeks I had got nowhere and, realising what a huge country Australia was and how few resources I had, I despaired and returned to England, having failed utterly in my quest to find my grandchildren. I was gutted.

But I had a sister-in-law in Colombia and though we live thousands of miles from each other, Natalia and I have remained friends all our lives and we correspond. She has been very supportive and, when times were really bad, encouraged me not to despair. A beautiful faith-filled woman, Natalia reminds me that with God nothing is impossible. I had a letter from her the other day, though I've mislaid it under a pile of papers on my desk, which I never find the time or inclination to tidy up. I often lose things and waste time searching for them – because sorting out cupboards and shelves is tedious and a low priority. My mother used to tear her hair out over the mess in my bedroom, but Julian's room never bothered me. I wonder if you keep your bedrooms clean and tidy – I haven't met many children who do.

I get carried away thinking of you as I type this letter – and keep forgetting that you won't be reading it. Perhaps one day I'll miraculously find you and send letters to you for real. Anyhow I'll keep on writing and perpetuating the illusion that you'll get them.

Let me tell you about Christmas in Dorset. I have lived in the village for two and a half years since the summer of 2010. My first Christmas as a new arrival was quiet, apart from an evening tagging along with local carol singers who cheerfully accepted my inability to sing in tune. My neighbours Bill and Lou kindly asked me to have Christmas lunch with them, when they discovered I had no family.

Last year, I decided to invite some of my new friends to eat Christmas supper with me. I'd met Doris Bugler some while before, after church. She's not one to mince words and says what she thinks, which other people often consider tactless, but I like her honesty and respect her intelligence. So that evening, I'd invited Doris and some others in the village whom I knew to be on their own or without family, apart from James Trevett, my landlord, who is unmarried but always goes to relatives in Scotland for Christmas and 'Hogmanay' – Scottish New Year's Eve.

There were nine of us crammed in round my kitchen table, including Doris and the Stickleys and Matt Tapper. I felt sorry for Matt, lonely and sad in his bereavement, but began to realise that he was a self-absorbed man who preferred to be on his own. He ate in silence and I don't think he smiled once, poor chap. Bill grinned a lot but said little, though his wife Lou chattered too much. I was unaware until that evening that she and Alice Diffey, who was another guest, dislike each other politely. Alice, who is a widow, considers herself superior as she is a retired schoolteacher. The other three round the table were John and Maggie Damon, who lived opposite (he's the man who was thrown into the pond last summer) and Harry Scaddon, a dignified man in his sixties who lives on his own near the church and is in poor health.

My intention was to bring together my new friends in the village for a cheerful Christmas meal. Cooking is not something in which I excel (what is, I wonder?) so though my modest efforts were not quite up to scratch, there was plenty of pleasant red plonk and I tried my best to be entertaining. But it was not a particularly successful combination of people or personalities and this made the meal less than harmonious.

On Christmas night many choose to go down to the local pub. George and Flora always decorate the Anchor with glitter, garlands and an overladen tree that is jammed in at a drunken angle because it is too tall for the low ceiling and beams. Lots of people drop in and this year so shall I. At least I won't be alone, as I suspect Matt might be, though he does go occasionally to the pub. Harry often goes and John will be there. Doris and Alice probably won't come – perhaps they were brought up by parents who didn't approve of single women going to pubs on their own. But those old-fashioned ideas don't constrain me – I'm a free spirit and what others think has never bothered me!

The weather is chilly, but I don't think we'll have snow this year. Just as well, because the cottage has no insulation and gets very cold, though I have a small wood-burning stove which helps to warm it up. It's getting late and Folly is nuzzling my leg – she wants a cuddle and a saucer of milk. I wish you both a very Merry Christmas tomorrow. I hope and pray that you will be happy.

With carols of love,
Grandmama

Josie hesitates. Her fingers hover over the keyboard. Which of her names should she choose?

Looking up, she stares out of the window, noticing the crazed patterns which the frost has traced on her windowpane. It is cold in the room and she needs to light a fire, but she's short of logs and wants to put it off as long as possible. It will be even colder tonight. Quickly she types: 'Josette Moreno'. It sounds more exciting. As she presses 'Send', she realises the doorbell has been sounding faintly for some while.

Few people use the front door as most of the locals know that the back door is always unlocked and the kitchen is where Josie is usually to be found. She walks through to the hall and opens the door. Her landlord James Trevett is standing with his back to her, gazing down the village street. He is wearing a smart but old-fashioned overcoat, though he is only in his thirties. He spins round when he hears her say, "Good morning."

"Ah hello, Josie. I was beginning to wonder if anybody was at home."

"I'm not anybody – I'm your tenant. And I think I know why you've come, Mr Trevett."

"Why don't you call me James?" He leans with affected casualness against the door frame and looks down at her.

"I don't like being familiar with someone when I owe them rent." She says this calmly with no hint of any embarrassment as she reaches up and pulls a coat and scarf off the hook just inside the door.

"Ah yes, I was coming to that. I'm not here to hassle you. Absolutely not! Just occurred to me you might have a little problem and I thought we could have a friendly chat and try and sort it out. Might I come in?"

"Actually, I was just off to visit Harry. He's unwell and I said I'd cook him a meal. He's expecting me and I'm late." Josie pulls on her old green coat and fumbles for gloves in its pocket. She glances in the cracked mirror on the wall and notices that her hair looks as if it hasn't seen a brush in a week. "So sorry that it's not a convenient moment," she says, emerging and pulling the door firmly shut behind her to conceal the unholy mess in her hall and sitting room.

"In that case perhaps we could have our little talk on the way there." James lives on his own in a large house further up the lane from Harry's cottage. He falls into step beside her.

Josie chooses her words carefully. "I'm well aware that I'm sometimes overdue with the rent. I know you've always been patient about this for which I'm grateful. However, on this occasion it's not a problem to find the money, though that often is the case. It's because I've had no response to my several messages about the broken guttering on the rear wall, which causes damp inside. I have to spend more on heating to try and keep it at bay." Inwardly wincing at this lie - electric heating is unaffordable and she never uses it - Josie keeps her eyes on the road.

"Isn't that fixed yet? I thought I'd asked Bill to mend it some while back," James says with a frown.

"Perhaps he hasn't had time yet. I could mention it to him when I next see him over the garden fence? Would that be all right?"

"Absolutely. And I'll tell him to do it as soon as possible. We can't have your cottage getting damp."

If only you knew, thinks Josie, what it's like to have no central heating. And not to have enough money to pay the bills.

At this point she catches sight of Alice Diffey walking towards them, snug in pink overcoat with pristine fur boots and a trim woolly hat. "Hello, Alice. Mr Trevett and I are just on our way to see Harry," says Josie with a cheery smile, attempting to deflect Alice from focusing on what she and her landlord might need to discuss.

Alice's eyes flick from one to the other and Josie knows that she has guessed instantly that Josie is trying to persuade her landlord to be lenient about the arrears in her rent. The villagers know that Alice has a nose for debt. She can always sniff it out.

11th February 2013

Dear Magpies,

We had our second major snowfall of the winter yesterday, although it was nothing like as heavy as the huge snowstorm which enveloped the country three weeks ago, causing hardship for many. But not to me – I piled on lots of clothes and managed fine.

My world is clothed in shades of white and black. The fields and hedges are frosted blue white, the roofs and gardens bleached sheet white, whilst in contrast the stone walls of the cottages are charcoal grey. Tree branches are ebony black where the wind has whipped off the snow and the slushy street has dark mud tracks. The sky is a blurred beige and a creamy mist swirls over the stream in the lower meadow. When the sun comes out everything takes on brighter warmer hues. The sky becomes pink, the trees a chill blue and the snow is almost golden in the morning sun. Who says winter has no colour?

In Australia it's summer, though autumn will come to you

soon as surely as spring will happen here. In Colombia, the seasons are different – hot, rainy and dry – and the sun sets at around 6pm. In April and May, the heat and humidity on the Caribbean coast saps a person's energy, but the blustery wind gives some respite. Barranquilla, where we lived, was an exciting and vibrant city. Each year, during the four days preceding Ash Wednesday, it has a world-famous carnival which is an amazing event celebrating a unique mix of different cultures with elaborate floats and energetic performers in flamboyant costumes dancing to Cumbia, dance music popular throughout Latin America. Noisy, raucous and colourful, the carnival is fun!

From time to time we visited Bogota, but it took ten hours by car and the mountains were not always safe, so then we had to fly. In the 1970s the country suffered from stagnant economic growth and high inflation and to make matters worse, Colombia's illegal drug trade grew steadily as the drug cartels or gangs amassed huge amounts of money, weapons and influence. There were also leftist rebel groups and violence ensued with some attacks on civilians. The 1980s were also unsettled times and Raul's parents were agitated about our living so far from them and persuaded their son to ask his company to transfer him back to their head office in the capital. In 1988 we moved back to Bogota with mixed feelings, leaving our carefree Caribbean lifestyle behind. Julian, now fourteen, attended a private school which my parents-in-law had offered to pay for if we returned. This was the Colegio Salesiano de Leon XIII, which had an excellent reputation and which we could not possibly have afforded ourselves.

I had always had a better relationship with my father-in-law than with his wife. Raul's mother had been unsympathetic when we discovered that I was unable to have any more children. A single child in a Colombian family is unusual – but Paola considered it a serious failure on my part. For Julian to have no siblings was a disappointment. I would love to have had more children. My name held a promise – Josephine from the Latin Josephina means: 'God will add another son'. For a few years I thought He might, but it did not happen.

Raul and I moved to a modest apartment in the Chapinero district of the city, not far from my parents-in-law's elegant house. Juan Carlos, who had seen little of his son and grandson during the Barranquilla years, was immensely pleased to have us living so close to him. He developed a real bond with Julian and he took him out to sporting events, activities and meals. Others thought him austere, but in the company of his adored grandson, the older man mellowed and they used to laugh and tease each other.

A few months after our return to the capital I had a frantic phone call from my mother in Kenya, where my father worked at the British Embassy. Whilst visiting a project, he had cut himself and developed septicaemia; he was dangerously ill. Raul, always decisive in a crisis, promptly arranged flights for me to Nairobi. I left within a day, but it was four weeks before I returned. He enlisted his sister Natalia, who was still single, to keep an eye on his teenage son, and she kept house for them during my absence.

My father died before I arrived, which distressed me immensely, as there were things I would like to have said to him, such as how much I loved him and how much he meant to me. My mother was devastated, and we mourned together as we arranged his funeral with help from embassy staff who were tactfully supportive. Afterwards my mother wanted to go back to her family in France and we spent a week packing up all her possessions to be shipped there. I travelled to Paris with her and we went to her brother's house just outside Paris. After a couple of weeks, I had to go home to Colombia and suggested that she might like to come and stay with us whilst she considered her future. But she was adamant that she would not leave France again. I discussed the future with my uncle Rémy, who seemed willing to look after his sister until she decided where she wanted to live. Then I felt able to leave and return to my own family.

I grieved for a long time, though I kept this to myself and got on with life. As ever, Natalia sensed my sadness and in her compassionate and gentle way, helped me come to terms with the loss of my favourite parent. She had finished a teaching job at a school in a deprived part of the city and had decided to work near Ibaqué, about four hours west of Bogota. Natalia felt God was calling her to work with the parentless and the homeless. She was persuaded by a friend to join the management staff of an orphanage school attached to a convent, where her skills and experience would be underpinned by the inner strength she derived from her strong faith. A month later she left for her new post and we missed her quiet wisdom and loving support.

I needed a job too and started working part-time for a commercial art gallery, which was run by a colleague of Raul's. I had no experience but my fluency in English and French as well as Spanish was an asset, which no doubt got me the job, where I began to learn about contemporary art.

In 1991, a new constitution came into force, protecting human rights and establishing rights to social security and healthcare. Things were looking up. In spite of this, Raul, my buccaneering husband, was not content in Bogota, away from the free-wheeling and vibrant life in Barranquilla. He pined for sailing and missed his friends, and he decided to change his job, but at this point his shipping company offered him a one-year position in their office in the USA in the Port of Houston, which handled huge amounts of cargo and shipping. He leapt at the chance and within a few weeks we had uprooted ourselves from Colombia and gone to live in Texas.

A year in a co-educational American school helped Julian become fluent with his English. He also learnt how to ride horses and drive cars. And he discovered girls. Julian was a fine-looking lad and I saw the admiration in the eyes of girls at school. Soon he acquired a stunning girlfriend called Abigail and his English improved rapidly!

I felt less at home in America – everything was too big and too fast – but Raul seemed to enjoy the hectic pace of life and work. Too soon our year came to an end and we had to return to Colombia. Julian was reluctant to return but he settled down to his final year at the Colegio and took his studies seriously. Raul, however, had become addicted to change, and without consulting me, he asked his company to transfer him back to their office in Barranquilla, where he started work after Easter in 1993. We did not wish to uproot Julian for a second time from his school when important exams were looming up, so reluctantly I agreed to stay in our apartment in the capital, to which Raul would return at weekends. It was the first time that the two of us had been apart on a regular basis and I pined for him. In the summer holiday, Julian and I went down to be with Raul in his cramped little bachelor apartment by the sea.

Raul relished being back in Barranquilla and promptly took up sailing again. He met up with a friend called Diego who kept a sailing boat, about twelve metres long, in the marina in Cartagena, a town further west, where winds were less strong. Raul was offered the chance to crew aboard *La Niña* (which means 'The Girl'). Sailing absorbed Raul's free time and sometimes he didn't come home at weekends. I tried not to feel upset by his selfishness.

It was in late 1993 that our family life was torn into tatters by a freak storm.

But I shall have to tell you about that tragedy another time, as I soon need to go and see Harry Scaddon, a village friend who is not in the best of health. He used to live overseas where he nearly died and, though he's recovered, his health is permanently damaged. He also wears dark glasses to protect his weak eyes from the sun, though he does not use them in winter. He lives in a small cottage at the top end of the village near the church, but not as far as James's house. Sometimes I take him a prepared meal, but he is a proud man and is reluctant to accept charity. From time to time he invites me for a meal in the pub, which I enjoy not only for the food but also because Harry is stimulating company. We talk about politics and art and books, which is a pleasant change from the subject of the weather which seems to obsess many of the villagers most of the time.

George produces good pub meals and Flora has decided to offer a limited lunchtime menu and a traditional roast lunch on Sundays. They have managed to attract new customers and so Flora has employed a Polish girl, called Lena, who lives in a nearby village. She works hard and smiles a lot, so some of the farmworkers nearby have taken to dropping into the pub. The new waitress is good for business and trade is looking up, which has put a smile back on Flora's face. George, kept busy in the kitchen, now has no time to squander their slender resources on acquiring junk, though I expect he still drinks because in a pub alcohol is readily available. George's cheeks are often red – though he does work in a hot kitchen. Also he is unsociable – shyness is a real handicap if you are a publican. He's lucky to have a wife like Flora who is chatty with customers! Lena's long and lustrous hair attracts people too.

Are children allowed in pubs in Australia? I don't know why I ask you questions because I know I'll never get any answers. But

I won't indulge in self-pity – my life is good. I may have no family but I do have friends.

The cooking smells from my oven have reminded me that my shepherd's pie is now ready to take round to Harry. I'm going to put on my coat and old boots and trudge up the icy street bearing hot food for my friend. I've lost my gloves again so I shall carry it there using my oven mittens. Let's hope I don't slip!

With snowfalls of love,

Grandmama

He leans against a tree to fuse his figure and the trunk together and render him invisible. He looks across at the sturdy mediaeval church with its square tower, a bastion against time and decay, oblivious of the changing seasons. A watery sunlight washes over the churchyard and its array of ancient headstones, some of them sunk out of alignment like a row of uneven rotting teeth. A hundred yards away two figures emerge from the church porch. Perhaps they have lit candles inside or they may have been praying - he considers both futile activities. He watches them walk down the path and stop halfway to the lychgate.

The short stocky figure is Doris Bugler and she turns to go to the part of the cemetery which is used for more recent interments. She is carrying a bunch of daffodils and he sees her lean down and place them against a headstone, which is probably the grave of her parents who both died a few years back.

The taller figure, who has stopped on the main path,

is Josie Cuff, easily recognisable by her mop of wild hair and baggy green overcoat. She looks despondent and, although she is cheerful when they meet in the village, he has found out about her tragic past history. She has given up the search for her two lost grandchildren, who have disappeared into thin air somewhere in the Antipodes, along with their mother, the wife of her dead son. Josie works as a carer – an occupation he considers dreary and badly paid. The woman seems poorer than the proverbial church mouse, but she is resourceful and manages to get by. He wonders how.

He is convinced that Josie Cuff has, somewhere in the habitual disorder of her cottage, the information that he seeks to obtain for someone else. He has watched her long enough and there's nothing he can glean from her external activities – her job, her social life, her regular walks. Therefore, the answer has to be somewhere inside her home. It will be risky, but he needs to gain access whilst she is not there. She rarely locks her door during the day – so conveniently careless! He watches the two women head off up the hill behind the church – they are clearly going for a walk. He turns and slinks out of the churchyard through a gap in the hedge. Now is his chance.

30th March 2013

Dear Magpies,

Tomorrow is Easter Sunday. As I write this in late afternoon, I realise it's already Easter Day with you. Wherever that is! I wonder what you'll do today. That I may never know is terribly sad. It's as if an old wound has reopened and is aching. Take a deep breath, Josie, and start again.

Earlier this week, together with others I helped decorate our ancient church with fresh spring flowers. I'm much fonder of the delicate beauty of snowdrops, crocuses, daffodils, and iris than the gaudier lustrous flowers that flaunt themselves in summer. Most of all, I love roses, which bloom gloriously from late spring all the way to late autumn. Tomorrow morning, I shall attend the Easter service in the church. It will be chilly – the heating is very erratic – so to celebrate I shall wear boots and gloves and a gaudy red overcoat I bought in a charity shop. The congregation is normally small, but Christmas and Easter attract more people including those who are muddled or undecided about their beliefs. Perhaps they find it comforting to listen to familiar prayers and sing well-known hymns. It will be good to see the church full for a change. Afterwards there will be hot drinks and biscuits inside the church and we will mill about and chat before going home to a slap-up Easter lunch…if you have a family. Which I don't anymore! Families with children often have Easter egg hunts in their gardens. Is this something that you do? I hope so.

This year I've been invited for lunch by John Damon, who has his sister and another couple staying. He has invited James to come along as well, so there will be six of us. I think he might want a hand with the cooking, which must be why I'd been asked. I'm happy to help.

When I woke up this morning, I lay in bed staring vaguely at the ceiling – the tiny cracks above the window and the small brown patch of damp in one corner. I then looked out of the window – I'd forgotten to close the curtains again – and tried to see the pale curled leaves of spring soon to appear on the trees. Closing my eyes again, I had a waking dream about you both. You were out of focus in a distant field, running across green grass, laughing and carefree. I cannot visualise what you now look like – my memories are blurred. I live in hope – a forlorn hope – of finding out. Where, oh where are you?

This reminds me of one of the finest poems in the English language: *Ode to a Nightingale* by John Keats. The final stanza (or verse) begins like this:

> Forlorn! the very word is like a bell
> To toll me back from thee to my sole self!

I rarely feel lonely and desperate but this is one of those days. My heart aches. Reading poetry helps resist the temptation to despair. I wonder if you like poetry and whether I will ever be able to share with you some of the poems I love most.

In my last letter I had no time to tell you how your paternal grandfather died. My mood is already sombre, so I'll do it now.

1993 began in optimism but ended in tragedy. This was twenty years ago, though it seems longer than that. I was forty-one and Julian was eighteen and had finished his final school term in late June. He did moderately well in his exams and wanted to go to study abroad either in America or Australia. He was keen on oceanography though he wasn't committed to any particular course at that stage. He wanted to fly the nest, spread his wings and see the world. Having just broken up with a girlfriend, Carolina, he took a holiday with some school friends travelling round the southern part of Colombia. I was a little worried because the political scene was still unsettled in the country with much instability and unrest caused by the leftist rebel groups who were still active. However, the Medellin drug cartel was broken in 1993 and key leaders were arrested. Julian reassured me that they would all take great care and the group set off in mid-July.

One evening a few days later, Raul told me that he would be taking two weeks holiday from work to go sailing. With his friend Diego, they would sail *La Niña* north-eastwards some 400 miles to the Isla de Andres, a large island belonging to Colombia but lying a hundred miles off the coast of Nicaragua. This ambitious voyage meant they would have to push the boat to get there and back in the time, so they enlisted another friend, called Miguel, to come with them. The voyage was imminent. Winds were blowing steadily from the north-east and no tropical storms were forecast.

I was upset by the sudden plan and hurt that it had not crossed his mind to ask me if I might like to come along, particularly as our son was taking his first holiday on his own. Raul said that I was not experienced enough, but as a concession he suggested that I take a two-hour flight from Bogota to San Andres Island to meet them. I should book up a small hotel so we could spend a few days together before they sailed back. I reluctantly agreed, though annoyed I had been excluded from the planning and the project.

I felt uneasy. This was a long passage over open water in an area where few sailing boats ventured. Raul assured me that the boat was fully equipped with a VHF radio, life raft and emergency flares, but I knew that he rarely bothered to wear a life jacket or safety harness in unsettled weather. He had never worn a safety helmet on his motorbike, proclaiming himself a free spirit who didn't like to be constrained. I sighed and had to accept. Colombian wives were not expected to criticise their husbands.

They set off on 4th August from Cartagena. Raul telephoned me before their departure to tell me that the weather was fine. I could hear the excitement in his voice. He loved the sea and being aboard a sailing vessel exhilarated him as nothing else did. They hoped that the boat would cover at least eighty nautical miles each day, but the first couple of days might be slower because light winds were forecast. The passage there would take about five days and Raul suggested that I book my flight to the island for 10th August. He said he had to go as they were leaving from the dock in half an hour. Though reluctant to say goodbye, I wished him fair winds and told him I loved him. He sang out that he adored me and, as I whispered, "Take care," I realised he had already ended the call.

I felt very low. My son, on the brink of adult life, was travelling with friends, and my husband was setting off on a sea voyage – both were moving away from me. My sister-in-law was living several hours away and I felt lonely so I decided to telephone my mother in France, something I rarely did. She was still living with her brother, which was more convenient than living alone. My uncle answered the call and told me she had gone to Paris for a few days. My mother, thousands of miles away in Europe, was as elusive as ever.

Also far away, but more threatening, was a tropical storm named Bret. The depression had formed about 1000 miles to the west of the Cape Verde Islands in the Atlantic Ocean off the coast of Africa. By 5th August it had strengthened and become as tropical storm with winds of about 60 mph. It didn't feature on the news until it crossed Trinidad on 7th August and later on the same day it made landfall in South America. Rainfall in Venezuela was heavy and widespread mudslides were reported which destroyed 10,000 houses and caused 173 deaths. It was coming in our direction! The next day it crossed briefly into northern Colombia and thankfully weakened in intensity over the mountains before it moved into the Caribbean Sea.

I was praying that the storm would decrease further and my beloved Raul and his friends aboard *La Niña* would make landfall and safety. I was horrified when I heard that Bret had strengthened again and would make landfall in southern Nicaragua on 10th August, the day I was due to arrive in San Andres. By 9th August I had not heard anything, but I received a call from the airline saying that my flight would be delayed or cancelled owing to bad weather in the area. Raul's parents were also extremely worried, though our son on his travels 200 miles to the south was blissfully unaware of the problem.

On 10th August, I was falling apart, pacing up and down our small apartment in Bogota, a sick feeling in my throat and a void in the pit of my stomach. There was still no word from the crew of *La Niña*. My parents-in-law managed to get in touch with the coastguard at San Andres, who were very busy dealing with various vessels that had been washed up on the shore, wrecked. They had no news of a lone yacht inbound from Cartagena. My heart sank when I heard that people had been drowned. The storm had destroyed almost 1000 houses in Nicaragua and 35,000 people were left homeless; twelve bridges had collapsed and Bret had caused millions of dollars' worth of damage.

I cannot recall how I got through the next week. I staggered in black despair through the days and endured achingly sleepless nights. Juan Carlos and Paola suggested that I move in with them, but I wanted to remain by our telephone, waiting and hoping that Raul might miraculously phone. I received a couple of postcards from Julian and was relieved that he had not telephoned. What could I have said to him? A week passed. Tropical storm Bret, leaving devastation in its wake, had crossed into the Pacific Ocean and dissipated.

Then, amazingly, on 15th August, I received a phone call from my father-in-law, who had been contacted by a coastguard in Puerto Limon in Costa Rica, to say that the yacht with the name

La Niña had put into the port under power. The yacht had been dismasted and was in terrible shape with two crew aboard. We waited, hardly daring to hope. A few hours later we were informed of the identity of the two men: Diego and Miguel. Raul had gone overboard and drowned a few days earlier. My world fell apart – I had lost my love.

A week later, I had a telephone call from Diego and he gave the full story. He wanted to spare me the details but I needed to know what had happened. It was far worse than I could ever have imagined. He said they had a pleasant but slow passage in bright sun for the first couple of days; then the wind had picked up, and they heard on their radio about the storm coming their way. On 9th August, they had only fifty-five miles to run to reach the island when the storm hit them. They were well prepared, had put on storm sails and battened everything down. The wind strength was phenomenal; the seas were huge with spume everywhere and no visibility at all. At the height of the storm, it was dangerous for any of them to remain on deck so they lashed the helm and retreated below for six hours, whilst the storm howled around them, pushing them westwards. The most terrifying moment was when the whole cabin became inverted and they found themselves thrown across the boat as the boat rolled over 360°. They heard an enormous crack and realised the mast had broken. The boat shuddered upright again but there was constant banging on the side of the boat and they realised this must be a part of the mast. They clawed their way up the companionway ladder, went on deck and saw that the mast had broken in two places and was half overboard, held alongside by the tangled wire stays. The jagged end was causing damage to the hull, so they had to cut away the rigging with bolt cutters and let the mast sink.

On the 11th August, the winds gradually lessened, and they tried to get the engine started. They had been pumping water out of the bilges and everything was soaked, but the next day they did eventually get it going. Relieved to have survived the storm, they set off to the south-west, towards the nearest landfall in Costa Rica to avoid the shallow waters off the coast of Nicaragua. The seas had abated somewhat but they made slow progress as the boat would only go about four knots under power. They prayed they would not run out of fuel. After two days, they calculated they still had fifty miles to run to the coast. Then they spotted the pirogue. A pirogue is a long, narrow wooden canoe, which local fishermen use in Central America and the Caribbean.

At this point in the story Diego faltered but I made him go on. The pirogue had an outboard on the back and four men aboard who were waving and calling out, seemingly in distress. But, as they came alongside the yacht, Diego and Miguel, who were on deck, realised with horror that the men wore scarves around their faces and had guns and knives. The pirates leapt aboard the yacht and, holding a knife to Diego's throat, demanded all the money there was on board. Raul had been sleeping down below but he woke and realised that his friends were in danger. He grabbed the handgun which the yacht carried to deal with situations like this, but as he emerged from the cabin the pirates panicked and shot him. He reeled back against the guard rail and fell to the deck bleeding profusely. He didn't move and one of the pirates leaned over him and said 'Muerto'– dead!

The pirates continued to threaten Diego and made Miguel hand over their dollars, watches and torches. Then they picked up Raul's body and dumped it over the side. Diego watched with horror as his friend sank beneath the waves. He and Miguel were convinced they would be thrown over the side too and their attackers would take the boat. But at that point a small cargo ship was spotted steaming in their direction. The pirates grabbed as many things as they could, slung them into their pirogue, jumped aboard and started their engine, making off at speed to the west. The crew of the cargo vessel, which stopped by the stricken yacht about fifteen minutes afterwards, were appalled by the violent attack and escorted the sailing boat into the harbour at the nearest Costa Rican port, Puerto Limon.

Diego was immensely saddened by the death of his good friend and knew how dreadful it must be for his family. He offered to come and see me when he returned to Colombia but he had to stay in Costa Rica while the incident, which had involved a death, was being investigated. I was stunned to realise that Raul had survived a horrific storm only to be killed by evil violence.

We contacted Julian, who returned to Bogota, distraught at his father's death. He did not speak for five days and I was so frozen in misery that I could not comfort him. Eventually he went to see his grandfather and they sat in the Moreno house, silent in grief together. There was no burial, no chance to say goodbye. Storm Bret caused 184 deaths – more than any other hurricane in 1993 – and my Raul was one of them. His parents never recovered from the pain of losing their son.

It's probably just as well that you won't receive this letter with its distressing details about the death of a man you never met. Your grandfather was the love of my life – lover, joker, husband and friend. We danced through marriage for twenty wonderful years. I have never forgotten him.

A few weeks afterwards Natalia, who had adored her extrovert brother, reminded me of the famous verses in the Bible (to be found in Chapter 3 of the Old Testament book of Ecclesiastes) which starts: 'There is a time for everything, and a season for every activity under heaven.' Among the various phases in life there is: 'A time to be born and a time to die' and: 'A time to weep and a time to laugh.' I thought I would never laugh again but I can and do.

I have picked up my Bible to reread the passage. The verse that leapt off the page and saddened me further is: 'A time to search and a time to give up.' I think I've reached the end of my inclination to write the story of my life in letters to grandchildren who will never read them. There is: 'A time to be silent and a time to speak.' But you will always be in my mind.

With oceans of love,

Grandmama

On Monday 1st April Josie is riffling through the papers on the table she uses as her desk, trying to find a letter she received a few days earlier from her sister-in-law in Colombia. Natalia is old-fashioned and still writes to her on thin airmail paper. Josie receives few items in the post these days and these occasional letters in Spanish keep her in touch with her earlier life. She has also mislaid her computer mouse and hopes to locate that too.

She hears the doorbell and, knowing the door is ajar, calls out, "Come on in." She's expecting Doris for lunch and, hearing footsteps in the room, turns to greet her. She is surprised to see John Damon standing there. He is smiling and holding out something in his hand. It takes a few seconds for Josie to realise that it is her woollen scarf that she left behind in his house after Easter Sunday lunch the day before.

"Hi, John." She stands up and walks across the room. "Thank you so much for a lovely meal yesterday. How kind of you to return my scarf. I'd no idea I'd left it behind." She notices he's looking over her shoulder.

Josie's eyes follow his gaze. The surface of her desk is crammed with books, documents, old packets and empty coffee cups. Her computer screen is turned on but the keyboard is completely swamped by a deluge of papers. The tower unit on the floor beside the table has a stack of CDs balanced precariously on top of it and next to it the printer is reposing on a battered armchair where her cat is contentedly asleep on an old cushion. "My desk is in a dreadful muddle – I want to read my emails but can't find my mouse." She ought to feel embarrassed but doesn't.

"Perhaps Folly can help – she's good tracking down rodents. Though today she seems unconcerned," John says while Josie takes the scarf from his hand and flips it over the back of the armchair.

Leaning over it, she strokes her cat's head. "Folly is used to my mess and mayhem. So long as I feed her, she loves me."

"They say the way to a man's heart is through his stomach, but it seems food might be the key to a woman's heart." John inclines his head on one side and grins.

"Not to mine," says Josie firmly. "Though your meal was utterly delicious and you're certainly a much better cook than I am."

"It seems I'm better at finding things too," John says. He walks across to her desk and pulls out the black mouse from below a crumpled brown envelope. "I caught sight of its whiskers." He hands it to Josie. "April Fool!"

"Brilliant. I want to check my emails before Doris arrives for a snack lunch."

"In that case I'll take myself off. But before I go, I wondered if you've heard anything from Maggie. She's gone quiet and won't respond to communications. I'm trying to move things along and get on with the divorce." Josie had been friends with Maggie and they were still in touch.

So that was why he called in, thinks Josie. "Sorry, John. I haven't had an email from her in months." This is true, although Maggie has telephoned her recently.

"Never mind. Not to worry. See you soon." He saunters off and Josie hears the door slam. John never leaves doors unlocked. He doesn't want casual visitors and only lets people into his house by invitation. Josie reflects on what his motive might be for asking about his estranged wife. What is it he really wants to find out?

She sits down at her desk and, shoving the clutter off her keyboard, she finds the mouse mat, and is soon looking at her inbox. Two minutes later she opens the third new email and becomes very still as she reads it. It is marked 'To Josette Moreno', and is from a sender in New Zealand. She gives a big sob and bursts into tears.

At this point the doorbell rings and Josie leaps to her feet, knocking over the chair, and runs into the hall. For an instant she has the mad idea that it's him ringing the bell. She flings open the door. Doris stands there, her friendly expression turning to one of surprised concern when she sees how agitated Josie is. "What's wrong?" she asks. "You look distraught. Have you had bad news?"

"No, no," Josie explodes. "It's good news. Wonderful news! I've just had an email from Tom. My grandson. For years I've searched for him in vain. But now he's found me!"

PART II

In Secret

1st April 2013

Dearest Tom,

I *am* Josette Moreno. You say you are the son of Julian and Melissa Moreno, and have a younger sister called Charlotte. You *are* my grandson.

I was ecstatic to get your email.

For ten years I tried to find you both and have been in despair because I could not. I now understand why I've been unable to trace you – I've been looking in the wrong place. I had no idea that you were living in New Zealand – and under a different name!

Your father Julian, as I'm sure you know, died when you were three years old. You were christened Tomas Raul (after your grandfather, my first husband) Moreno. But now you seem to have a different surname – Brown. I wonder why.

How did you manage to track me down? I too have changed my name from Moreno. I remarried and my name is now Josie Cuff. Josie is a shortened version of my full name, Josephine. I live in the south-west of England in a county called Dorset.

Where in New Zealand do you live? Please let me know as soon as possible because I never want to lose touch with you again. Do you have a telephone number?

How are your mother and sister? Tom you must be sixteen now and Lottie about thirteen. I am sixty and I haven't seen you both since the year 2000 when my world fell apart after your father's death.

Tom, do please email me back as soon as possible. I'm breathless with excitement and cannot wait to hear more about you and Lottie and your life in New Zealand. I'm thrilled to bits to be back in contact with you and I thank you immensely for finding me and getting in touch. Do give my love to your mother and sister. This is so amazing!

With love and gratitude,

Your grandmother Josie.

There are few lights in Winterborne Slepe. All is quiet except for the sighing of the wind through the trees on the hillside above. The residents have all gone to bed. Except for him. Behind closed curtains he has watched a film on his computer, been on online for a few hours and then written an email. He leans back and reads it through:

> I have little to report on the matter which you contacted me about. I have carried out various discreet and careful searches, but have not yet uncovered anything relevant.
>
> The whole village is aware that the eccentric Josie Cuff has re-established contact with her long-lost grandchildren. She's been going around the village with a radiant face announcing the news to one and all, though why she assumes we're interested in her family saga I cannot imagine. It seems the kids live in a different country from the one where she was searching. I heard it was the teenage grandson who traced her and made contact. I expect the reason she was unable to track them down herself is that

she hasn't got much clue when it comes to the internet and search engines. Everyone knows Josie is disorganised and always loses things, so it doesn't surprise me that she lost her grandchildren ten years ago, although it seems monumentally careless. Of course, when she told me I responded politely and said I was pleased for her.

I don't think this event has any relevance to the enquiries I am making on your behalf but I am going to remain vigilant, listen to any village talk and keep an eye on Josie's correspondence. It might give me some leads. I expect she likes to keep in touch with old friends. For this reason, I propose to make entry to her house again but this time I'll take a look at her computer – she trusts people and is slapdash, so she might not use a password.

He sends it, switches off the computer and goes to bed.

4th April 2013

Dear Tom,

I'm still brimming over with happiness since your extraordinary, unexpected email. Though I was a bundle of nerves until I got your second one in reply to mine. I now understand the situation. I had no idea that your mother knows nothing about your contacting me, and for the present I will keep it between you and me, since you want it that way. I hope you don't mind if I ask why you don't want your mother to find out.

Here is my address: The Haven, Long Lane, Winterborne Slepe, Dorset, England. 'The Haven' is the name of my small cottage which I rent. It's halfway down the main street of the village where I've lived for about three years.

What is your address in New Zealand? I should be so grateful if you would let me have it. I promise not to send any letters to you through the post, since you've asked me not to do this. It's very easy to write emails to each other and I'm happy to do that. Does your sister know that we are in touch?

You mention that your mother remarried, to a farmer called Robert Brown. I'm glad you like your stepfather. Is he an Australian or a New Zealander?

Thank you for asking the name of my second husband – he was called Oliver Cuff. He was in poor health at the time I married him and sadly he died almost six years ago. I'm now on my own again. He was a lovely man who came from Dorset and we discovered we had briefly attended the same primary school.

Where do you go to school? There are so many things I want to ask you but I don't want to deluge you with too many questions. I would so love to have a photograph of you and your sister if you were able to attach one to an email. Not to worry if you can't manage this. I'm happy to wait. Is there anything you'd like to know about me and my family?

I'm puzzled as to how you managed to find me. I haven't used the name Moreno for a while and I know it's a very common surname in Colombia. You are a real sleuth to have managed to track me to my small Dorset haven. I'm impressed.

By the way, do please call me Grandma or Grandma Josie or just plain Josie rather than Mrs Moreno, which is far too formal.

With love and curiosity,

Grandma Josie

12th April 2013

Dear Tom,

Thanks for your email which I received on Wednesday after a gruelling day at work. I replied yesterday but it seems I forgot to send it. I found it still in my draft folder this evening when I got back from work. I work on Tuesdays, Wednesdays and Fridays in another village a few miles away.

I'm so relieved that you sent me your address so that, if for any reason we lose contact by email, I will know where you are. And yes, I promise to contact you only by email. I'm glad you are going to tell your sister that we are in touch. Don't underestimate her – I'm sure she's able to keep a secret.

You say that your mother never talks about your father and is reluctant to answer your questions about him. Perhaps that's a little understandable, as the shock of his early death must have been dreadful. Discussing him may bring back painful memories of that sad time thirteen years ago. I so glad she's found happiness in her second marriage. And I was pleased also to hear that you have a little half-sister called Rebecca, who is known as 'Bex'.

I'm surprised Melissa never mentions me. I find it strange that, when you asked her if she had my address, she said I had broken off contact because I didn't want to have anything to do with you all ever again. Please believe me when I say that this is not true. I never wished for this estrangement and indeed I have spent years trying to find your family and re-establish contact. Clearly there has been some big misunderstanding.

In any case you and I are now in communication and that's simply wonderful. I was fascinated to hear how you managed to trace me. How lucky that you came across a book of English poetry on a bookshelf and saw your father's name inscribed in it. You must have known that you were half Colombian and I was astonished to realise that your mother did not tell you that your surname was originally Moreno. So when you were about five years old you moved to New Zealand and at that time your surname was Jones, which I know was your mother's maiden name, before her marriage to Julian. Then you all took the name Brown when your mother married your stepfather.

What a lot of name changes! But you're not the only one. I too have changed my name three times. My mother was French and my father English and I was born in France. My first name was Josephine Hansford. After my marriage to your grandfather, Raul Moreno, in Colombia, I became Josette Moreno. (Josette is the diminutive of the French name, Josephine.) After he died I returned to live in England, and some years later I remarried and became Josie Cuff. I used to be called Josie when I was at school, so it's a name I feel comfortable with. How unfortunate that Moreno is such a common surname in Colombia! I'm not surprised you didn't have any luck trying to track down other members of your father's family. I'm so glad you then tried to track down any Morenos in England. It was an impulse on my part to put my Colombian name on an article that I wrote five months ago and which was published in a Dorset magazine. I did it because both my husband and son loved poetry and the article was about a poem by a famous English poet called Thomas Hardy, who lived in Dorset. It was the first time I had used 'Josette Moreno' for a long while. I am amazed that you came across it and put two and two together and made seven. I'm in awe of your perseverance.

I understand completely why you want to know about your father Julian. He must be a mysterious figure, if your mother refuses to talk about him. Do you actually remember him? You were three when he died, but Lottie was only six months old and won't recall him at all. He was a good-looking young man – but I expect you know this because no doubt you have seen photographs of him. I should so like to see some photographs of you.

Forgive me, but it's getting late now and I need to feed my cat, Folly, who is mewing in hunger. My stomach is rumbling too. I'm not quite sure what I've got in the fridge to eat but I expect I shall find something edible. I promise in my next email to tell you about your father. And you must promise me to share this with your sister. I mean Lottie of course, not Bex. How old is Bex?

Still lots of questions. And I'm glad that you have questions for me too. I look forward to sharing memories of my son with my grandchildren. But please be patient.

With love and excitement,

Your grandmother Josie

Josie enjoys lunchtime at the pub, with the subdued murmur of conversation punctuated by the occasional ripple of laughter and the clinking of plates, cutlery and glasses. It is a pleasant change from the soothing quietness in her solitary home, from which she sometimes likes to escape to meet people and talk with friends. She looks around her, noticing the pub is fuller than usual.

She is pleased that the Elfords' business has improved. George is a competent chef and is kept busy enough in the kitchen to keep him away from the bar, which is Flora's domain and where she dispenses drinks and friendly chatter. Their new waitress, Lena, darts between kitchen, bar and tables with graceful efficiency and an easy smile that makes her customers feel well looked after and prompts them to tip accordingly.

Josie watches Harry lean across the table and pour her another glass of red wine. "Thank you. The boeuf bourguignon is delicious," she says as she skewers a dripping shallot on her fork and pops it into her mouth. She can see the look of satisfaction on his face as he watches her eating. Josie is hungry – she often is – and savours the novelty of eating food prepared by somebody else. It's kind of him to invite her for a pub lunch as he has until recently been too ill to leave his house.

"It's good to see you looking so well, Harry."

"It's a nice change to take you out for a meal," he says. "I often relied on the food you cooked for me when I was poorly in the autumn. Extraordinarily kind of you."

"No problem. I'm no great cook but I can do plain meals with simple ingredients. It's what I do in my job as a carer, so I've plenty of practice." She does not mention that her larder and fridge are always void of expensive ingredients and choice meat.

"I'm feeling more energetic too – and I'm taking advantage of the spring weather for some walking," Harry tells her. "I was up in the woods above the village last Sunday and I was surprised to run into your neighbour,

Matt Tapper. He had some binoculars with him and told me he was a birdwatcher. He mentioned reported sightings of a bar-tailed godwit, which can fly non-stop further than any other known bird, and he hoped to spot one. It was good to see him opening up about his hobby, because he's normally a very reticent fellow."

"I agree. I've tried hard over the last couple of years to be affable and friendly, since he lives next door, but he's not an easy man to get to know and it's hard to engage him in conversation."

"Naturally we all feel terribly sorry for him because he lost his wife a couple of years back," Harry says as he waves at Lena, who comes over. He orders coffee for them both.

Josie is surprised that he didn't ask her whether she preferred tea, which she does. "I hardly ever saw Ann, who was terminally ill when I arrived in the village. What was she like?"

"Pale and beautiful. Gentle too. But very shy. None of us could see what had attracted her to Matt who, although a nice-looking chap, is somebody without any smooth edges. I find him socially inept. He looks awkward and he makes you feel awkward. Not an easy man to chat to - which was why I was surprised when he told me about his hobby. Now I come to think of it, he has some of the compulsive behaviour that twitchers seem to have. He was obsessive about his wife too. His over-protective behaviour during her illness raised a few eyebrows." Harry frowns. "He didn't encourage anyone to visit her."

"He must have been devastated when she died of breast cancer. I gather she was only in her thirties."

"Tragic to die so young. But cancer is no respecter of age. You've told me that your second husband also died of cancer. He was a Dorset man, I understand?"

"Yes, but Oliver was nearly sixty when he died. We had only five years together and he was ill with cancer for most of that time. I still miss his courageous sense of humour."

"What happened to your first marriage? Did it end in divorce?"

Josie feels a strange disinclination to talk about Raul to Harry. With a mental shrug she banishes her reluctance. "My first husband was Colombian. We married young and had twenty wonderful years together. He loved sailing and was lost at sea. Our only son died at the age of twenty-seven. He was married and had two small children in Australia." It's safer to give the basic facts.

"I assume they were the grandchildren with whom you lost touch and are now back in contact. I'm delighted for you."

Josie nods. "It's the best thing that's happened to me in a long while. A wonderful Easter present – I'm a very happy bunny."

Lena arrives with the coffee. She gives them a beaming smile and asks them if they have enjoyed their meal. Her dark hair is tied back neatly behind her head and Josie thinks her a delightful hard-working young woman.

They see James Trevett enter the pub and walk across to the bar. He sits on a stool, and Flora serves him a pint of beer. James is a young man who owns a fine house and land. He is clearly a 'good catch' but doesn't seem to have a steady girlfriend. He turns on his stool and surveys the others in the pub. It becomes clear to them both that he is watching Lena as she flits around the dining tables. Harry raises his eyebrows and Josie smiles in complicity.

Half an hour later they are still at the table, discussing the former prime minister, Margaret Thatcher, who has died of a stroke a week earlier on 8th April. Harry has been singing her praises but Josie is not a fan.

"You must admit, Harry, that she was impossibly autocratic. An impressive lady, I grant you, but arrogant, with a hectoring style in parliamentary debates. However, I was living in Colombia in the 1970s and 80s so I was less affected by her disastrous policies."

"You're misguided. I considered her a superb politician. I was appalled when I heard there had been street parties in some towns to celebrate her death. How tasteless and cruel! So was a song I heard on the radio, a parody from *The Wizard of Oz*: 'Ding dong! The Witch is Dead'. Whatever is this country coming to?"

Josie manages to suppress a smile. "Oliver admired Maggie too and in fact I've got his copy of a biography of Margaret Thatcher on my bookshelf. I'll give it to you, if you don't have it already."

"Thanks so much. I don't get to bookshops much these days and I've read almost everything on my shelves. Perhaps I could come over sometime and have a look through your books, if you don't mind my borrowing the odd one."

"I'm fine about lending my books. But I warn you

my shelves are crammed full. Very disorganised – like most things in my life." She shrugs and makes a mock-apologetic face, hoping that Harry does not detect, in her honest self-criticism, a hint of worry about her inability to keep things under control.

On their way back up the lane towards their respective houses they pass Alice Diffey out for her Sunday afternoon walk. She greets them with a coy knowing smirk, which sets Josie's teeth on edge. Rumours of village intrigues emanate from Alice like bad smells.

21st April 2013

Dear Tom,

Thank you so much for your email yesterday and the photograph attached of you and Lottie taken last Christmas on holiday in Milford Sound, which looks to be a glorious place. I have been reading lots about New Zealand and it seems that South Island, where you live, is particularly beautiful and remote. You appear to live quite far from any major town.

The photograph is wonderful but you and Lottie have changed so much – from toddlers to teenagers – that I hardly recognise you. You are quite tall and have dark hair like your father. I can't see the colour of your eyes but they seem to be dark too. I see that Lottie has fair hair like her mother, but she has a look of Julian's aunt Natalia, who is Raul's sister. Natalia lives, of course, in Colombia and she and I have kept in touch over the years. She works as head teacher of a school which was set up by the local Catholic church, and many children attend from the orphanage where Natalia used to work. I'm very fond of her. I hope you don't mind that I've told her about being back in touch with you. She adored her nephew and will be very pleased to know that his children are safe and well and living in New Zealand. She has no other close relatives.

I attach the photograph of myself taken a couple of years ago in a friend's garden. I look a bit windswept but then my hair always looks a bit wild and woolly. I've hardly any recollection of my own early childhood so I don't expect you to remember me. Do you have any memories of your father? I'm surprised that you have only seen two photographs of him. Although over the years I have mislaid most of my photographs, I will try to dig out a couple and get them scanned by a friend to send to you. Julian was a handsome young man though he was less flamboyant than his father. When young he was quite shy. He often had a rather serious expression on his face, particularly when he was concentrating on something or studying for exams. He had a habit of stroking his right eyebrow and frowning when he had a problem. But when he smiled the look in his eyes softened and it was like the sun appearing from behind a cloud.

I promised I'd tell you about your father. You also asked about my family and your father's Colombian family, so I think I'll start with a bit of background history.

I was born in Paris in France in 1952. My mother was French and my father English. His name was Miles Hansford and she was called Marguerite. He was a diplomat and when I was young we lived abroad in the various countries to which he was posted. We often stayed in Dorset when we came home to England on leave, because this was where my father had grown up.

It was whilst my father was working at the embassy in Colombia in South America that I met Raul Moreno and fell in love. I already spoke Spanish. I was only twenty-one when we married and at first we lived in Bogota near Raul's parents, Juan Carlos and Paola. Later we moved to Barranquilla on the coast where Raul landed a good job in the shipping business. This was where your father was born and where he went to primary school. Later we returned to live in the capital, Bogota, and his Colombian grandparents paid for him to go to an excellent Catholic school in the city.

After he left school, he went to Australia to study where he met your mother, who was a student at the same university in Western Australia. They were married in 1996 and I flew out for the wedding. When you and Lottie were born, I came out to Australia to see you both and stayed with your family for a few weeks on each occasion. I adored getting to know my grandchildren. I was then living in England and the airfares were quite expensive or I would have come more often.

After your father's sudden death whilst on a visit to Colombia, I came to Australia to visit you and your mother. It was a sad occasion and your mum was very distressed. After my return to England, I continued to write to Melissa, though she rarely responded. It was around 2002 when a letter was returned to me, as undeliverable – this may have been the time you all went to live in New Zealand. Your mum's parents, Mr and Mrs Jones, moved soon afterwards, so there was nobody to ask where you were. You can imagine how desperate I felt and how hard I searched for you. At last we are back in contact and reunited. What a blessing!

It's Saturday today and I'm going to help a friend plant seeds in her vegetable patch. Later I plan to go for a walk in between the rain showers. I may ask Harry to come with me – he's dropping by after lunch to return a book he borrowed. I feel sorry for him since he is somewhat frail and less active than he would like to be. Do you play sport at the weekends? If so, what games do you play?

I keep forgetting that although it's spring here, it's autumn where you are. You mentioned that your school term has ended so I hope you have a good break.

I always like weekends and the prospect of three days off before I go back to work on Tuesday. I do twelve hour shifts on three days a week caring for an elderly couple, who are infirm and unwell. I'm really fond of both of them because, in the midst of all their problems, they manage to smile and think positively. Like them I try to be optimistic so that, even when I feel wistful and lonely, I can always find something good and beautiful to be thankful for. We should hang onto hope and remember that nothing is more important than love.

I expect Melissa has told you about the day you were born – an event always embedded in the mind of a mother. In my next email I will tell you about the extraordinary day in 1974 when, during a horrendous storm, your father was born.

Please give my love to Lottie. I do hope you are showing her these emails.

With love and hope,
Grandma Josie

The cottage is silent and passively accepts his presence. He has reached the doorway to the front room and looks around. His heart seems to be knocking on his chest. The clock on the mantelpiece, however, has stopped - probably because Josie never remembers to get a new battery for it. There is a faint floral smell in the air - it cannot emanate from the dead flowers in a vase on a small table - so it must be some perfume she wears.

There are some dust motes twirling round, generated from the slight draught caused by his illicit entry through the rear door, which as usual Josie has left unlocked.

There are no net curtains so he has to be careful when he moves to the table she uses as a desk in front of the window, as he might be visible from the road. He glances up and down the lane and sees no one. It is the middle of the day on a Tuesday and the village is quiet. Josie is out at work several miles away. He looks quickly through the piles of paperwork on her desk. He comes across an air letter with a South American stamp, glances at it and sees that it is written in Spanish. He pockets it so he can get it translated and return it - on a later visit. She'll never miss it - or she might think she's mislaid it. The woman is so untidy.

He crouches down in front of the table to check the box file on the floor, as he did the last time. He knows he's not visible through the window when he does this. But it seems that she has not opened it since the last time he looked - quite possibly she never puts things in it any more. It's covered in dust. He straightens up and glances out of the window. No one. There is a green light at the bottom right-hand corner of the monitor on her desk, which probably means she has left the computer on - again. He knows her password but he rarely needs it. He sits on her chair and quickly forwards her emails to his own computer, and then erases all trace of having done so.

He is about to leave when he hears a clunking sound from the kitchen and, in a moment of panic, thinks the owner of the house has returned early. He turns slowly, mind racing with excuses and apologies. His body sags with relief. It is Josie's dratted cat who slips into the room, having come in through the cat flap in the back door. The animal jumps up onto a chair, from where it sits like an inquisitor fixing him with an accusing stare.

He was going to check along the bookshelves, where Josie often puts little memos and notes, but he is slightly unnerved by the cat's unwavering yellow eyes. He can hear a car coming down the road so he swiftly moves out of the room and out of sight. Checking the rear gardens for movement, he exits and slips down the garden and through the broken fence at the rear. It was easy – he's getting better at this.

10th May 2013

Dear Tom,

Your email arrived on 8th May which happened to be my birthday. It was good to hear that you think you do remember me when I came to Australia. You were three and I remember reading you stories whilst your mother was trying to get Lottie down for the night. She was only a baby and I recall she had colic and cried a lot. But then all of us cried buckets at that time, because we missed Julian so much.

On Saturday, as a birthday treat, a friend took me out to the cinema in the local town, and yesterday was a glorious spring day, crisp but sunny so I went for a long walk after church. Today I'm at home as I don't work on Mondays, so now I've time to write and start telling you more about your father.

Your father was born on 13th August in 1974. Raul, and I were living in Barranquilla, a lovely place on the Caribbean coast about ten degrees north of the Equator. August is the warmest month but also one of the rainiest. Raul was working as usual and, heavily pregnant, I waddled around at home, feeling tired and nervous. When I went into labour a neighbour drove me to the hospital. It was extremely windy, because a tropical storm, named Alma, had hit Venezuela the day before where it had caused landslides but, although it had abated before arriving in northern Colombia, there was heavy rainfall.

These days men are encouraged to be with their wives when they give birth. I expect your stepfather was with Melissa when she had Rebecca. (I'm not sure I like the nickname 'Bex'!) Back in the 1970s in South America, it was the custom for the husband to come to the hospital, wait whilst the wife gave birth and then come in to see wife and baby afterwards. I had telephoned my husband's office and left a message for him. During the day, I kept asking the nurses if Raul had arrived, but he had not. Later that afternoon, the skies darkened, thunder growled and torrential rain deluged the city. I was having a turbulent afternoon too, with my own waters breaking and a quick transition into the final stages of labour. Still Raul did not come. In the midst of painful contractions, I asked the midwife to get an urgent message to him to say the birth was imminent. The storm raged outside and I raved inside at my husband's absence.

As Raul told me later, he had left his car at the office and was at a warehouse in the port when he was summoned by his secretary. In the downpour there were no taxis and as the hospital was closer than his car, he set off at a run through the flooded streets, arriving at the maternity unit about five minutes before I gave birth. The nurses summoned him in a few minutes afterwards and he dashed in soaked to the skin and hugged me. He picked up our son, who got wet and began to wail. A nurse hastily grabbed the baby and gave him back to me. I felt unbelievably happy, and when the sun eventually broke through the dark thunderous clouds, everything was covered in a golden glow.

We named your father 'Julian' because this was a Colombian name as well as an English name and similar to the French name 'Julien'. His second name was to be Carlos, after his Colombian grandfather, Juan Carlos, who was delighted to have another boy in the family.

I had given up my job but I was happy to be at home with my son. But my angelic baby soon grew up and became a demanding little toddler. He was curious and adventurous and liked to explore. He enjoyed putting things into holes, such as pencils into electric plugs, and he pulled things out of cupboards, grabbed keys and money out of my bag and ran off with them. He liked to wander off and hide from me, which turned into a game of hide and seek. A frightening episode happened when Julian was less than two years old. It was a Sunday morning, when we were all in our bedroom upstairs, I had turned on the hot water tap of the bath in an adjacent bathroom and gone back briefly into the bedroom. Julian wandered into the bathroom and pushed the door closed, managing to shoot the bolt and lock himself in. When I returned a couple of minutes later to add the cold water to the hot and have my bath, he was already trying to push the door open and finding he couldn't get out. I tried to explain to him that what he had to do was to push the bolt back, but the more panicky I became the more distraught he got, crying and hammering with his little fists on the other side of the door. I realised the hot water would soon start to spill over the edge of the bath tub and Julian might burn his feet or slip and hurt himself. Not to mention the problem of the water flooding the floor and the room below! Raul soon realised he would have to break the door down. This was more difficult than we thought so Raul ran downstairs to the toolbox and found an axe. Julian had been shrieking in panic but was now whimpering. I tried to keep my voice steady as I called to Julian to stand back away from the door as his father swung the axe and hacked a hole through the panel, so we could rescue our little son, turn off the tap and mop up the water.

We never teased Julian about this mishap. This was because, when I was about seven, I was with my parents standing on a railway station platform in England, waiting for a train. I had asked to go to the toilet and my mother had given me a penny, which was to put into a slot so that I could get inside the cubicle. Unfortunately, when I wanted to leave, I was unable to open the door and started crying because I thought the train with my parents would leave without me. My mother found me in time, but for years afterwards I was teased about it and my brother used to jeer at me and sing,

"O dear what can the matter be? Dear, dear what can the matter be?

Poor little Josie got locked in the lavatory. And nobody knew she was there!"

I hated them laughing about something which had frightened me so badly.

That's enough memories for the moment – more about your father's life in my next email. Now about you and your sister: I'm glad to hear you play rugger – and of course I've heard of the All Blacks. There was a time when I used to go to rugby matches and I still like to watch the occasional match on the TV in our local pub. What other sport or activities do you do? I'm pleased that Lottie plays netball – I used to do that at school but was never very good, in spite of being quite tall. You don't say much about your sister – I'd like to know more. Is there any way she can use your laptop and email me herself? Just an idea.

Our pub is called the Anchor and is at the lower end of Long Lane and is run by a couple called George and Flora Elford. She works in the bar and he does the cooking, and there's a Polish girl called Lena who is the waitress. She is a breath of fresh air in our village, which has few newcomers and rarely one as pretty and as lively as Lena. Business has picked up because George produces good pub food and because Lena serves customers with a smile. Some of the younger men in the village have been trying to get to know her better, as the saying goes, but she remains breezily aloof. My landlord, to whom I pay rent for my cottage, is called James. A single man in his thirties, he has been going to the pub more often and trying to chat to Lena who is busy serving meals. But he has a rival, who happens to be my neighbour, Matt Tapper. I'm quite surprised about this because his lovely wife Ann died a couple of years ago and since then, he has been very solitary and does not socialise with the other villagers. We have all tried to be friendly, but he keeps himself to himself. Now and then he goes into the pub for a pint of beer and sits there watching everyone and doesn't engage in conversation that much. But it seems he has taken a shine to Lena, and is now exhibiting signs of jealousy and anger towards James, whom he thinks is making better headway with the girl than he is. It is clear to the rest of us that Lena is not really interested in either of them. The villagers watch the drama with amusement.

This is a mammoth email so I'll end now. I hope you don't mind if I just sign off as 'Josie'. The title 'grandma' makes me feel proud to have grandchildren, but it also makes me feel a bit old. And I don't feel old at all. It occurs to me that you might prefer me to sign off with initials if you want to conceal the name of the sender of the email. I could sign off with GMJ for GrandMa Josie. Let me know.

    With love and secrecy,

    Josie

Walking down the lane towards her house, Josie sees Alice Diffey standing outside the Stickleys' cottage talking to Louise, who is holding a broom. She's surprised because Lou does not care for Alice and tends to avoid her. Alice is aware of this but it does not deter her from telling Lou titbits of village news when they happen to meet. When Josie is about thirty yards away, Alice finishes her chat and walks off.

Lou sees her neighbour returning and walks towards her. "Hi, Josie. Weather's getting warmer. Had a nice walk? I was sweepin' the front path when Alice saw me and came over with some interestin' news."

Josie, reluctant to listen to malicious village gossip, does not respond.

"It seems that our landlord has applied for planning permission to put up a wind generator. One of them tall white jobs with turnin' blades."

Josie is puzzled. "I cannot imagine why George would want to get involved with wind power."

"Not the pub landlord. Not George. I mean Mr Trevett, who owns our cottages. It seems ee wants to put it up in the top field on the 'ill behind us. Alice says they're noisy nasty things and we should all oppose it."

"I suggest we wait until we get more information and see what's proposed. There'll be plenty of time for villagers to put in questions and objections." Josie is dismayed but won't show it.

"Alice says that if we let 'im put one up, before we knows it, there'll be a wind farm with lots dotted all over our 'ills."

Josie sighs. "I think that's scaremongering. We need to see what the planning application actually says. That's not too difficult – the local council will have all the details available."

"I expect Harry will 'ave them already. Alice told me that ee's dead against it. I expect my Bill won't object, seein' as ee works for Mr James and won't go against 'is boss. I expect I'll be told about it when ee gets back from work. Anyhow, must go in and get 'is tea ready. Bye, Josie." Flora walks back to her cottage.

Josie enters her house through the back door and as she throws the keys down on the kitchen worktop the telephone starts to ring in the front room. She goes through to answer it.

"Is that you, Josie? Are you alone?" It's John's wife and she sounds anxious.

"Hi, Maggie. Yes, I'm on my own. As usual. Did you get my message?" Josie had left a phone message a few days before, saying that John had been asking if she knew where Maggie was.

"That's why I rang. You mentioned that John had been trying to find out if you knew where I was. That's not allowed! He knows he has to communicate with me through my solicitor regarding the divorce."

"Keep calm, Maggie. John was fishing for information but I didn't tell him where you are. And I gave him no hint that I knew. And I didn't say that we're in touch by telephone either."

"The latest development is that he's told his solicitor, who told mine, that he believes I'm in a relationship with another man. I'm furious."

Overcoming the inclination to ask if she is, Josie says, "That's a bit much, since you left him because of his infidelities."

"And his physical abuse." Maggie sounds angry. She has already told Josie that John had treated her badly in the months before she finally left him. "I couldn't stay in the house any longer."

Josie is reluctant to stoke Maggie's injured feelings but feels she must put her friend in the picture. "You ought to know that during the past month John has been insinuating that you were the one who'd been having an affair, and it was the reason you left him and not the other way round."

"How dare he spread rumours like that! I'll tell my solicitor."

"John is probably trying to get some leverage in the divorce proceedings by shifting some of the blame for the break-up of your marriage onto you."

"That's the sort of underhand tactics he would adopt. Thanks for warning me, Josie. You're a good friend."

By now, Josie is distinctly uncomfortable. She is not

quite certain whether she is entirely in Maggie's camp. Initially, when Maggie told her about John's treatment of her, she was outraged and all her feminine sympathies were aroused, but now she is not so sure. John is a large man but he does not seem aggressive. Who knows where the truth lies? She is certainly not going to ask John. She had lunch at his house over Easter and is affable with him when they meet. She does not want to take sides. The divorce is something the couple will have to work out between themselves and their solicitors. But she does know where Maggie is living and feels obliged to conceal this from John.

She says awkwardly, "Take care and good luck with the divorce. It's always upsetting."

"Too right. Must go. Bye." Maggie is always abrupt with her goodbyes.

As she replaces the receiver, Josie wonders if Maggie is on her own. Which one of them is lying? Or maybe they both are. She does not want either of them to think that she will help them shop the other. She must gently retreat from their confidences. Why is it that married people try to enlist her sympathies and think she is willing to listen to all their troubles? The assumption is that, because she is on her own, she does not have any relationship problems. Since she has no members of her family in the world's northern hemisphere, that is a fair assumption, but she has other mundane but more pressing concerns. How is she going to pay this month's rent? And is there anything in her fridge to eat for supper?

But first she wants to see if Tom has emailed her. He

is a teenager so his emails are brief and arrive at irregular intervals. But at least they are in contact. She is worried that he may not have told Lottie about their clandestine correspondence. She aches to be in touch with her granddaughter too.

20th June 2013

Dear TMB,

Thanks for your email which you sent on Sunday. I went into the local town this morning to do some shopping. I managed to get a friend of mine to scan a couple of photographs on her office scanner and I attach them. One is of your father taken when he was about nine and he is wearing roller skates. This is a popular activity in Colombia and Julian loved roller-skating with his friends. Later on he was keen on football – and played for the school team. Football is the most widely played team sport but rugger is far less popular, though they do have a national team in Colombia. Cycling is also a national craze. The other photo of your father was taken when he was very small – I believe he was two at the time – which was taken at Raul's parents' house. Juan Carlos adored his grandson and he and Julian would spend hours on the patio or in the living room playing games and swopping stories. Grandparents and grandchildren can have special times together, but I have missed that rapport with you and your sister so I hope you have developed a close relationship with your mother's parents.

You said you had looked up the tropical storm Alma on the internet and had found a map tracking it for the dates around your father's birth. How enterprising! I'd no idea that one could look up details of past storms and hurricanes. You will no doubt have seen on the map that Barranquilla is not far from the border with Venezuela where Alma unloaded lots of rain and finally blew itself out.

You mentioned about being accidentally shut in a schoolroom with the door locked. That must've been scary. Being locked in a room is almost as bad as getting lost outside in lonely places or in the midst of a crowd. Your father, when he was about nine, managed to get separated from us during the Barranquilla Carnival with masses of floats, music and dancers. One of the biggest carnivals in the world, it runs for four days and the entire city is swamped with thousands of visitors. It can be wildly exciting but, for some of the children, a little overwhelming. Julian used to love watching the day-time parades, but that year he ran off to look at some dancers who were juggling and I lost sight of him in the huge jostling crowds. For one of the worst hours of my life, Raul and I searched for him – we were utterly distraught because some people who come to this Carnival are not very trustworthy. I was terrified he might be harmed but we finally found him in a café, with a family who had seen him on the road running in and out of the procession of dancers. He was very distressed and in tears when they rescued him, but calmed down when they told him they would locate his parents. After that experience he never liked being in the midst of huge crowds.

Being separated from those we love makes us feel so vulnerable. I was worried to hear that Lottie likes to wander off on her own round the farm, but assume she knows how to take care of herself. How much land do you have? Does your stepfather have a lot of sheep? A huge amount of New Zealand lamb is sold in the UK though I rarely eat it. Do you ride horses too? In his teens your father became keen on riding and went on trekking holidays on horseback.

Tomorrow is 21st June and the longest day of the year, and it is strange to think that it will be the shortest day for you in New Zealand. The weather here is set fine, which is good because on Saturday we have our annual village Midsummer fete. It's always good fun, and takes place at the end of the village near the pub and the pond. Last year we had a very entertaining incident when one of my neighbours was thrown into the duck pond by an angry young man. It wasn't much fun for John who got very wet but it made us all giggle. I was surprised that he didn't retaliate or try to pick a fight with the guy who did it. He just stomped home to dry off. Usually he's a friendly man but recently he's become more secretive – this may be because he is going through a difficult divorce. His wife left him about a year ago. I don't think anybody will end up in the duck pond this year, but you never know! James Trevett, the gentleman who owns most of the land round here, has put in plans to erect a tall wind generator on his field overlooking the village. Many residents are horrified and Harry is quivering with anger. Perhaps James should be warned, if he decides to attend the fete, not to walk too near the pond or set the ducks quacking!

So you were both given mobiles though Lottie got hers only recently. I don't have a mobile phone – only a landline. Good to hear that Lottie loves reading books – but I expect the mobile encourages her to spend more time texting or talking to her friends. I understand why you don't want her to borrow your laptop, but she must have access to computers at school – unless they're only to be used for schoolwork. I would so love to hear from Lottie. Please tell her that I think about her and send her my love. Does she have any messages for me?

Thank you for explaining that you don't normally use email for keeping in touch with your friends and always contact them on Facebook or other social media. I am touched that you set up an email account in order to write to me, though I think you will find it useful for other communications.

I was interested to hear that you have learnt about acronyms in a lesson at school. Not all initials are necessarily acronyms. However, as you signed off your last email with 'TMB (Tom Moreno Brown)', I shall reciprocate.

Love and Laughter (LAL) from,

GMJ   BFN (Bye for Now)   KIT (Keep in Touch)

Silent observation comes naturally to him. He finds it hard to talk with people when his motive is to elicit information. He prefers to be economical with words and it takes an effort to engage in casual conversation. He can glean a little from what people look like, but much more from what they say. This village is awash with gossip. Certain residents enjoy passing on titbits about other people's business to anyone who will listen. All that is required is a prompt in the right direction and the floodgates open.

Only yesterday, by casually mentioning to Lou Stickley that he heard the pub was now doing much better, he was regaled with the story about how George Elford bought an old croquet set at the local auction for more money than it was worth, and how his wife was furious because they have no flat expanse of grass on which locals could play. Lou giggled as she told him that Flora Elford had threatened to hit her husband over the head with a mallet but Josie, who happened to be in the pub, managed to calm things down and Lena arrived for work and had them all laughing within minutes. At the end of Lou's story, he smiled but didn't give any comment on the Elfords, Josie or Lena, though he admires the beautiful Polish girl and enjoys her funny stories. When the pub is less busy, he likes talking with her. Flora often chats with Lena too, and Flora is a good friend of Josie's.

What he needs to find out is information about Josie's real financial situation and who she is in contact with.

As she sips her tea Josie looks around her. Everything in Doris's small kitchen is clean and tidy. The work surfaces are empty of clutter apart from a breadboard and a kettle. A single shelf displays Doris's collection of pottery jugs. The cooker is shiny and sleek, unlike hers with blackened food burnt on to the gas rings. Everything here is put away in drawers and she can see sparkling glasses and floral crockery through the glazed window of a wall cupboard. How do people manage it?

Josie knows that Doris banishes books and newspapers to the sitting room, but even there they are marshalled with precision into a bookshelf and a magazine rack. The cushions on the chair and small sofa are all plumped up - a far cry from her saggy furniture - and the remote control for the television will be placed at right angles to the coffee table edges. The only similarity is that they both will have a bunch of flowers in the room, though Doris arranges hers carefully in a vase, whereas Josie just jams them in and lets them be 'natural'. This is an excuse; the truth is that she chooses to give no time to 'enhancing' flowers and disparages attempts to 'gild' creation. She has the same philosophy when it comes to weeding flower beds and pruning.

Yet in spite of the differences in their homes and attitude to possessions, the two women have a lot in common. It has taken a while to get to know Doris Bugler, who is a retired nurse with a slightly starchy set to her broad face. She wears good quality sensible clothes and is fastidious about cleanliness. Some of the villagers say she is reserved whilst others think her unfriendly but they are all agreed that she is an honest woman who keeps her opinions to herself. Some men refer to her as an elderly spinster, which irritates Josie, who remembers Doris telling her on one occasion that that she "never had time for a husband" and on another, "God didn't choose to send me a husband and I didn't choose to seek one."

Josie is often outspoken and their friendship has dissolved Doris's reticence. Although Doris tells the unvarnished truth, she never voices any criticism of the way her friend lives. For this Josie is very grateful, as she is weary of certain people in the village who seem to think that Josie's precarious and disorganised way of life is something reprehensible, about which they have the right to comment and offer advice.

Others may think Doris prim and fussy but Josie knows that, underneath her austere demeanour, there is a keen intelligence and a compassionate heart. Doris is one of the kindest women she has ever met. Essentially, they both have the same aim – to help other people or as her friend puts it, "to serve humanity". They have different personalities and different ways of achieving what they believe they must do, but there is a real sisterhood in their common endeavour. And they both share a deep faith.

They live in a rural English village where it has long been the custom to be reticent about one's faith. This tradition says that it's alright to go quietly to church and it's acceptable to pray in private, but one really must not flaunt one's spirituality in public or discuss one's religious beliefs with others. Neither of them approves of this attitude but, in order to live in a small village without offending others, Doris complies to the extent that she does not talk about her faith unless invited to do so. Josie is less conformist and knows that she has surprised and alienated a few people by her embarrassing habit of being outspoken about her core values and beliefs.

She does not like secrecy but she is involved in keeping secret something that is very important to her. This is what she is discussing with Doris, seated at the latter's tiny but pristine kitchen table.

"My grandson and I have been exchanging emails for over three months which I'm thrilled about, but I'm concerned about two things. Firstly, Tom is adamant that he doesn't want his mother to know that he and I are in touch. My daughter-in-law Melissa severed all communication with me over ten years ago and took active steps to ensure that I was unable to trace them.

"Why was that?" asks Doris, sympathy in her calm brown eyes.

"It may be because she was jealous of the very close relationship I had with my son. Julian kept in good touch with me - and this annoyed Melissa."

"Jealousy between a mother-in-law and a daughter-in-law is not uncommon."

"I know that. Tom seems to be aware of Melissa's animosity towards me and, like all teenagers, doesn't want a confrontation with his mother, so he'd rather not mention it to her. Perhaps he puzzles over what caused the estrangement. Obviously, he loves his mother - all kids do - even if he doesn't always agree with her. He may have heard her side of the story and now he wants to hear mine."

"Then he can make up his own mind."

"Precisely. Meanwhile, I'm wondering whether it's in some way unethical for me to carry on this correspondence in secret, and whether I should be trying to persuade him to inform his mother about it."

"How old did you say he is?" Doris pours them both a second cup of tea from an elegant teapot.

"Seventeen later this month. He's communicative for a teenager - though he's obviously an active boy too - keen on rugger. He made it plain right from the start that he didn't want to upset his mother by revealing that he has managed to track me down. Do you think I should continue to respect his wish to keep our emails a secret?"

"For the time being. If you felt this was causing him problems, then I think you would be obliged to tell his mother. What about his sister?"

"Lottie. That's another thing I'm concerned about. I've sent messages to her via Tom, and asked him to show my emails to her but, although he's implied that he will, I'm unsure that he really has."

"Why do you think that?" says Doris as she puts down her bone china teacup carefully on its saucer.

"Tom's worried Lottie is not able to keep a secret. She doesn't have her own laptop and he doesn't let her use his. He may be proud of his coup in having found me and doesn't want to threaten his secret by sharing it with a younger sister. Teenage boys can be quite selfish."

"Doesn't he realise that you must be keen to know more about your granddaughter?"

"I told him a few times that I'd love to hear from her. But so far I've no confirmation she's even in the picture."

"Josie, I think you must insist that he share his new-found grandmother with his sister. Tell him that it's selfish not to give her the pleasure of knowing you and what you have to say about their father."

"Tom gave me their address but made me promise not to use the post, so I can't write to her."

"You told me they have a stepfather. Perhaps you ought to be prepared for the possibility that she considers him as her daddy and might not be interested in hearing about someone who died when she was a baby."

"True." Josie frowns. "She probably has a close relationship with her stepfather and feels loyal to him."

"All this is speculation. You should insist that Tom tells Lottie about you, and let her decide whether she wants to make contact. She may not want to disobey her parents."

"Obviously I don't want to undermine her relationship with Melissa." Josie glances at her watch, gulps the rest of her tea and gets to her feet. "I've lost track of time. I must go."

Doris gives Josie an enquiring look. "Why do I get the feeling that the antipathy Melissa feels for you is not one-sided?"

"How astute you are!" Josie gives a wry smile. "I'd best keep my opinion of Melissa to myself. It's possible that she may have changed for the better." She does not add that she thinks this unlikely. Does a leopard change its spots? Does an obsessional control freak become tolerant and relaxed?

She scoops up her bag. "Thanks so much for the tea and the chat. See you soon."

24th July 2013

Dear Tom and Lottie,

When I received your email a couple of days ago, I was thrilled to hear from my granddaughter for the first time. I was very pleased that each of you wrote half.

Lottie, thank you for telling me about your stepfather, the farm and the Romney variety of sheep. I understand there are lots of sheep farms in the Canterbury region where you live. How big a flock do you have? Perhaps some of your sheep are sold for export and end up in England where we eat a lot of New Zealand lamb. Tom has told me that you like to ride and that the farm has horses. Where do you ride? I'd love to hear more from you.

Thanks, Tom, for letting Lottie use your laptop. So glad

you had an enjoyable 17th birthday last week, and, as it fell on a Saturday, you were able to have lots of friends with you.

I was concerned to hear about the earthquake in Cook Strait a few days ago which affected Wellington, and I'm so glad it wasn't felt in your region in South Island. We all remember the severe earthquake in Christchurch three years ago which caused a huge amount of damage to the cathedral and the city. I'm thankful we don't have them here. A week ago, we had a severe heatwave which is rare in England. Outside in the garden I drooped like a wilting flower and inside the cottage the heat made me want to lie down. Earthquakes are very different – you need to get up and run outside. I love walking and feeling the earth solid beneath my feet and I would find it horrific to have the ground swaying and rippling. Colombia, where I lived for nearly thirty years, lies on the Pacific Ring of Fire and has earthquakes. Probably one of the worst earthquakes in Colombia in recent years was in 1999 in Armenia, a city in the centre of the country's coffee growing region. Thousands of coffee farms were ruined and the quake toppled tower blocks, hotels, and historic churches in Armenia. But within fifteen years the city was rebuilt. Luckily, I was living in England at the time and you and your parents were in Australia.

Twenty years earlier in 1979 I was in living in Colombia during one of the most violent earthquakes in the history of the country, which had its epicentre just offshore near the port to Tumarco. Your father was five years old and Raul and I happened to be staying with his parents in their home in Bogota, the capital. It happened in the middle of the night and was felt throughout the country. I remember being jolted awake by the shuddering in our bedroom. Raul switched on the light and we saw the hanging overhead light swaying. We jumped out of bed, grabbed Julian who was crying and were running downstairs with Raul's parents when the shaking subsided. We all went out into the garden and, trembling with fear, waited for after-shocks. I remember thinking how fragile life was – one minute we were asleep and secure in bed and the next minute the whole house was rocking about us. One's confidence in a calm benign world is shaken to the core. But we were lucky – Bogota was little affected compared with Tumarco where many buildings fell down and lots of people died. Perhaps the worst thing was that there was a dreadful tsunami with a tidal wave of over five metres which destroyed villages along the coast and washed houses away. For several years afterwards, Julian was terrified of being caught in another earthquake.

Thank you for telling me about Midwinter Carnival in Dunedin, further south than you. The carnival procession sounds wonderful with its hundreds of exotic hand-crafted lanterns, some of them gigantic. I still find it hard to get my head around the fact that I'm enjoying summer here whilst you have winter in New Zealand. Does it snow much in the southern part of South Island? Here our Midsummer fete was lucky to have warm dry weather. This year we had an excellent band and we all ended up dancing beside the pond. I'm amazed that nobody fell in.

When does your holiday end and the next term start? In England the school year ends in July after which there is a long summer holiday. In Colombia, your father used to attend a private college, where the school year started in September and finished in June. Confusingly, there was a different calendar for state schools including the primary school that he attended in Barranquilla, which started in January and finished in November.

We don't have a primary school in Winterborne Slepe, which is a shame as I love to hear the sound of children playing at break time. Younger children attend school in a village only a few miles away, whereas older children are collected from the village in a bus and driven to the secondary school in the local town. How far is it from your home to your school? As you live on a farm it's probably some miles away. Does Mummy drive you there daily? Do tell me a little bit about your school and your friends. And about Bex, your half-sister – what is she like? There's still so much that I don't know about you and your life in New Zealand. Do send me some more photographs – I'd love a family shot of all five of you.

With love from midsummer to midwinter,

From GMJ xxx

The clear morning sunlight filters through the foliage as a breeze rustles the leaves. The sky is an unblemished blue though the air is still cool. Later the day will become very warm, so Josie has decided that now is the best time for a walk. After the exertion of climbing the hill behind her cottage, she is now ambling through the wood at the top. She watches herself pass in and out of shadow as she moves along beneath the trees, singing to herself. She is so absorbed with the quivering patches of light and shade and with her melody that she is taken by surprise with the discovery that she is not alone. She hears footsteps on the path behind her and stops, disappointed that her solitude is about to be broken. She turns with a smile on her face and the sun in her eyes so it takes a few seconds before she registers the identity of the other person with whom she is sharing this particular patch of woodland. It is Matt Tapper. Her spirits sag.

"Hi, Matt." She waits while he catches up with her.

He's wearing his usual baggy army trousers, a green wax jacket round which hang his binoculars, and as usual, there is a faint sour and unwashed smell emanating from him. "Lovely day," she says brightly.

"Not bad."

She recalls that he often takes Sunday walks to go birdwatching. "Seen anything unusual?"

"Not yet."

Making conversation with Matt is like wading through treacle. She searches her head for another topic. "Do you think the field beyond this edge of the wood is where the proposed wind turbine is going to be sited?" Surely the man has heard about this.

"It might be. Doesn't really concern me."

He starts to walk on and she feels obliged to accompany him. She doesn't want to seem unfriendly, even though she is certain he would also rather be on his own, and says, "I'm not that bothered about it either but I won't admit that to some of the villagers, who seem up in arms about the plan. I've always thought using wind power is a modern, clean method of making electricity."

"Wind turbines are noisy."

"True. But I don't think they're as unsightly as people say. Coal and nuclear-powered generating plants are ugly and produce unpleasant emissions and waste. A tall white tower with the wind vanes lazily turning is not so very bad."

"S'pose not – if you don't have to live under it."

They have reached the fence round the field in question. "I'm going this way," she says.

As she predicted, he indicates with a wave of his hand that he is heading in the other direction. They are clearly both relieved to be going separate ways.

"Bye," she says, and with a nod of his head he turns and walks off.

She remembers that he and Ann used to like going for walks together before she became so ill, but she's been dead now for over two years. He is still a comparatively young man who goes out to work each day and comes back to an empty house. She wonders what it is he does – he has probably told her and she has forgotten. She feels guilt and sympathy for this lonely man who is her neighbour. He is never troublesome but neither is he friendly. She has never repeated her invitation to him for a meal in her cottage after the awkwardness of the Christmas lunch he attended. But she recalls that in recent months she has seen him about more often, watching the dancing at the fete and drinking in the pub. Flora says he has been hovering around Lena, but drones of men in the village appear to be attracted to the honeypot. There are bets on which one of them will succeed.

Josie starts to head back home. She raises her head, sniffs the air and listens to the birds singing – she loves summer. Her other neighbour, Bill, has given her some raspberries and she is going to make jam. She loves the process – the stirring and the bubbling and the filling of glass jars with hot crimson fluid, pulp and pips. The fruit is free and sugar is cheap, and she enjoys giving jam to friends who are often so generous to her.

Perhaps her grandchildren have emailed her. She

quickens her pace but resolves not to be disappointed if they have not. They are teenagers and have many other preoccupations. She feels so honoured that they want to have a relationship with a grandmother who lives half a world away. She wonders what will happen when their mother finds out about their emails. But for the moment, secrecy is alright.

18th August 2013

Dear Lottie and Tom,

This is just a quick email to say that I've had a glorious Sunday and that I'm thinking of you both. I've just finished making some delicious raspberry jam. I always find this satisfying, especially pouring the hot jam into clean jars. I like to write labels and stick them on. Do you ever make jam? I prefer raspberries to strawberries but I'll make it from any fruit – gooseberries, apricots, plums. Strangely enough I don't eat a lot of jam myself though sometimes a spoonful stirred in with some yoghurt is yummy. Pots of home-made jam make marvellous gifts and are often sold at village fetes to raise money for church repairs, library books or local charities. I often give mine away.

In the morning I went for a walk in the woods on the hill overlooking the village. I met my neighbour who is a man in his forties called Matt Tapper. He doesn't say much but I think he watches a lot of television and probably spends hours on his computer. What a solitary form of entertainment! I'm all for communicating with others and having shared experiences – much more fun! But he does have a redeeming hobby – he likes birdwatching and walking. In England people who are obsessive about trying to spot rare birds are called 'twitchers'. Matt doesn't seem to twitch that often but I'll bet he knows a lot more about birds than I do. I like the small robins and blue tits and I know a buzzard when I see one – and anyone can recognise a magpie.

That reminds me of something that happened when I was visiting your parents in Australia when you were both very small. Your father had given you some gloriously large black and white towels. Tom, you started running around in the towel flapping your arms. Lottie, you were just a baby and lay on the towel kicking your legs. I laughed and said you looked like a pair of magpies, so Julian and I started calling you our 'Magpies'. As a child in France, when we spotted a magpie we used to say: 'Bonjour, Monsieur Pie'. If it's all right with you, I might revert to addressing you both as Magpies.

Summery greetings from Dorset.

And warm love to my Magpies from

GMJ xxx

15th September 2013

Dear Magpies,

It was good to hear from you both – it's very kind of you, Tom, to let your sister borrow your laptop occasionally so she can write to me as well.

You are both obviously keen on team sports. Lottie, I'm very glad you've been picked for the school netball team in your age group. When I was at school, we played hockey and netball – but

I wasn't much good at either. In hockey I used to miss the ball and clout people's shins which was very unpopular, whilst in netball I kept missing passes or dropping the ball at critical moments. I never made it into the team. The only thing I was moderately good at was tennis.

Tom, it was good to hear about your rugby game against a school in Christchurch and I'm glad you won this time. Raul always told me that he thought rugby a brutal sport, where hard tackles could cause real injury. I hope you don't get too battered and bruised. At least you are a winger and not in the scrum so I expect you can run fast. My second husband Oliver and I used to like watching rugger on the TV. The head gear and the mouth guards which players wear make them look very primitive and fearsome. But nothing is quite as awe-inspiring as watching the All Blacks do their Maori Haka War Dance before matches.

Your father used to have terrible falls on his roller skates and cut his knees and arms, so we bought him some kneepads and elbow pads. In his late teens, he got inline skates which enabled him to go even faster. Colombians are passionate about roller skating – inline speed skating is a national sport, which is widely practised in all the main cities. Raul and I used to go and watch Julian occasionally; it was exciting but also nail-biting to see him racing along at a breakneck speed. Did you know that Colombia wins the World Roller Speed Skating Championships regularly? I read in the newspaper recently that they won most of the medals again at this year's world championships held in Belgium. Colombians are also mad about motor racing and crazy about speed.

Going fast is something that the landowner in our village, James Trevett, likes to do. I think I told you that he owns my cottage and I pay him rent. He has just acquired a trendy sports car in an electric blue colour. Very flashy! He is now often to be seen driving down the lane showing off his new acquisition. The man has more money than sense. Tom, you tell me you drive yourself and your sister to school in one of the farm pickups. I hope you take lots of care whilst you gain experience. I was surprised to hear that you can drive aged sixteen in New Zealand – it's seventeen in the UK – and that you have driven quad bikes and the tractor on the farm for some years.

I'm glad, Tom, that you like science and maths and plan to study engineering at college or university. When I was at school many of the girls chose not to take much interest in science. Maths was not seen as an attractive subject and was considered far too difficult. Such a narrow minded and short-sighted view! I was permitted to discontinue science and was not encouraged to continue with maths because I was told that I had no aptitude. So now I feel very ignorant about physics and chemistry, and my lack of ability with figures is such a disadvantage in life. Too silly! I think it hugely important for children to learn as much as they can on as wide a range of subjects as possible.

I suspect that this is what James Trevett did not do. Harry Scaddon, who lives near him and knows him rather better than I do, is not as discreet as he should be. I wouldn't repeat what he said to anyone else, but since you are in New Zealand, there seems no harm.

Apparently, James went to a minor public school in the West Country and is not academic. There's no shame in not being clever – one can't help that. But he is lazy – and one can do something about that! According to Harry, James admits that he didn't bother to work and didn't pass many exams. After he left school, he went to London and for about fifteen years worked in a variety of jobs. One was as a negotiator with estate agents and another was a junior post in a firm of stockbrokers. He was probably just a general dogsbody, because I can't see that he has the aptitude for the cut and thrust of stockbroking or selling houses. His parents originally came from Dorset but now live in Scotland. His father's older brother, Charles Trevett, was an accountant by profession who also farmed a small estate in Winterborne Slepe, which he had bought some years earlier. Divorced with no children, he used to invite his nephew to stay with him for weekend exeats from school, because the boy's parents lived so far away. James says that his uncle was fond of him, treated him like a son and made him his heir, having no other close relatives. Harry's view is that Charles Trevett decided to leave the estate to James, because although the lad wasn't the sharpest knife in the block, he didn't want his ex-wife to have it. The older man became unwell and thought he would have time to teach James how the estate worked, but he developed an aggressive form of cancer and died very quickly.

James inherited it all and, having achieved little during his career in London, at the age of thirty-five, he decided to move to Dorset to live in the house and run the estate. He has only one employee, Bill Stickley, who lives with his wife next door to me. Various farm contractors come in to do certain jobs, such as harvesting the arable crops. Bill does all the other jobs, including gardening. It's clear to everyone in the village that James knows little about farming or life in the country. It was never a full-time job for his uncle and, because James is lazy and inefficient, he dreams up schemes to occupy his time and strolls around wearing brand-new wellington boots and a pristine tweed jacket. He owns my cottage and the Stickleys' in Long Lane, and he has a third one on his land which was an estate worker's cottage. Last year he decided to renovate this old dwelling and rent it out for holiday lets and apparently it now looks trim and cosy. I believe he managed to get some lettings over the summer. Maybe things aren't going quite so well with farming, and he's trying to raise some extra income. We'd all like to do that! GLTH (Good luck to him)!

I'm not quite sure why I have rattled on so much about James Trevett, but perhaps it's because I have this uneasy feeling that he doesn't really want me as his tenant. At times I'm a bit late with paying the rent but he always gets it in the end. And I'm a bit untidy – but that's no crime. Anyhow, his uncle gave me a lease for five years which has more than two years to run. So I should be OK. I've settled snugly into Winterborne Slepe and I like the place and its inhabitants. I've grown quite fond of my dilapidated little thatched cottage and I can't face the thought of moving again. I want to put down roots. I have always dreamed of buying my own home one day but it's never happened yet and I can't see any prospect of it happening in the future. I have no rich uncle to leave me a large house and an income, but I am content to rent and only ask to be left in peace.

We all like to believe that everybody marries for love and this may be true most of the time. But it's obvious that there are some selfish people who marry for money and there are those who might even think James Trevett and his smart sports car a good catch. He's the opposite of tall, dark and handsome, being of medium height, pale and plain, but he tries hard to be friendly in spite of his awkwardness and I hope one day he'll discover the satisfaction of doing work he enjoys.

I enjoy my work, menial and repetitive as it is. And poorly paid. As you know, I'm carer to an elderly couple whom I like and respect. They suffer from pain and are often anxious about their lack of mobility yet they are always asking me how I am. Some people have life so easy and others so hard. I expect you both have friends who always seem to be dragged down by problems and others who sail through life without a care. I try to eradicate self-pity and complacency from my life, as both are bad news.

I have just looked out of my window to see Alice Diffey trotting up to my front door. She has a resolute expression on her face and is carrying a collecting tin. I know I'll be unable to resist her request for contributions to yet another of her charities. I wonder if I have any coins in my purse. My bell is ringing. Must go.

With love and with modest expectations,

GMJ xxx

The mug of coffee sits on the table, steaming gently, but with less resentment than the drinker. He is sitting in the kitchen, glowering at the calendar pinned on the wall opposite. The surveillance and information gathering are taking too much time. And he's getting nowhere. The woman appears to be as transparent and extrovert as ever with her neighbours, though he knows only too well that outward behaviour is capable of masking a need for concealment. He has been surreptitiously listening to village chatter but heard nothing particularly useful and, during his visual inspections of her cottage, he has not yet seen anything relevant. Her regular correspondence with her grandchildren has not yet revealed any pertinent information, although she mentions Colombia occasionally. She sends few emails to other people and when she does they are short and perfunctory. He has been through her bank statements, which she keeps in an old folder on the bottom shelf of her bookcase, and they reveal what he expected - which is that Josie seems to live on a slender income from her caring job and her state pension, both of which come in regularly. From the bank account it seems she has very little money.

There is of course a financial incentive for him to find out the facts. He will have to let the Colombian know soon that so far he has drawn a blank. How irritating! He picks up the coffee, which is now cooled a little, and drinks it slowly. Then he gets up and walks over to put the cup on the draining board. The sink is full unwashed crockery half submerged in cold greasy water. How good it would be to have a woman in his life again. He hates household chores.

19th October 2013

Dear Magpies,

A litter of five puppies – how delightful! Thank you for telling me about your dogs. I don't have one myself, although I do have my little cat, Folly. She is a good mouse catcher, supplementing her diet constantly with dainty rodent morsels, so she doesn't require much food, except in the winter. I like large dogs but they eat so much! I couldn't afford dog meat since I can hardly afford meat for myself! After paying rent and utility bills and the costs of running my little car which I need to get to work, there's not a lot left. But I manage fine and I grow vegetables which I eat. My neighbour, Bill, gives me some seeds and seedlings which I plant in my little plot and in the summer, I pick fruit. Free food! Bill and Lou have a very friendly dog called Pilot and sometimes I join Lou when she takes him for a walk.

Dogs are companionable. I got to know a very bouncy black Labrador who lived in the house opposite, where John Damon lives. His wife Maggie moved out about a year and a half ago and the couple are now in the middle of a rather messy divorce. She and I were friends and used to go to for walks together with their dog, whose name was Bailey. He was a beautiful dog with a gentle expression and a shiny coat, but I have a hunch he wasn't too bright – he was always running off. The dog adored Maggie, but when she left, she didn't take him and he pined for her. John went out to work each day and didn't fancy taking the dog for long walks early in the morning or after he got home when he was tired. I offered to walk the dog on the days when I wasn't working. Bailey and I got to know each other quite well.

But about a year ago he disappeared. John didn't seem to be too bothered, which I found rather strange, but I was quite worried about the poor animal. I asked John how he had managed to escape from the house and he shrugged his shoulders and said he had no idea. I thought perhaps the dog had died and John had removed the body. Though the last time I'd seen Bailey, the dog looked fit and well. Then about a week later, John put a note through my door to say that he had received a letter from Maggie, who told him that she had returned to the village, let herself into the house with her key, collected a few items that she considered belonged to her and taken Bailey too. I think John was more outraged that she had come into the house in his absence than he was about her removing his dog. He instantly changed all the locks and complained to all of us that Maggie had returned and kidnapped his beloved pedigree Labrador. I didn't make any comment, but I certainly think the animal is better off with his mistress than with his master. She will look after him well but I do miss my four-legged walking companion.

About a month ago, Maggie telephoned me late at night. She has always been a night owl and used to stay up late watching television or waiting for John to come home from one of his many business trips (which Maggie found suspicious) and one sleepless night I remembered seeing their lights on at about 2 am, when all the other lights in the village were out. She told me on the phone that she was divorcing John for infidelity and physical abuse, but was worried that she had put herself at a disadvantage by leaving the marital home. She regrets not telling the police at the time. She is now sharing a flat with a friend. She is angry with John for not responding quicker through his solicitor, as she wants to get things settled regarding the divorce. I feel very sorry for her though I never witnessed any abuse and I have only her word for his infidelities. I don't want to be involved in the marital quarrel or the divorce proceedings. It's particularly awkward as John lives opposite me and we are on friendly terms. Although he's told other people in the village that it was Maggie who was unfaithful and not him, he has never said this to me, because he knows Maggie and I were friends. I don't know the truth and I'm not going to take sides. But I do get the feeling sometimes that he is trying to find out if I know where she is and if she is on her own.

I expect that you have some friends at school whose parents have relationship problems. Children always find quarrelling parents very distressing and fear a marital break-up. But I have been very blessed. There was only one occasion in my life when I doubted my husband's fidelity.

In 1988, Raul and I had left Barranquilla and went back to live in Bogota, in an apartment in the Chapinero district quite close to his parents' house. At that time, Raul's unmarried sister, Natalia, was living with her parents and teaching at a school in Bogota. Over the years she and I had become good friends and she adored her nephew. Julian was about fourteen when he started attending the Colegio Salesiano de Leon XIII, a good school for which the fees were paid by my parents-in-law. Julian loved the school and became close friends with some of the boys there, one of whom was called Mateo. One Saturday when Julian and Mateo were in our apartment playing loud music and behaving just as noisy teenagers do (I expect you know what I mean!), Natalia called round. Whilst she and I were trying to talk in the sitting room, the disruption and noise level reached new heights, so Natalia got up and spoke strongly to them. Mateo made a face at her and muttered some insult under his breath, but they left the house and went to kick a football outside in the street. I sighed. Natalia seemed to manage to discipline them when I could not. She told me that Mateo was not a suitable friend for Julian, as he was a wild boy who might lead her nephew into trouble. Many years later her words were to prove prophetic.

Soon after we returned to Bogota, my father died suddenly whilst working in Africa, and I had had to leave Colombia for some weeks to help my mother and resettle her with relatives in France. During that time Natalia, who was in between jobs, had kept an eye on my husband and son, cooking meals and generally looking after them. Shortly after I got back home she went to work in a small town in the Los Nevados mountains where, four years earlier, there had been a major volcanic eruption causing horrific landslides that had buried the town of Amero and 20,000 people under a sea of mud. This appalling disaster caused huge problems in the ensuing years. Natalia decided to move to the area to work in an orphanage and school which served the local community.

I was working in a contemporary art gallery in downtown Bogota. From time to time we held exhibitions to which foreign visitors came, so my languages came in useful. Often a new exhibition began with an evening Private View, to which many potential buyers were invited. I was put in charge of organising these events and had to ensure everything ran smoothly, while the owners of the gallery persuaded wealthy clients to invest in contemporary art.

Your grandfather Raul worked in the head office of a large shipping company and he was good in his job. But in 1991 he wanted a change and the management sent him for a year to their office in Houston in the United States. We went with him and we had an amazing time, though Julian got into a few scrapes whilst he was there!

Anyhow, six months before we left for the USA, I had to work late for a couple of evenings, helping to hang the exhibition and arrange the private exhibition evening. Then Raul announced that he could not come to it, because he had a business meeting and dinner. I was disappointed because he had always supported me by coming along to art events in the past. Julian was nearly sixteen, so he was happy to stay at home and amuse himself. During the evening, he had a phone call from his school friend Mateo, which really upset him. When I returned at around 10 pm, having cleared up and closed the gallery after the guests left, I found him moodily sitting on the sofa. When I asked him what was wrong, he refused to tell me but eventually I managed to persuade him to explain why he was distressed. He told me that Mateo had called him to say his parents had been dining in a restaurant in the city and they had seen his father, whom they knew from school events, enter the restaurant. He was with a good-looking woman and they had sat down together for a meal and chatted animatedly throughout it.

When Mateo's parents had finished their meal, his father could not resist sauntering over to Raul to say hello. Raul immediately introduced his companion as his sister. With a broad grin Mateo's father wished them an enjoyable evening and left. Mateo was at home when his parents returned and was told that they had met Julian's father dining with a woman who was not his wife. They didn't for a moment believe the old excuse that she was his sister. Mateo, who had a streak of devilment, telephoned Julian and gave him this salacious morsel of gossip and, inevitably, Julian had been really upset. But not as upset as I was when he told me! I knew perfectly well that Natalia was working far away in Tolima province so it could not possibly have been her. Perhaps Raul's business meeting had included a woman, but it seemed unlikely that he would take her out for dinner on his own afterwards. I tried to come up with a better solution than the obvious one but the green-eyed monster, Jealousy, began to torment me. I packed Julian off to bed with a confident smile that belied my inner turmoil, saying that the woman was probably a business colleague and no doubt Raul would explain it all in the morning. I waited up for my errant husband and became angrier and more agitated as the minutes went by. My imagination ran riot with what might happen after the secretive dinner Raul had enjoyed with this beautiful woman. I sat on the sofa growing more and more miserable, jealousy chewing away at my peace of mind, my hands fidgeting with my house keys. In a spurt of rage, I threw them onto the carpet. It was then I noticed a red flashing light on our flat telephone answering machine (very few people had mobile phones at that time). There was an unheard message. Trembling, I dialled and listened. Then very quietly I put the receiver down.

Raul had called at 8 o'clock to say that his meeting had finished and that he was taking Natalia out for dinner. His sister had paid an unexpected visit to the capital to sort out some financial problem with the orphanage and was staying for a couple of days at their parents' house. She had wanted to ask Raul's advice and, as Juan Carlos and Paola were out with friends that evening, she suggested they eat together. He would drop her back at their parents' before coming home to his Josette. My resentment evaporated like steam from a kettle and, when a few minutes later I heard his key turn in the lock, I felt disgusted with myself for not trusting him. I was immensely relieved that I had listened to the message before he arrived home and was able to stand up with my arms open and a smile on my face as he came into the room.

The next day, Natalia came into the gallery and we had lunch together. She is indeed a good-looking woman and an immensely kind one. Apart from you two, my New Zealand Magpies, I have lost every other member of my direct family, but I still have my wonderful sister-in-law. Though we live thousands of miles apart, Natalia and I have remained friends all our lives and write airmail letters to each other occasionally. She lives in Colombia and has immersed herself in her work with children. I think she is now running the school. I had a letter from her the other day – she does not care to send emails. This reminds me that I must reply when I can locate it, as it appears to have gone absent without leave. If you two have a tendency to be untidy, then you can blame it on me and my genes. Your father never cared a hoot about cleaning his bedroom, and with me for a mother and witnessing my chaotic housekeeping, who could blame him? As far as I'm concerned, ignoring dust is not a crime and tidiness is an overrated virtue. I've got more exciting things to do with my time. From my son I demanded kindness and respect for others, but I didn't mind about minor faults such as a messy bedroom.

This incident goes to show that we should trust people we love, especially if they love us. This was the only occasion I was torn apart by jealousy, but then happily I have not been given cause. It eats away at peace of mind. Stress can be totally self-inflicted. When I was young and living with my parents, my mother used to fret about so many things and was frequently consumed with anxiety about her health and her possessions. She was always concerned about what people thought of her, and whether she was wearing the right clothes or saying the right things. Oddly enough she didn't really worry that much about her husband or her children. She was fond of my brother Henri, when he was small, and paraded him like a trophy in front of acquaintances. When he grew older, he managed to elude her possessiveness and opted out of the family. My father was a capable man, a tactful experienced diplomat and, although my mother liked him to be there when she needed him at social or diplomatic gatherings, she never listened to what he had to say. This must have been difficult for him, although he rarely showed any obvious disquiet and often resorted to his daughter for family conversation and companionship. We used to talk together for hours and the same things made us laugh. Sometimes we would look up and find my mother staring at us with a puzzled expression on her face, at a total loss to understand what we found so funny. At times like this I almost felt sorry for her.

I hope you get on well with your stepfather. What is he like? Tell me more about your half-sister, Bex. I hope your mother is well and enjoys life in New Zealand. It's sad that she never mentions your father or me. I don't know why this is and it may be unwise to ask.

The trees are flaunting their foliage in a glorious myriad of colours. The wind is stronger and now that it's cooler, leaves will soon be swirling down to the ground. Dusk falls earlier and winter is on the horizon. With you, spring is coming.

With love from autumnal England,
GMJ xxx

Josie is sitting hunched in her old armchair, enmeshed in her thoughts, eyes unfocused and with arms folded. The New Zealand emails seem to be coming from Tom alone now. Lottie appears to have dropped out of the correspondence. Josie is perturbed about this and speculates as to whether it is because of pressure from her brother. She is still writing emails addressed to both Magpies and hopes that Lottie is reading them even if she isn't replying. It is over six months since she established contact with her grandchildren, and she worries that the link is tenuous and could be broken at any time. She cannot call because has no telephone number for them and the children can not afford to call her on their mobiles. She does have an address for them but has absolutely no funds to travel out to New Zealand, even if it were wise to do so which it probably isn't. It's likely that Melissa would not welcome her reappearance in their lives.

Tom has mentioned that his mother is quite fussy and strict, especially about the food they eat, the clothes they wear and the friends they visit. Josie is convinced that her daughter-in-law is still a controlling person, who aims to dominate every aspect of family life. She tried to do this with Julian. On the few occasions when she visited them in Australia, Josie had been dismayed by Melissa's habit of ordering him around and making constant demands on his attention and his time. She exerted pressure through tears and entreaties, making him feel guilty when he wanted to do things on his own or go off with friends for a few hours. However, when he announced his intention of flying to Colombia to visit his ailing grandfather, she was unable to dissuade him.

He was adamant that he would go. Melissa was never to forget that it was Josie who had told Julian that the old man was seriously ill and wanted to see his grandson for the last time. So Julian went. And never came back.

Josie is also feeling uneasy about the fact that her life seems to have become more disorganised and the house massively untidy. Sometimes her solitary life makes her feel low and saps her enthusiasm to deal with things that ought to be done. Especially today when thoughts of her son and his early death intrude and disrupt her habitual cheerful attitude to life. She shivers and looks across at the fireplace. Next month she will have to light the wood-burning stove in the evenings to keep warm. She wonders how she is going to get logs for fuel and whether she will manage to obtain some for free as she did last year.

Something catches her attention on the mantelpiece. A letter has been stuck behind one of the pewter candlesticks. She gets up and walks across to pick it up. It is an airmail letter from her sister-in-law, Natalia, which arrived some while back, and which she had mislaid. She frowns – she has no recollection of putting it there. As she walks through to the kitchen to make a cup of coffee, she unfolds the letter and, whilst the kettle boils, she adjusts her mind to Spanish and rereads it. Natalia has expressed her delight that Josie has found her grandchildren – the precious children of her nephew Julian, who died so tragically thirteen years ago. She is asking whether Josie has seen photographs of Tomas and Charlotte, and if they look like their father. Josie has indeed seen a couple of photographs and believes that Tom is like Julian whilst Lottie seems to be more like her mother. Or maybe there is a little of herself in Lottie.

She is grateful that her teenage grandson continues to be interested in what she has to say. The kettle clicks off and Josie makes the coffee. As she wraps her cold fingers round the warm mug, Josie's optimism returns. One day she and her granddaughter might become friends.

31st October 2013

Dear Magpies,

Three days ago, southern England was struck by a massive storm with torrential rain and winds of over 70 mph. Falling trees – many had not yet shed their leaves – caused most damage and disruption. In London two high cranes came crashing to the ground and in Devon, to the west of Dorset, a tall wind turbine was blown down. Needless to say this has fuelled the anti-wind power campaign in our village. We lost a couple of trees up in the wood and an ash tree came down in a garden, but luckily no power lines were brought down, though elsewhere there were many power cuts. There has been some damage to my thatched roof, and I hope my landlord has it mended before the damp patch gets too bad. The storm was named after St Jude as it happened on his Saints day. He is the patron saint of desperate cases and lost causes, which gives me some hope about my leaking roof.

So you want to know about your father's escapades during our year in Houston.

This city is the largest in Texas and the most important port in the Gulf of Mexico, not only for shipping but also for industry. Houston has a number of swampy rivers, which are called 'bayous', flowing through it and a vital waterway called the Ship Channel which links to the sea. We knew the area was extremely hot and humid in the summer but the rains in the winter could cause flooding. Only when we got there did we discover that it's a highly polluted city with high ozone levels and smog. Fortunately, we were assigned an apartment and a company car, both of which had air conditioning.

Julian was almost seventeen and it was a good opportunity to radically improve his English. Without mentioning this to our son, we thought an additional benefit was that it would take him away from the poisonous influence of his school friend, Mateo, with whom our son had already got into trouble.

Julian was sent to an American school for a year – this was a huge change for him because it was co-educational. He was at first stunned and then delighted to have girls in the classroom studying alongside him. It took a while for him to get used to a new system and having all his lessons in English. Raul and I took to talking English whilst he was in the house, so he had total immersion in the language, which is the only way to learn. Julian enjoyed the lack of restrictions which had been imposed by his Colombian school and soon made friends. One of them, Daniel, invited him back for a weekend at his family ranch, where there were horses. Luckily Julian knew how to ride and was delighted to escape from the big city into the open Texan countryside.

Daniel's family introduced Julian to an event that really caught his imagination – the Houston Livestock Show and Rodeo, which was held every year in March and ran for two weeks. Over a million people attended this annual jamboree. As well as live entertainment with well-known singers and bands, there were livestock exhibitions, parades and carnivals, pig racing and barbecues and the biggest event of all – a stunning rodeo in the Astrodome Stadium. Just before this event, the city hosted a 'Go Texan Day' where everyone was encouraged to dress up in traditional Western costume. Children took part and Julian persuaded us to buy him cowboy boots and hat so he could strut around with his friend.

Different trail rides set off from outlying areas and participants rode in a cavalcade to gather at a park to camp and party before joining the big Rodeo Parade through downtown Houston. Daniel invited his friend Julian to join him on a trail ride of about 100 miles, during which the two boys careered wildly around on their horses and were reprimanded by one of the older men for being too boisterous and forbidden to join the parade. In spite of this setback it was a huge adventure for Julian, although the day after he returned he was so sore he could hardly walk! But he went to see the rodeo and this event really stimulated his lifelong fascination with horses.

This wasn't his only passion. Julian was now interested in girls. He had been catapulted into a society of carefree confident young people – unshackled by the restraints of Colombian families and Catholic traditions. The girls he met fluttered their beautiful wings at him and he was captivated. Julian had grown up tall and was a good-looking young man. Although not so strikingly handsome as his father, he had the Latin looks which always seem to impress women – raven black hair, creamy skin and melting dark eyes. He began to date a girl from his school called Abigail. This demure name was misleading as Abi was neither modest nor shy. Drama was her favourite subject and Abi, with peachy complexion and corn-gold hair, declared her intention of becoming an actress.

This ambition was stimulated by the active performing arts scene in Houston. With indulgent parents, Abi, also seventeen, had her own large car and swanned around town with her friends. In Colombia and in some states of America, kids were allowed to drive on provisional licences at the age of sixteen, though in Colombia fewer young people had cars. Julian soon acquired a provisional licence and Abi let him drive her car.

One evening, with another friend called Ryan in the car with them, Julian was teased about driving slowly and being overcautious. Embarrassed by his inexperience, he began to drive faster, beyond his ability. He failed to brake in time behind another car at a red light and shunted into it, and an angry scene ensued with the other driver. When it was discovered that he was uninsured, Julian was fined and had to pay for the damage. To Julian's dismay, Ryan gleefully recounted the incident at school. Abi, who had misled Julian saying that he was covered by her policy, generously offered to pay, which was just as well as Julian certainly could not have afforded to do so.

Ryan came from a wealthy family. Always dressed in the most expensive pair of Levi's, he possessed a hi-fi system, which was the envy of many of his school friends, and he also acquired a hand-held mobile phone. In 1991, these were beginning to appear more often but because they were expensive, most students could not afford them. Ryan strutted around with his big mobile and was the envy of his school friends. Showing off was harmless but Ryan was keen on gambling and at weekends his obliging parents allowed him to invite friends around to play music, drink in moderation and play cards. On one occasion Julian was invited and became involved in a game of poker with five other boys. They may have lured him in because they thought they could fleece him (we gave him a student allowance), but what they didn't know was that in Colombia Julian had played a lot of poker with Mateo and his crowd and he had become quite adept at the game. Julian later told me what had happened. On one hand, when everyone else had thrown in, he was left betting with Ryan who, after a run of bad luck, did not have enough money to bet further. Because he was convinced that he had the better hand and Julian was bluffing, Ryan threw down his mobile phone as his bet. When the cards were put down, Julian had a full house but Ryan only had three aces so Julian acquired the mobile phone. Ryan was stunned but tried not to show how upset he was. The next day when Raul discovered Julian playing with his trophy, he elicited the full story, forbade him to gamble ever again – and made him return the mobile to Ryan's parents. Ryan got his mobile phone back but was angry because everyone knew he had lost it at poker and then been handed it back.

A week later he picked a fight with Julian at school. They were both reprimanded after being forcibly separated but Julian had come off better with fewer bruises. Ryan got his revenge by stealing Abi from him. Though sad about this, Julian soon recovered and went out to spend a week's holiday with Daniel and his family on their ranch. Daniel had very pretty younger sister called Emily!

When we returned to Colombia in 1992, Julian returned to the Colegio for his final year and had to work hard to catch up on the syllabus for his exams. He was pleased to be reunited with his Colombian friends but, providentially, Mateo was no longer at the school. Rumour had it that he had been expelled. Without the distraction of his rebel friend, Julian managed to settle down and work towards his exams. His ambition was to become a vet and to work with horses and large animals. A year later he graduated and asked us if it was possible for him to study abroad, perhaps in the USA. But at this time tragedy struck, and his father – my beloved Raul – was lost at sea in a sailing accident off the coast of Nicaragua. This changed our lives forever.

Today is Halloween – do you celebrate this questionable tradition? This evening I shall probably stay at home and arm myself with sweets and biscuits to hand out to children with ghoulish face masks who rap imperiously on my door demanding 'trick or treat'. I prefer to give treats rather than suffer the ignominy of having to undergo punishment. One year I'd opted for a trick and had to sing a song. I began on a very loud rendering of 'Rule Britannia' during which they scampered away in horror.

With love and patriotism,

GMJ xxx

6th November 2013

Dear Tom,

I'm glad you liked the story of your father's year in Texas. You are about the same age now as he was then – and I'm sure you sometimes run wild, though I don't expect you to tell me about it.

So you went to a bonfire night and firework display yesterday evening. It seems strange to me that New Zealand on the other side of the world has any idea about the significance of the gunpowder plot on 5th November in London 400 years ago. But clearly you do celebrate it. I was surprised to hear that the sale of fireworks is illegal in New Zealand except during the first five days of November, but it must limit the accidents, and it occurs to me that, as it's quite warm 'down under' at this time, fireworks might start bushfires. It is rather a shame that rockets are banned. I really love the whoosh and the exploding stars fanning out in the night sky. I was horrified to read in your email about an overexcited dog running madly round and round the bonfire and that, when a child threw a stick onto the flames, the dog was stupid enough to follow it. Just as well there was a water hose on hand! But I'm not surprised the animal's fur was a bit frizzled.

I don't blame your stepfather for being adamant about not allowing fireworks on his farm. With barns and livestock, you can't be too careful. You say he's strict about late nights and noisy parties, but lots of parents are a bit stuffy about teenage behaviour. Perhaps he doesn't reprimand Bex as much as you and Lottie because she's a lot younger. Have you tried talking with him about his rules and pointing out that you are now seventeen and would like more freedom and a chance to show him that you are more responsible than he thinks? Might be worth a try. Explain to him that it's not unusual of someone your age to have a girlfriend and to want to spend time with her. By the way, what's her name? And what's she like?

It's early in the morning here and I'm typing this before I go to work. I hope the elderly couple, for whom I work, were able to sleep last night. There was a firework display in their village and two years ago a rocket set fire to a thatched roof a few doors up from them. Although it was put out and the cottage survived, they have been nervous about fireworks ever since.

Much love to you and Lottie,
GMJ xxx

Darkness has fallen and nobody will notice him while he lingers in the unlit car for a few minutes. He has just arrived back in the village and parked in the lane. He's not in any hurry. There are no lights in her cottage. The woman doesn't usually get back from work until around 7 pm but he wants to pinpoint a more accurate time for her return. He hears footsteps approaching and averts his head to conceal his face so the person will not see anyone sitting in the dark car. A woman trots past on the other side of the road and he can see Alice Diffey's sturdy back as she heads down the lane towards her house. He assumes she has been involved in one of her 'good works' up at the village hall near the church. She is such a pain in the neck! The last time they met, she tapped him sharply on the shoulder and demanded that he make a donation to the Royal British Legion Poppy Appeal. Once he had paid up, she picked up a poppy and tried to stick it into his sweater. When he grabbed it from her and stuffed it into his pocket, she looked offended. He wonders if she has any idea how much she offends other people. After a while he sees the small headlights of Josie's car wobble their way up the road and stop outside her gate. His watch shows that it is 6.18. A little earlier than usual. She won't notice him - she's too vague. After she has gone in, he continues sitting there for a few minutes before moving. His empty house does not attract him. He might go to the pub for a drink.

29th November 2013

Dear Magpies,

I'm at the end of an exhausting week. David and Jean, the

couple I work for, have both been unwell. The other carer is on holiday, so I've been working on her days as well as mine and the hours are long. Jean has been sleeping a lot but David, who can't walk very well, became chatty today and told me about a time in their lives when they lived in Scotland. He asked me about my life and listened with interest when I told him about my first marriage and my years in Colombia. This evening, though physically tired because I've been on my feet all day, I feel restless and so decided to write to you.

Last weekend I learnt something extraordinary from someone who, for whatever reason, seems to take an interest in me. Harry Scaddon lives near the church in an attractive seventeenth-century cottage called The Old Rectory. He's a few years older than me and he's as pallid and thin as skimmed milk. His face is full of creases and when he walks, he moves with an almost fussy precision. His eyesight is poor and he wears glasses in square black frames. He talks knowledgeably about politics and art and architecture, all of which are subjects I enjoy debating. But his real passion is church architecture – even though he is not a man of faith. I know this because we have discussed our respective beliefs, and it is quite clear we differ in that I believe and trust in God and he does not.

Last year he was ill for a long while and some of us who live nearby cooked meals for him and kept an eye out for him, as he lives alone. Happily, he has recovered sufficiently to take a more active role in the village, though I suspect his underlying health is poor and he gets out of breath if he walks too far. As a traditionalist he's very opposed to the wind turbine project – and calls it 'an abomination'. Harry has a car, though it is seldom driven, and he used to keep it in a barn belonging to James Trevett. Recently he had decided to remove it from there because he doesn't want any favours from James at a time when he plans to be vociferous in his criticism of the wind tower that James proposes to erect if he gets planning permission. His car now sits outside in the rain as do many vehicles belonging to residents of the village. Most of the cottages in the lane were built two hundred years before cars were invented – so there are few garages.

Anyhow last Sunday he telephoned me to ask if he could drop by and have a look at my books, as I've offered to lend him any that he finds interesting. I had made a carrot cake the day before and so I invited him for tea. Having munched his way through two slices – I'm pleased his appetite is much better – he embarked on the topic of the wind turbine. I am heartily sick of being accosted by all the villagers trying to enlist me in the protest campaign and I'm irritated by the residents' stuffy opposition to change in general. I'm not opposed to wind power and renewable energy, so I've refused to become involved. To deflect Harry from giving me a detailed update on the parish council action plan, I suggested he browse through my books. He hovered alongside the shelves, peering at various titles and pulling some out to look at them. After a few minutes, he asked me why some of the books had different names written inside them. I explained that over the years I had bought many books in jumble sales and from second-hand book stalls, and often the names of previous owners were inscribed in them.

He picked up a book of poetry by Thomas Hardy and read out the name 'Miles Hansford' on the flyleaf, mentioning that it was a Dorset name. I told him that the book had once belonged to my father and had been given to me by my mother after his death.

"Your maiden name was Hansford?"

"That's right," I said. "My father came from Dorset."

"I was at boarding school with a boy called Hansford. We

were quite good friends. His name was Henry as mine is, so we were often called Henry I and Henry II. I heard he later became an archaeologist."

I was amazed. "Your school friend must have been my brother unless there are two archaeologists with the same name. How extraordinary! When was the last time you met?" I said.

"We kept in touch for a few years," Harry said. "But the friendship lapsed. He was a solitary man and I remember him as shy and not easy to talk to. But he knew his stuff and I recall he published a couple of scholarly books."

I told him that Henri, as he had been christened by our French mother, had been older than me. We had never been particularly close and saw little of each other during our adult lives. On one occasion when he was in South America on his way to work on an archaeological project, he had come to visit Raul and me and to meet his nephew, Julian. Harry listened quietly as I mentioned that my brother had gone missing about ten years ago. Whilst I was in France sorting out my mother's things after her death, I came across a Christmas card that Henri had sent her, but there was no address in it nor could I find one amongst her papers. Though I tried, I was unable to trace him or tell him that our mother had died. I contacted the Royal Archaeological Institute and the British Archaeological Association but neither had any address for him. No one had any news of him so I assumed he had lived and died abroad.

As I told Harry all this, I saw him looking at me thoughtfully. Afterwards he said, "I recall reading in a newspaper a few years back that the archaeologist Henri Hansford had disappeared and was presumed dead. How very sad for you."

I said, "My brother never took much interest in my life and I knew little about his."

After Harry had gone, taking a couple of books with him, I continued to think about my brother. It was sad we had drifted apart after childhood and never really known each other or shared any deep affection. Henri had never got married and he was probably alone when he died. What a bleak picture this creates in my mind!

I do hope that, wherever you are, you two will remain good friends and keep in touch with each other all your lives.

Folly, who has been curled up asleep on the sofa whilst I've been typing this, has just stretched and jumped onto the floor. I know that in a few minutes she will disappear through the cat flap in the back door and go on her nightly prowl. She is alert but I am tired. I must send this and go to bed.

Goodnight, my loved ones,

GMJ xxx

Josie leaves the parish hall, escaping from the high-pitched voices and bustle of activity to go outside into the cool December evening. She has been helping with other members of the village to decorate the place for a Christmas event. Everybody was offering opinions and issuing orders, so she decided to just get on with doing whatever she was asked to do. She pulls her coat around her, wraps the scarf round her neck and sets off down the lane to her cottage. She is glad that James Trevett found a thatcher who has repaired the damage in her roof - it has taken long enough. But the bedroom still smells damp.

She reaches home a few minutes later and goes

round the back to the kitchen door. It is dark and, whilst fumbling for the keys, she hears a light thudding noise. It is Folly who has jumped over the fence and now materialises beside her, winding herself through Josie's legs. They enter together. As Josie dumps her bag on the table and puts the kettle on, the cat stalks round the kitchen sniffing the air. With her mug of coffee Josie wanders through to the hall and realises that she has not yet picked up the post from the floor below the letter box. She leans down, scoops up half a dozen envelopes and glances at them. The one with the Scottish stamp is a Christmas card from her stepdaughter Emily, there are two other Christmas cards and a couple of window envelopes that look ominously like bills which will need paying. The postman has been in too much of a hurry with his bigger load and one letter is addressed to John Damon, who lives opposite. She looks out of the window and sees lights in his house.

She remembers that John has offered to lend her a dehumidifier to help dispel the damp upstairs and so she decides to walk over, collect it and hand him his letter. Her house is not warm and she's still in her coat, so she unbolts the front door, crosses the road and presses his bell. Standing on the doorstep, she hears voices inside and assumes that John must be on the telephone. Deciding not to wait, she turns away. There are footsteps and the door opens a crack. John's plump face appears in the gap and registers who has rung his doorbell. She catches his frown - he's already regretting he answered it.

She launches in. "Hi, John. Sorry to bother you. I just

wondered if you had that dehumidifier which you said you'd lend me. I can't seem to get rid of the damp upstairs. But if it's not a good moment, not to worry. Also, here's a letter which got popped in my letter box rather than yours." She holds it out to him.

"Thanks, Josie. Can't get the machine right now but I'll bring it across later on." He takes the letter awkwardly. The way he is standing, in an attempt to block Josie's view of the hall, gives her the strong impression there is someone within. Nothing wrong with that. But it is John's shifty expression which indicates that John does not want her to know the identity of his visitor.

"That's fine. No problem." His embarrassment makes her keen to leave, so she turns to scurry back to her own house. Just before he closes the door, she hears a muffled woman's voice but the sound is nipped off as the door clicks shut.

Josie tries hard not to be inquisitive but she is naturally curious. Back in her kitchen, she heats up some soup. Does John have a girlfriend? He's in his fifties and not a bad looking man, a little on the heavy side. His wife has gone and he probably gets lonely. She wonders if the woman is Lena, as this is her day off from the Anchor. He has been flirting with her in the pub - but then, so have many men in the village. Lena is friendly to all but keeps her distance. Anyhow John is too old for her. Josie sternly reminds herself that it's none of her business if he has a lady friend. She wouldn't be the first. Then a thought strikes her - could it be Maggie who has returned to discuss the divorce or perhaps to seek a reconciliation? It's unlikely - and that's none of her business too.

The soup is ready and Josie goes to the cupboard to reach for a bowl and almost trips over her bag which is lying on the floor. Not on the table. Where she left it. She stops still and examines this thought, whilst stamping on her panic and trying to find a rational explanation. She hears the clock ticking. Folly is sitting on a kitchen chair, her huge eyes staring intently at Josie. Could the cat have knocked the bag off the table? The kitchen door is still unlocked. Is the room perceptibly cooler? Josie licks her lips and walks across to the door and shoots the bolt. The clunk breaks the tension and Josie tries to convince herself that, when she came in tonight she must have dropped the bag on the floor, as she sometimes does.

An hour later she has eaten the soup with bread and is sitting on the sofa trying to read. There is a loud knocking on the front door. Josie catches her breath, stands up and calls out, "Who's that?"

It is John Damon looking less furtive and more confident, and he is carrying the dehumidifier. She thanks him and bolts the door after he is gone, and checking the back door once again, goes upstairs with the machine to face her damp bedroom and her uneasy imaginings.

23rd December 2013

Dear Magpies,

As you swelter in sunny weather over Christmas, spare a thought for southern England where storms have caused floods and power cuts. In Dorset lots of people have been rescued from cars trapped by floodwater and a number of homes are without electricity. Winterborne Slepe has been unaffected although the stream running through the meadows below the lane is very swollen. And snow is forecast for Christmas. But don't worry about us – Folly and I are snug in our 'Haven', with a roaring fire in the sitting room to keep us warm.

There's a little mystery that I've not been able to solve. About ten days ago, I came back from work in the dark and was surprised to see a large pile of logs that had been delivered and stacked outside the front of my house. No one can tell me who arranged for them to be delivered or maybe people don't want to let me in on the secret. All I can say is that I'm enormously grateful for this anonymous and generous gift which has enabled me to have a lovely warm house at Christmas. Bless them.

The following day, which was Saturday, I realised I should get the logs stacked in the rear garden shed before it rained. I was wondering how I was going to go about moving them all, when my neighbour Matt came out of his house and saw me standing there looking at the pile. Without any preamble, he said that a wheelbarrow would be the best way of shifting them and that if I didn't have one – which I didn't – he would lend me his. When he came back with his wheelbarrow he mumbled, "Might as well give you a hand – bit of a job on your own," and started to help me. I was quite surprised, as Matt is not the friendliest person. Together in silence, we moved them all, one barrow-load after another until the last one which we emptied outside the kitchen door ready for me to take through to the sitting room fireplace. I thanked him profusely and offered him a cup of coffee but, shaking his head, he said, "You're welcome," and took himself off back to his own cottage. Strange lonely man! Could it be Matt who gave the logs to me? Who knows?

Tom, you mentioned that over the Christmas holidays you will all be spending some time by the sea in the 'batch' belonging to your cousins, the Taylor family. That sounds fun. Though Ethan is a bit older than you and is already at university, I'm glad you get on well. I trust, when you both go out in their dingy, that you will wear life jackets. Sailing is exhilarating but can also be dangerous. I hope that Lottie and Bex have fun with Lucy and Georgia. Spending time with family at Christmas is very special.

In Colombia during your father's childhood, the Moreno family used to gather together at Christmas. Although Raul and Natalia had no other siblings, they had many cousins. Julian may have been an only child but he loved spending time with family and friends. All this came to an end in August 1993 when my husband drowned.

Julian was so distraught by his father's death that he did not utter a word for five days. In the weeks that followed, I wallowed in a morass of misery whilst Julian, unable to comfort me, went off to his grandparents' house to alleviate his anguish by sharing it with them. They were deeply distressed over the death of their only son and it was Natalia who managed to keep the family from falling apart. She loved her brother but, concealing her own grief, resolved to help us with ours. She spent much time looking after her distraught mother, Paola, and during this strange time of emptiness and loss, your father and your great-grandfather, Juan Carlos, developed a real bond. They had often enjoyed time together when the old man had taken his grandson to various football games and Paso Fino horse fiestas, where Julian developed his love of pedigree horses. They used to play chess together – and listen to jazz. Now they sat together in the house in solidarity and in silence, remembering and mourning Raul.

The emotional pain caused by the death of a person you love can take a long time to heal, but with someone as young as Julian, at nineteen on the threshold of adult life and full of optimism for the future, the recovery can be quicker. During that autumn he formulated plans to go to university and discussed things at length not only with me but also with his grandfather. Finances and funds for further education would be difficult without Raul's salary, although there was a small pension for me from his company. Juan Carlos persuaded his wife that they should sponsor their grandson's further education and they put a sum of money into a savings account for him, to be used for his fees and maintenance at university. Finally Julian decided he wanted to study veterinary science and to do this in an English-speaking country abroad. The USA was too expensive, and in any case their degree courses began in the autumn, whereas in Australia the fees and costs were less, and the university year began in February. His grandparents were a bit shell-shocked on discovering that he wanted to study so far away, but he persuaded them by saying that he would come back and visit them at least once a year, during the main vacation over Christmas. He was unable to get into the University of Sydney but managed to get a place at Murdoch University near Perth in Western Australia to start in February 1994.

Christmas 1993, twenty years ago, was therefore a quiet reflective time. Raul's absence extinguished any possibility of merriment. Soon afterwards, Julian started making preparations for his departure to Australia and a lengthy university course. It can take six or seven years to become a vet. He made me promise that I would come and visit him in Australia and even hinted that I should move out there too. I was not ready to do that and so he left at the end of January for his new life in another continent. And of course, had he not done so, you two would never have been born. For it was in Western Australia at university where he met your mother, Melissa, and fell in love. More about this in another email.

But now I must wrap up a few gifts for friends in the village and I hope tomorrow, Christmas Eve, will bring a bit of sunshine so that I can walk round and deliver them. The rain has been torrential. Doris has invited me round for Christmas lunch the next day after church and in the evening Flora and George have planned entertaining Christmas activities at the pub. I expect many of us will go there. We might even need snowshoes!

With love and blessings at Christmas time from your

Grandma Josie xxx

2nd January 2014

Dear Magpies,

Happy New Year to you both. I hope 2014 will bring excitement and let there be peace as well. Did you have fun on New Year's Eve?

Tom, I hope that the last year of school inspires you to work sufficiently hard to get those exams at the end of it.

Lottie, I really want to get to know you better during this year as I think we have much to share on life, love and art.

Talking of love, or it might be lust in this case, I must tell you that jealousy ignited a fight in the village pub late on New Year's Eve. Many of us were there to see in the New Year and it was crammed. George had finished in the kitchen after cooking New Year's Eve dinner and was in the bar helping Flora serve drinks. Lena, their pretty Polish waitress, was flitting from table to table collecting glasses and wiping surfaces. Harry Scaddon, John Damon and I were sitting at a table with Bill and Lou Stickley, and Matt Tapper was sitting at the bar on his own. About half an hour before midnight, James Trevett came in with a couple who were staying with him. They bought drinks and stood near the fire because it was a cold night and all the tables were occupied. With background music and the babble of conversation it was noisy, but everyone was in good humour. Or so we thought.

As the clock sounded the midnight hour, we all stood and linked hands to sing 'Auld Lang Syne', after which various people hugged each other in friendly village fashion. Lena, who was wearing a skin-tight black and white dress, detached herself from the circle to return to the bar and get on with her work. Before she'd moved more than a pace or two, James, who likes to drink and who had clearly had a few too many, made a lunge and grabbed the waitress around her slim waist. He pulled her close and deposited a smacking kiss on her unwilling lips. Lena, quite understandably, pulled away with a shriek of dismay, whereupon Matt Tapper strode forward and landed a serious punch on James's face. James, who was a bit unsteady, staggered backwards and fell to the floor. But he got to his feet quick enough to lunge back and score a retaliatory blow on his opponent. Matt, who is a strong fellow, was surprised but he swung another punch which James managed to dodge, whilst delivering a savage kick at the other man's legs. Matt howled in pain, but at this point George intervened and pushed Matt aside, whilst John Damon grabbed James by the arm and pulled him away.

The rest of us, initially paralysed in surprise, looked on in fascinated horror. Lena watched with dismay as the two men fought over her – perhaps it wasn't the first time. Within three minutes, George had thrown them both out of the pub, and James's friends had scuttled out afterwards, no doubt to take him back home. Matt had to stagger home on his own. He hadn't been as drunk as James, so he'd have been miserably aware that he had behaved atrociously in front of everybody. When I went home, about an hour later, all the lights were off in his house. I hope he hadn't lurched into a ditch, but it was more likely that he was inside, sitting on his own in the dark, burning with humiliation. I felt sorry for him.

As for me, I ended the year happier than I began it. 2013 brought me back into contact with my grandchildren. After my ten-year search with no success, it was you who found me. We may live 12,000 miles apart, but it takes only a second or two to send an email winging its way across the world. Amazing!

With love – and hope for the future,

GMJ xxx

"You should buy yourself a new coat in the January sales," says Doris to Josie, as they walk on the sodden grass in the meadow beside the stream. "Your boots don't look in very good shape either."

"They don't leak as badly as the last pair," Josie says as she cranes round to see where Pilot has disappeared to. The dog, a delightful mutt of uncertain parentage, has a habit of dashing off when he is let off the lead. She calls him and soon the dog comes bounding back, wet tail wagging.

"How are the Stickleys?" Doris asks, fending off Pilot

as he enthusiastically cavorts round her feet. The dog belongs to Bill and Lou, but he is at work and she has a chest infection, which means that she cannot take their dog for its usual walk. Josie has offered to exercise the animal. Pilot's lack of aggression and his disarming innocence commends him to Josie and she is glad that he poses no threat to her cat. Folly's imperious gaze often stops Pilot in his tracks and a well-directed swipe with her paw can make him whimper and retreat.

Josie coughs and wraps her scarf tighter round her neck before replying, "Getting better," hoping that she won't watch their infectious cold.

They are now on the footpath that leads from the meadow up towards the church, and they admire the ethereal white snowdrops beginning to appear in the wintry grass beneath the bare trees. Josie tries in vain to stop Pilot from bounding through the fragile flowers. They can see Harry's cottage up ahead but won't pass too close, to Josie's relief.

Doris says, "A lot of people in the village think Harry's sweet on you. What do you think?"

"I've no idea," Josie snaps. "And I don't like gossip when it's unfounded. He's a friend with whom I occasionally have a meal and talk books. I don't always agree with his views and don't like his dogmatism. He's given me no indication that he has any affection for me." Josie bangs the gate shut as they leave the churchyard and walk up the road towards the Trevett estate.

Doris raises her eyebrows, purses her lips and changes the subject. "I saw Mr Trevett driving through the village yesterday. He stopped outside your cottage and carefully looked at it from his car. But when he saw me on the other side of the road, he gave a watery smile and drove off. Rumour has it that, with the success of his holiday cottage last summer, he's trying to find another of his dwellings to convert. I should watch out, Josie."

"Thanks for your concern, Doris. Harry tells me that, as long as I pay my rent, he can't get me out. He explained to me that, with some tenancy agreements, the landlord can give the tenant a month's notice to leave, but not with mine. I have a five-year lease with nearly two years to run. James could put up the rent but I hope he doesn't. He's not a bad person."

"He seems to have conveniently forgotten his disgraceful behaviour in the pub on New Year's Eve," says Doris, who knows about the fight even though she was not there.

"Whereas Matt, on the other hand, seems to have shrunk into his shell, suffering from loss of face. He hardly puts his nose outside in the village. He leaves for work before dawn, gets back after dark and he hasn't been back to the pub at all."

"I'm not surprised, since he was thrown out."

"George doesn't bear grudges and anyway, for obvious reasons, he's quite sympathetic about over-indulgence with alcohol!"

They turn down the lane and trudge back towards their respective homes. As they pass John's house, Josie says, "I feel sorry for John. The divorce is taking a long time to resolve, and meanwhile, in an effort to appear squeaky clean, he has been concealing the fact that he's got a girlfriend. I just wish he could get on with his life and let Maggie get on with hers - with her new man".

They reach The Haven and before she continues on to her house, Doris says, "See you on Sunday at church."

Josie nods. "I'd better go in - I have a slight sore throat. I don't want to croak like an old crow singing the hymns on Sunday."

"There's nothing wrong with old crows," says Doris with a smile as she turns to walk off.

16th January 2014

Dear Magpies,

Message for Lottie: HAPPY 14th BIRTHDAY tomorrow. I hope you are celebrating with your friends this weekend. It's summertime where you are – much more fun when throwing a party! The only bright thing here in a wintry January is the snowdrops.

Tom, I expect that wild kangaroos couldn't drag you to your kid sister's party, so I hope you have something else arranged. You could go and see a film or perhaps you need to get some practice for when the school rugby season starts.

This weekend, John Damon who lives opposite has invited me over for a drink to meet his friend Caroline, whom he calls 'Caro'. I think she's been around for a few months but he's been keeping her secret. I hope she's good for him – he's been on his own for a while now.

Love from me amid the snowdrops,
GMJ xxx

21st January 2014

Dear Tom,

Thanks for letting me know the good news that Lottie now has her own email address and for sending it to me. I assume she will be able to send and read her emails on your computer, since she doesn't yet have one of her own. I expect your mother does, but obviously it can't be borrowed for this purpose, because our being in contact by email is still a secret. I feel a little uneasy about this and wonder whether it is now time to tell your mother. I'm anxious that, if Melissa were to find out, she might be very upset. Can you give this some thought?

Another earthquake! You reassured me that it was in the south part of North Island and a magnitude of 6.5. I'm glad the damage to the town of Palmerston wasn't too bad and there was no loss of life. How fortunate you'd come back the week before from a visit to North Island, so you weren't anywhere near when it happened.

So, you have another week of holiday before the next school year starts in early February. You say you're dreading it – but don't. It's your final year with the 'NCEA' Certificate exams coming up and there's going to be lots of studying to do. Just take it one week at a time and remember that amidst the slog it's important to relax and have some fun.

With quaking love,
GMJ xxx

25th January 2014

Dear Lottie,

Wonderful! A whole email just from you. I'm so pleased you've now got your own email address set up, so that, when I want to write to you separately, I can do so. You say your mobile is not the type with access to the internet to receive emails, so I hope that you will be able to read them from time to time on your brother's or a friend's laptop. Or in an internet café – I assume you have these in your local town.

Your birthday BBQ party obviously went well – it's always amusing when people dress up in costume – what gave you the idea for a clown theme? Are Emma and Sophie your best friends? I'm not surprised you had a big sleepover at the farm since you live in the middle of the countryside far from other houses. Tom has been brilliant in his emails to me, but he hasn't really told me a lot about your farm – the house and the layout. So perhaps you might describe them to me in your next email. You told me about the sheep and I know you have horses and are keen on riding.

Tom told me that since he passed his test he drives to school, takes you with him and collects Emma on the way. I hope he's a good driver. When I was young, I got frightened when driven at speed by boys who wanted to show off by accelerating and braking hard. Young people often drive faster than is wise, given their inexperience. In two years, you will be able to get a provisional licence – now, that is frightening!

I have a small car, which I bought second-hand two years ago. It does the job of taking me to work in a nearby village and back again and it gets me into town to shop. I admit that I'm rather careless about tyre pressures, checking the oil and getting the service done. But I've got current insurance, which is obligatory. The other day I was driving back through country lanes to Winterborne Slepe and a sturdy grey badger trundled into my path. I caught sight of his white flash in the headlights, jammed on all the brakes and just managed to stop in time. Sometimes I see deer dart into the trees and a fox slink across the road. Dorset is a rural county – and a beautiful place. Many villages have ancient churches – ours is unusual because two of its arches have curious carved heads surrounded by foliage, and there's a pulpit with fine carvings dating from the seventeenth century. On the edge of the village are some prehistoric standing stones, cold and mysterious.

Do tell me what your favourite subjects are at school. Do you like science, as Tom does? Or are you into languages or geography? I know these are questions that all adults ask teenagers, but I really would be interested to know. I like reading books – both prose and poetry – and I wonder what you read. I prefer fiction to non-fiction because I find works of the imagination are more powerful – and sometimes more truthful – than facts and figures. I was not particularly academic and never bothered to work very hard when I was at school. I spent much of my life regretting this and I've been trying to educate myself ever since.

So Bex is only four years old and your mum spends lots of time at home looking after her. When did your mum marry your stepfather and had he been married before? Tom told me about your cousins – and I expect the two girls came to your party. He tells me he's good friends with Ethan who likes boats. I once liked sailing but not anymore. I used to play tennis quite a bit but these days I'm more interested in walking through woodland and talking to people. I have friends here although some of the villagers are hard to get to know and a few are reclusive. There's an elderly man who lives beyond the pub and wears a black patch over one eye. He puffs away on evil-smelling cigarettes and spends most of his day pottering about and muttering. His Dorset accent is so thick that few can understand him, but he seems content to have all his conversations with himself. I once baked him a cake and when I gave it to him, he gave me a suspicious look as if I was trying to poison him. He probably fed it to his dog, a mangy mongrel who looks almost as dotty as his master. And just as dirty! You don't want to get downwind of old 'Smokey'!

He is one of the few residents who, along with myself, seem to be quite unperturbed by the dispute over James's wind turbine project. Some people in the village feel strongly that this village does not want a tall white windmill to be erected on the hill above the village and even go so far as to refuse to talk to James in the pub. That's unnecessarily rude and I hope all this anger will die down when the planning authorities make their decision one way or the other. Do you have these things in your part of New Zealand? I happen to think they're elegant and beautiful, though I don't want one sited in my back garden!

Rumour in the form of Alice has it that Lena, the Polish pub waitress, has set her sights on land-owner James and is hoping to hook him into marriage. She might be lucky as he does appear to be keen on her. They have been seen driving around in his sports car and sometimes he drives her home after she's finished her shift at the pub. Poor widowed Matt has retired from the battle and must be chewing his nails in frustration that he's lost his chance with her.

You asked me to send you a photograph and I plan to take one on my camera and download it onto my computer. But I've mislaid the small cable which enables me to do this – and that isn't the only problem. I fear my camera has gone AWOL (absent without leave). Sometimes I think there is a vindictive poltergeist in the house that moves my things around because they seem to disappear and then pop up in the most peculiar places. But tidiness eludes me and to be honest the place is a mess. I'm not proud of this.

What's your bedroom like? Or Tom's? Teenage boys' rooms always seem to be the worst.

Perhaps this weekend I might attack the house and give it a thorough clean, but alternatively I might decide to go for a walk and afterwards sit down and read a good book. The only advantage of being on your own is that you can please yourself. Best of all is to be with someone you love. In my next email to you both, I'll tell you about how your father came to marry your mother. From what Tom has said, I doubt whether she's told you the story.

bfsjdo08iparew h.i3748yu,/ My cat Folly has jumped onto the keyboard and her paws have created this incomprehensible code. I interpret this to mean: "You have been ignoring me too long and I demand you stroke my back." I oblige. I wish there was somebody to stroke mine! Julian used to love having his head massaged when he was a boy. As a father he loved to cuddle you, though sadly you won't remember that. I think you may have inherited your beautiful eyes from him.

With love from me and purrs from Folly,
GMJ xxx

"I tell you, Josie, I'm almost at the end of my tether!" Flora is red in the face and near to tears. They both glance across at the door leading to the kitchen. "He's sitting in there, being bloody-minded and drowning his sorrows in cider."

"Why is he so miserable?" Josie asks.

"He says it's because there are no customers, no meals to cook, no money coming in and bills keep flooding in. But that's just an excuse."

There's nobody else in the Anchor as it is lunchtime in February. Lena only comes in for the evenings during the weekdays, so Flora is on her own. It is Thursday – a day when Josie does not work – so she is ensconced in her favourite corner of the pub, chatting to her friend.

"It's always quiet at this time of year and though finances get a bit tight, we can weather it OK," Flora continues in a quieter tone. "Things perk up at weekends and we usually manage to keep the ship on course until business improves in the spring."

Josie looks at her friend's worried face. "Cheer up, Flora. Things could be worse." She winces at this trite remark - comfort is not bestowed that easily.

"No, they couldn't! My husband is an alcoholic. There, I've it said it last!" She glares across at the kitchen door and Josie pictures George skulking in there with his jug of cider.

Josie casts tact aside. "Why do you think he drinks? What's the underlying problem?"

"I don't know. Perhaps he's disappointed in life or else he finds me a drag to live with. Maybe he doesn't love me anymore. It could be I'm the disappointment." Flora looks down at her feet as if her scuffed boots might be the cause of his disapproval.

Josie won't let Flora indulge in self-pity. Her friend needs encouragement. "I'm sure that's not the case. Alcoholism is an addiction but it can be cured."

"It's no good. He won't admit he's got a problem and he won't seek any help. I know him – he's pig-headed."

The telephone on the bar rings. With a sigh Flora gets up to go and answer it. In the corner the television is switched on with the sound turned down and Josie can see that it is showing the day's events from the winter Olympics in Sochi in Russia. She shivers at the thought of snow but so far this February has been windy rather than cold. Recently a sea wall in Devon supporting the main railway line was washed away in a powerful storm and thousands of homes had no electricity. She is not listening to Flora's conversation on the telephone and her thoughts roam and settle on her grandchildren. She wonders what they are doing at this moment in New Zealand, so far away. She wants them to have limitless opportunities in their lives. She is not averse to young people undertaking risky activities or dangerous sports, but when Tom told her in an email that he had been bungee-jumping near Queenstown, something that he hadn't admitted to his mother, she was swamped by a landslide of terror. She can bear no more accidents to those she loves, and no more loss, especially now when she has found a new focus for her love: grandchildren to fill the void in her life.

The telephone call has ended and Flora walks back to join her. Josie feels sorry for her and George. A pub landlord who drinks is not an uncommon occurrence but it's a difficult problem for the stability of his marriage and his business. Before Flora reaches the table there is a loud crash in the kitchen followed a few seconds later by a terrified bellow from George. Flora spins round and runs toward the door, whilst Josie leaps to her feet and follows her.

There is blood everywhere. George is kneeling on the floor cradling his wrist to his abdomen and howling. The front of his white apron is a lake of spreading red and there is an arc of blood across the floor and one wall. Flora wails in horror, frozen for a few seconds, before she darts forward to help George. Josie realises that George has severed his artery in his wrist so she grabs a kitchen towel and gets Flora to help her tighten it around his upper arm.

"Go and ring for an ambulance," Josie says to Flora. "Go on. 999. They need to come as fast as they can."

Flora dashes through to the telephone in the bar, whimpering, but makes the call. Meanwhile Josie tries to recall a first aid course that she did a long while before, as she keeps the tourniquet tight. She needs to remember how long she can leave it like this before loosening it. George has stopped shouting but is in a state of shock, half lying on the floor leaning against a kitchen unit, and she is holding onto his arm with the sodden towel. There is blood everywhere. There is also broken glass - George must have dropped a glass jug of cider, which shattered on the tiles. Being unsteady he has slipped on the liquid and fallen heavily onto the jagged broken pieces.

Flora comes back, "They're on their way. It'll take about fifteen to twenty minutes." Her voice wobbles as she sees the lake of blood and cider and Josie crouching beside her husband, whose face is white with horror.

"Get me another cloth," Josie demands. When Flora

hands it to her, she packs it round the wound. "Telephone Doris. With a bit of luck, she should be at home only two minutes up the road." She sees Flora hesitate and raises her voice. "Doris is a nurse. Do it, Flora. Now."

Five minutes later, Doris comes in carrying a first aid kit and extra bandages. Within a few minutes she has adjusted the tourniquet and managed to get some bandages over the wound. She explains what she is doing in a measured tone to calm George who is moaning in pain at this point. She helps him to take couple of codeine and asks Flora to find something to put round his shoulders. Josie finds a broom to sweep away some of the glass debris.

At this point the ambulance arrives and the paramedics take control of the situation. Within twenty minutes they depart with their patient on a trolley in the back and an ashen-faced Flora accompanying him. Josie has reassured her that they will close up the pub.

"Thank you so much, Doris. You were brilliant."

"You didn't do too badly. What a nasty accident! Poor Flora - it's clear she can't cope with the sight of blood."

"I'm going to clear it all up before she gets back," says Josie looking at the blood spattering the wall.

"I'll give you a hand." Together she and Doris sweep up the broken glass and mop up the gory mess.

When they have finished, Doris carefully washes her hands. "So how did it happen?"

"George was on his own in the kitchen and got drunk. Flora should stop selling draught cider."

"That won't stop him. Nor would closing the pub. You can try to put temptation out of reach but an addict will find a way. There's another way of tackling the problem of alcoholism - and that's to get professional help."

Josie looks doubtful. "I don't think George would admit he's got a problem or agree to do that."

"Perhaps this nasty accident will convince him," Doris says as she puts on her coat.

When she has gone, Josie writes a 'Closed' note to pin on the pub entrance door, locks up the pub and leaves by the rear exit. She will try to ring Flora later. As she walks home, she prays this accident will be a wake-up call for George.

23rd February 2014

Dear Magpies,

It's a chilly February in Dorset and the village has snuggled down into its valley to wait out the spring and I have retreated to my sitting room with its wood-burning stove to keep warm and write to you.

It's a couple of months since I last wrote about Julian and the episode of his life when he decided to leave Colombia and go to study in Australia. Since you have expressed a wish to know more about your father, I think I'll continue the story from there. Although I wasn't in Australia with him, he was good at writing letters and sending news.

Apparently, he settled in well at Murdoch. He arrived in Perth in February 1994 to begin his course in veterinary science. He knew no one but soon made a few friends, mainly those on the same course and the ones with whom he was sharing accommodation. After his year in America and having an English mother meant his English was up to standard, so he didn't have many problems there. I think he found it difficult to adjust to the easy-going Australian lifestyle, after the structured and strict family and school life he had led in Colombia. But your father was an adaptable young man and after a while it was apparent that he was enjoying himself in the big country where he had chosen to study. He took up new sports – such as swimming and tennis but he also managed to contact an equestrian centre, where he was able to get free riding by helping out with the horses and mucking out stables at weekends. He could not afford a car, but friends gave him lifts and he managed.

Which was more than I was doing back in Colombia. I was still shell-shocked by the loss of Raul and, to compound my sense of bereavement, I now had to cope with the absence of my son. The fact that he was so far away made things difficult and I found myself unable to concentrate on tasks and, much worse, unable to smile. The joy had gone out of my life and I was lonely. Following the death of her brother, Natalia had taken time off from her job in Tolima province to be with her parents and with me. But in time she had to return to her work and her home, some hours west of Bogota. I was still living in our small apartment in Chapinero, close to my parents-in-law's house. I no longer had my job and was living on a small widow's pension from the shipping company, which had employed my husband.

About this time my mother-in-law, Paola, to whom I had never been particularly close, fell ill. I discovered that for some time she had concealed the fact that she had cancer. With a wide circle of friends and acquaintances, she did not want them to see her when she was looking less than her best, so she withdrew from society. She left the house only to have her treatments at the hospital. Inevitably, with little else except loss to occupy my mind, I made myself useful by looking after her. Though I tried hard to be caring, I know she resented my presence and the fact that she had to rely on me. Her husband, Juan Carlos, was unable to help because of his age and anyway he was still inconsolable from the death of his son. When Paola's condition deteriorated, Natalia again took leave from her teaching post and came back to Bogota. Together we nursed her mother until the poor woman finally died on a searing hot day in August.

Julian flew back to Colombia for her funeral – his grandfather paid for the ticket. But it fell in the middle of term and so he stayed only for a week before going back to Perth. Whilst with us, he spent much of this time consoling his grandfather and inevitably had less time with me. When he had gone my spirits plummeted. I knew I'd not see him again until he returned towards the end of the year for the longer summer holiday. It was too expensive for him to return to Colombia for the shorter holidays, so during these he stayed in Australia and got temporary jobs to help add to his maintenance allowance from his grandparents.

Juan Carlos was devastated by the death of his wife and gradually became reclusive. He missed his grandson and began to rely heavily on his daughter. But not on me. Although the old man was fond of me, he often gave the impression that he thought I was a jinx on the family. Natalia and I had a discussion and she decided it was her duty to give up her job in Tolima and return to find another job in the capital. She would live with her father and look after him. The rest of his family closed ranks and politely elbowed me out of their lives. My son was studying abroad and I had become dispensable to the Moreno family, who, with the exception of my sister-in-law, still regarded me as a foreigner. Kind-hearted Natalia was as loving and supportive to me as ever and always full of hope.

This feeling of redundancy and a sense of being no use to anybody set me thinking that I might leave Colombia and return to Europe. My mother was still living in France in a small house on the estate of her brother. In the same way that Raul had found his relationship with his mother problematic, I too had never been friends with my mother. It may be more accurate to say that she had not wanted a close loving relationship with her daughter.

In October that year, I planned to pay her a visit in France. Then I would go on to England to where I had spent some of the happiest moments of my childhood – Dorset – and see if I could start all over again and build a new life. I wrote to Julian and told him of my plans, but he pleaded with me to stay in Colombia until early the following year, because he would be coming back to spend the Christmas vacation with the family in Bogota. So I stayed on for another three months and he and I had Christmas with Natalia and Juan Carlos. In January my son and I went back to our apartment for three weeks, during which he saw some of his friends and spent time with me. He told me about his life in Australia and said that he had met a girl he liked very much. Like him, she was a first-year student and they had started dating. She was called Melissa.

In my next email, I'll tell you about your parents' marriage and my first visit to Australia. But before I finish, I must tell you about something dramatic that happened here about ten days ago.

Our local pub is called the Anchor, which is a strange name for one in the middle of a rural village, although nowhere in Dorset is that far from the sea. I'm good friends with Flora who runs the pub with her husband, George. I was there on a day off from work, chatting to Flora. We both heard a huge crash in the kitchen and dashed through to find that George had dropped a glass jug and fallen onto the broken fragments. He had severed the artery in his right wrist and was in deep shock. Flora telephoned for an ambulance and contacted a local nurse called Doris. I cannot tell you how awful it was with blood everywhere. The ambulance arrived and the paramedics took George to hospital. Soon he returned home (they live over the pub) with his arm in a bandage, but he cannot work. This poses a problem because the pub serves meals and he is the cook. I have been helping Flora in the bar or the kitchen on the days when I'm not working, and the waitress Lena has been marvellous and is working extra hours. So together the three of us have been managing well and soon George's arm will be healed enough for him to resume work. I must say I'm quite enjoying working there though it's hard work standing on your feet all evening.

Tom, like many students of your age, you will have worked part-time as a waiter. But what are your plans when you finish school next December? I expect you've discussed this with your mother and stepfather. Have you decided yet about further education? I should be so interested to know. It's been a while since I've heard from you. I'm writing to you together this time but sending it to your separate email addresses.

Lottie, thanks for your email last week. I was sorry to hear that you've had an argument with Sophie but I expect it will blow over in time. It's never worth bearing grudges for too long. It hurts the person who feels the anger and it damages peace of mind. Let it go, that's my advice. Concentrate on your netball and see if you can get into the school team. What position do you play?

I lost track of time! I must leave now and go to the pub for my Sunday shift.

With love from a barmaid,
GMJ xxx

He is sitting at a table in the company of a farmer and a couple of locals, listening to the usual banter and desultory conversation. It is Saturday evening and the pub is crowded. His eyes follow Lena as she flits like a moth amongst the tables, chatting and smiling to customers, her dark hair swinging in a loose plait down her back. Flora is in the kitchen with George who has to take things more slowly since his accident. Drunken fool! Josie is working behind the bar, a job she has clearly taken to like a duck to water, and has become adept at pulling pints, opening bottles and chatting to customers at the bar. Her presence here during the last couple of weeks has meant that her cottage is invitingly empty on three or four evenings a week.

He recalls how nervous he was on the first few occasions that he made his illicit entry over a year ago. But now, as Josie spends many evenings working in the pub, he has become used to 'visiting' her home in her absence. He has even managed to overcome his uneasiness when confronted by the accusing stare of her weird cat. He can read the woman's emails in the comfort of his own sitting room, but he enjoys the excitement of creeping warily around her cottage in the dark with a small red pencil-light torch. He has even ventured upstairs and he anticipates the excitement of slinking around her rooms in soft shoes, flicking through her personal papers and fingering her possessions. He fears detection but the acid tingle of apprehension has become almost like a drug during the past months.

A man at his table laughs at some remark that has

been made. Joining in, he grins at his companions, picks up his drink and drains it.

Yes, he likes sleuthing.

15th March 2014

Dear Magpies,

At last there is a hint of spring in the air – the birdsong is more exuberant, daffodils are beginning to unfurl and the fields glisten with dew, washed in the rays of a luminous sun. It's early morning and I'm at my table with the new day dancing outside my window. What a delight! Equally delightful is the fact that I'm feeling close to you as I write this.

I will continue my story and your father's too: I was at the point where both he and I left Colombia in February 1995. He returned for his second year doing veterinary science at university in Australia, and I went to Europe to try and find respite from my loss. It was now a year and a half since Raul's death and I was still searching for inner peace and my lost smile. I was only forty-three, a widow with half of my life before me. I didn't want just to exist – I wanted to live again.

Back in Colombia, Julian's grandfather was becoming a sad introverted old man and I don't think he noticed I had gone. Natalia was the only one sorry to see me depart but we knew we'd always be sisters and promised to keep in touch. I flew to France where I arrived in the middle of winter and realised how few warm clothes I possessed. I travelled from Paris to Normandy where my mother lived amongst her relatives. Although I had seen little of her since our time together following my father's death, my mother did not invite me to share her small house and so I stayed with my uncle in the big *manoir* on his estate. It was strange speaking French once again – the language was submerged in my mind and I now had to pull it out, polish it off and start to re-use it.

My French cousins teased me about my English and Spanish accents and tried to rouse me out of my habitual sadness. Though I felt like a refugee it was comforting to be amongst my family again, even though we had been apart for many years. I had forgotten how witty French conversations could be and how delicious the food always was. I had become rather thin during the previous year and, now I was eating brioche, baguettes and pâté, I put on some weight. My mother, your great-grandmother, talked a lot about her health and lamented the deprivations of living in the country and having no access to civilised life in the city. The constant complaints enabled her to avoid addressing difficult topics such as my bereavement and my disorientation. I could not discuss my son with her and share how much I missed him. She was not interested in my life in Colombia and recoiled from any of my attempts at intimacy. Nothing had changed – she was as distant from me as ever.

I stayed with my uncle and his wife for about six weeks and although they were happy for me to stay longer, I was embarrassed to accept further hospitality. I was also restless. Not feeling ready to return to England and face the daunting job of trying to build a life for myself there, I decided on a whim to go to Spain. I had a few savings left in a bank account in Colombia and I still had the small pension from the shipping company, so in April I took a train south and west. Raul and I had always dreamed of going to Andalusia in southern Spain and I decided that this was unfinished business. This region is blisteringly hot in the summer months but is warm and delightful in the spring.

As I started on my travels, I imagined that I was accompanied by my beloved husband, serenaded by his deep voice and embraced by his love. I began to feel comforted in his remembered presence. Together we walked through the pillared perfection of the Moorish Alhambra Palace – a place of exquisite beauty in the mountainous Granada. He paced along beside me as I wandered through the Alcazar castle in Seville and he was with me as I climbed the Giralda – a great bell tower of the city's mighty cathedral – and then we knelt and prayed together in the chancel within. I talked to him about the amazing effect created by the strong arches in the powerful Mezquita, Córdoba's mosque-cathedral. We wandered together in the hills and along rivers and visited the Alcazaba, an eleventh-century fortification in Malaga.

Please don't think that your grandmother was out of her mind. In fact, I was regaining control over my grief and allowing it to dissipate, as this Spanish interlude enabled me to place it in its proper perspective. With Raul 'beside' me, I learned to appreciate the rich culture and fine architecture of Andalusia. And I also learned to accept that in future I would always be able to draw on the strength of my memories and the happiness we had shared. On my last day before I crossed over to Gibraltar, from where I would fly back to England, I wandered barefoot along the seashore at Algeciras. I felt the waves flow around my feet and when they receded, they took my pain with them. I met another woman walking in the other direction and, when she raised one hand in greeting, I managed a smile. I was ready for the way ahead.

Meanwhile, whilst I was warming myself in Spain in the imaginary presence of the love of my life, in an autumnal Australia our son Julian was fanning the flames of his first love. He kept in touch with me by the occasional letter and told me more about Melissa Jones. A year younger than him, she was attending the same college, studying geography and they had met at a student party the previous November. He had seen a vision with long golden hair from across the room and 'her laughter had chimed in his heart' – very poetic, your father! He had pushed his way through to her and introduced himself in his charming accented English. (When I met her the following year, I found that he had not exaggerated and she was indeed a strikingly good-looking young woman with blue eyes and sun-tanned skin, gleaming with health.) Clearly, she found Julian attractive with his raven hair and melting brown eyes and with his being an exotic stranger from South America and with a Colombian family wealthy enough to send him to study in Australia.

They had much in common. They were studying at the same place. They were both young and beautiful. Julian discovered that Melissa enjoyed riding and they would often spend hours in the outback riding on a couple of horses from the stables where he did part-time work. He admired her energy and extrovert personality which made her popular with others and she appreciated him for his graceful sincerity and delightfully old-fashioned courtesy. She threw a party for him on his twenty-first birthday in August that year and they spent all their spare time together. They were in love.

Your father was an only child and so was your mother. Her parents lived in a small town in the fertile south-west corner of Western Australia; he was a pharmacist and his wife worked in the local community hospital. Apparently, when Julian first met them, they were suspicious about their daughter's strange foreign boyfriend but he soon won them round with his charm and gentle manners. When he needed a job during the two-week short break in October, they invited him to stay and he got temporary work in the town. In late December at the end of the second year at Murdoch, true to his promise, Julian flew home to Colombia and spent a month there to please his grandfather. I was unable to join him in Colombia for Christmas, because my mother fell ill and I was summoned to France to nurse her. One evening whilst I was in my uncle's house in Normandy, Julian telephoned me from his grandfather's house. I could hear the elation in his voice as told me he had asked Melissa to marry him and she had said yes. They wanted to have the wedding in a couple of months which seemed very hasty to me. I was about to mention that they were very young to get married but recalled that I was married at the same age and that I had not wanted to wait either. My protest died on my lips. Julian told me her parents were happy about it, so I had to go along with their plans.

Thankfully, my mother recovered from her illness, which enabled me to return to England and then fly out to Western Australia for the wedding, which was held in Melissa's home town. Julian met me at the airport and gently revealed to me the wonderful news that he and Melissa were going to have a child in the late summer. I was delighted about becoming a grandmother for the first time. Quite a young one too! It was immediately apparent that the wedding had been arranged as soon as possible to avoid embarrassing older members of the family.

Julian had bought a battered second-hand car with some of his earnings and together we drove south to Melissa's family home. She was already there, and Julian and I had been found accommodation with some kind friends of her parents. I only met your maternal grandparents two days before the wedding, which gave me little time to get to know them. Julian looked relaxed and happy, though I had detected a slight apprehension about the future and how he was going to be able to provide for a wife and young child. But on the day both he and Melissa looked radiant.

I wonder if your mother has ever told you about her wedding day. As Julian was a Catholic and Melissa's parents were Anglican, a church marriage had been arranged. The marriage ceremony began in a catastrophic way – with the bridegroom nearly missing his own wedding! It is the bride who often arrives late because she is nervous or her hair needs to be rearranged or simply because it's her prerogative to keep the guests waiting in anticipation. But it was Julian who caused huge embarrassment by his late appearance. Traditionally the groom does not stay at the same house as the bride on the night before the wedding, so it had been arranged that his best man would collect him from where we were staying, take him for a light lunch and then deliver him to the church in good time before the start of the 2 pm wedding service. I was given a lift to the church by friends of the family but Julian was not there when we arrived. I confidently expected that he would turn up well in advance of the scheduled time and well before his bride. When 2 pm came and went, there was some consternation amongst the guests because there was no sign of either the bride or the groom. I was subsequently told that Melissa was waiting for fifteen minutes outside the church with her two bridesmaids and her father who was to give her way.

At ten minutes past two, everyone was squirming uncomfortably in their pews when the wail of a siren was heard, immediately followed by the shriek of brakes and the banging of car doors. The two young men in dark suits appeared at the church door, the groom with a face of desperate panic and the best man grinning with relief. Their car had broken down and eventually they had flagged down a police car that drove them to the church. They cantered up the aisle and stood at the front with chests heaving from exertion and stifled laughter. A minute later the bride entered the church with an expression on her face which said 'We are not amused'! Poor

Melissa – she may have feared that Julian had jilted her at the church. He would never have been that cruel, but without doubt he upstaged his bride. A cat did too, but that's another story.

After the wedding I returned to England and your parents returned to university and it wasn't until April during the two-week vacation that they had a brief honeymoon at a hotel by the sea. A few months later, Tom was born.

After the initial euphoria of becoming parents, Julian and Melissa realised that having a small baby and trying to be full-time students was a difficult task. Money was tight. They both had to get part-time jobs and they juggled the childcare between them, since her parents did not live close enough to help much. With the responsibilities of parenthood came the realisation that their previous carefree student life had gone forever.

In England I was also struggling – to find work. With no qualifications I was able only to get part-time work as a shop assistant or a carer. Eventually I had managed to get a job working in a residential care home in a large town in Dorset, where I found a bedsit to rent. In September I took two weeks' holiday and flew out to Australia to see my grandson for the first time. Tom, you may be a tall strong young man now, but then you were a small baby. When I first held you, a deluge of emotion swamped me and I knew that a bond had been established that would remain all my life. I like to feel I was some help to Julian and Melissa during my stay. I slept on a sofa in their tiny student apartment, sharing the room with my grandson. Melissa had stopped breastfeeding early to enable her to go to lectures, and I was sorry for her because her final exams (for her three-year course) were looming up later that autumn. She was overtired and stressed out. Julian was loving and supportive but we all knew that he had three more years of studying before he qualified as a vet and could earn any significant salary.

I returned to the UK elated by my visit but dismayed by the prospect of seeing very little of my son and his family in the future. Before I left Julian told me he had decided to stay in Australia after he qualified. He hoped to visit me in England and promised to go back to Colombia to visit his grandfather and aunt occasionally. He was immensely grateful to his grandfather for supporting his education and I believe he wrote to the old man from time to time. Sadly, financial and family circumstances never enabled him to travel to England.

During the next three years the family trio had a happy life in Australia. Tom, do you have any memories from this period? I came out for another visit when you were two years old and we had some lovely days together when I basked in the warmth of my family like someone deprived of the sun. However, it was at this time that your mother's attitude to me changed. Commendably she had a job and was keeping the family income going whilst her husband continued his long course of study. She was not enjoying her teaching post, which was tiring and demanding and allowed too little time with her own child. I had the feeling that she resented my presence and was jealous of my close relationship with my son. Naturally, because I visited Australia so rarely, Julian spent a lot of time with me during my stay. Melissa, who had the advantage of seeing her parents regularly, did not appreciate my need to spend time with him. She had decided not to take any holiday during my visit so, when she was at work, I looked after my grandson and loved getting to know him. When she arrived home in the evening, she found the two of us laughing and playing together whilst Julian studied. Perhaps she felt left out and, even though I tried to get her to join in, I knew she would be glad to see the back of me when I left. Resentment festers, I'm sorry to say.

This email is longer than intended, my dearest Magpies. It's hard to condense years of life into a few paragraphs. But I shall have to break off as it's time for me to go to church because the Sunday service starts at 11 am and I have to walk there. I sometimes sing on my way. Some people find this eccentric but I find it fun. I'll be thinking of you on the other side of the globe and I'll sing a bit louder so you can hear me.

From your loving extrovert,
GMJ xxx

As Josie lays the fire in her wood burner, placing logs on top of paper and kindling, she is wondering if it was alright to reveal to her grandson that he was conceived before his parents' wedding. It's a minor issue and there's nothing unconventional about it these days. In all probability he knows already and it won't shock him if he doesn't. Why is she always so outspoken? As she looks around for the matches, she hopes the truth won't embarrass him. Is this a secret that Melissa and Julian kept from their son? She has no way of knowing and hopes that Tom does not blurt it out and cause his mother to ask how he found out.

Josie finds the box of matches on the floor under the table and kneels down to light the fire. The paper ignites and the flame runs along it, curling and burning the edges beneath the wood. As she watches a thin spiral of smoke waft upwards, she remembers how sceptical she was when Melissa told her that her pregnancy was a happy accident. In any case, Julian loved her and did the honourable thing, insisting they get married without delay. Her precious Magpies are the children of that marriage and they are the only family she has left.

She gazes at the smouldering fire and sees a little flame lick round the edge of a log. At last. She hears a creak and glances round but there is no one there. Perhaps it is Folly who is in the house somewhere. She does not believe in ghosts or evil visitations. But yesterday she caught her breath when she found the dusty footprint of a shoe on the carpet in her bedroom. She stared at it for a few moments hoping it might be one of her own. Cautiously she placed her own foot into it and saw it was far too big to be hers. She had shuddered – there was no warmth in it such as the page had found in Good King Wenceslas' footstep in the snow. She was gripped by an icy conviction that an intruder had been in her house.

And now as she watches the fire warm her sitting room, she thinks she might have overreacted. Perhaps her landlord, James, who has a key, came in to do an inspection, or sent in one of his workmen during her absence. Unlikely but just possible. In any case the footprint tells her that a real person has been in her home without her knowledge. The cottage does not feel like a safe haven any more.

19th April 2014

Dear Lottie,

I'm so glad you liked my account of your parents' wedding day and want to hear the story of the cat in the church. I am surprised that your mother brushed aside your questions about her first wedding – maybe she found it awkward to tell you about it because Robert was in the room. I'm sorry I forgot to describe the wedding dress. I recollect that it was long, lacy and white. In order to refresh my memory, I have tried to find a box of old photographs which include some of the wedding, but I seem to have mislaid it. It will probably turn up in a place that I'm not expecting it to be. Anyhow, all of us thought Melissa and Julian a very handsome couple.

What I do remember clearly was a curious incident during the ceremony when Julian and Melissa were standing at the altar taking their vows. A black cat had found its way into the church and with tail erect it began to walk up the main aisle. Some of the congregation smiled as the cat trotted past, but when it arrived at where Julian and Melissa were standing, it began to walk through and round Julian's feet, nuzzling his ankles. Though this was a little distracting, Julian tried to ignore it. Eventually it was Melissa who bent down and gave it a gentle smack to send it away. Whereupon the cat gave a yowl of protest and hissed at her. At this point one of the two bridesmaids, both friends of Melissa's, ran forward to pick up the mewling cat and carry it off into a side aisle of the church. Later at the reception some guests said they found the incident entertaining whilst others thought it unfortunate. Someone remarked that a black cat would bring good luck to the married couple. Most of us hoped the marriage would be blessed.

I was touched when you said that you are more interested in me, your grandmother, than in your father – a man whom you never knew because he died when you were six months old. Tom wants to know about his father and that's understandable. Boys need to respect and admire their fathers. You pointed out that

Tom doesn't have a close bond with his stepfather and resents the discipline that Robert imposes. Lottie, of course you and your mother are dismayed when he argues with Robert. But I don't know many teenage boys who don't argue with their fathers from time to time about restrictions and reprimands. I'm sure their disagreements will only be temporary. I'm glad that you really like Robert and often accompany him when he goes out on the farm.

You admitted to me that you get angry with your mother because she's always telling you what to do. Again, that's normal – it's unusual to find any mother and daughter who don't have the occasional tiff. She just wants the best for you.

It's nice to know that you all get on fine with Bex, even if she is a bit of an attention seeker. You shouldn't resent being an unpaid babysitter – that's part of being in a family. Just think about the many things your mother does for you and try to help her – with love and without complaint.

I'm sorry that you were unable to get to Christchurch on April 14th when Prince William and his wife Catherine came to the city as part of their Royal tour in New Zealand. I'm sure it was disappointing not to see them and their little baby boy, Prince George. I too have only seen photographs of him, as I hardly ever go to London and the Royal family rarely come to Dorset, except for Prince Charles who often visits a town called Poundbury, with which he is closely involved.

I must tell you something strange about the cottage where I live. It's built of stone, has a thatched roof and is over a hundred years old. It's very similar to the house next door where my neighbours, Bill and Lou, have lived for years. I was chatting to Lou the other day and she told me a curious story about my cottage. Apparently, over many years various people had seen or sensed the unmistakable presence of a young girl carrying a baby. Lou said that until five years ago, whenever she was in my cottage, she had felt accompanied by this girl and her baby. It seems no one ever felt frightened by the apparition. When old Mr Trevett undertook renovations to my cottage before I moved in, he asked Bill to put in a new door. After this was finished, he and Lou had been standing there and they suddenly felt the girl and her baby glide past and out of the door. Nobody has ever encountered them again, but the memory of their gentle loving presence still lingers in the cottage and the garden.

I don't believe in ghosts, but I do think that's a beautiful story. There is no doubt that there are things in the spiritual world about which we know very little and which we can't explain. I expect you study Shakespeare at school, and in his most famous tragedy, the main character Hamlet says this to his best friend:

> There are more things in heaven and earth, Horatio,
> Than are dreamt of in your philosophy.

I happen to believe in a good and loving God and I trust that He guides and protects me. We all encounter evil people and the suffering they cause. We live in a broken world but there is always hope. And love conquers all.

It is of course Easter Sunday tomorrow, probably the most meaningful day in the Christian calendar. After going to church I'll come back here, where I have invited some friends for lunch. Today I must prepare a big chicken casserole and attempt a lemon cheesecake. I don't seem to have the knack of making a dessert that looks pretty as well as tasting nice. Just in case I get it wrong, I've bought a large chocolate egg that we can all share!

I hope that you, Tom and your family have a lovely Easter.

Do you have an egg hunt in the garden amongst the autumn leaves? I do love getting your emails, dearest Lottie.

> With love and Easter blessings,
> GMJ xxx

11th May 2014

Dear Tom,

You write that you have decided to take a year off between school and university to go travelling in Asia for a few months. I expect you call it a 'gap year' as we do. To save up enough money, you said you'd find some work after leaving school early next year. That's a good plan but right now you need to concentrate on those all-important exams. I'm pleased to hear about your girlfriend and that you might go travelling together but don't think you should be planning this in order to get away from your stepfather. And I really don't approve of you referring to your stepfather as a 'fat tyrant'. A tendency to exaggerate does run in our family – but that's over the top. My advice is to be polite and helpful at home and to avoid getting into any arguments if he is, as you say, oppressive and opinionated. Julian used to have the odd disagreement with Raul but in general they respected each other. How dreadfully sad that your natural father is no longer alive! He adored you and Lottie.

Thanks so much remembering my birthday three days ago. I have made a note that you've changed your email address. I'm sure your reasons for doing so are valid – privacy is important. I realise that in your final year with much studying to be done you need to have access to your own computer all the time. I'm very pleased to hear that your sister's friend, Emma, is letting Lottie use her laptop to send and receive emails. Lottie tells me she is no longer friends with Sophie.

Whilst on the subject of privacy, I'm going to tell you something that I do not propose to tell Lottie because she is three and a half years younger than you and it might worry her, whereas at nearly eighteen you are an adult. I am uneasy about odd things that are happening to me and I need to share this with someone who cares about me and won't think that I'm overreacting. You might even be able to give your grandmother some advice. This is the problem:

It has become apparent to me during the last year that somebody – probably a man – has been infringing my privacy and spying on me in my cottage. I have always had an open-door policy in this village, as many of us do. We are a rural community and we trust each other. We lock the door at night, but many of us leave the front or back door open during the day, and there is a tacit understanding that we don't go into each other's houses unless invited. We certainly don't enter if it's obvious that the owner is absent.

I don't think this person is a thief although, by robbing me of my peace of mind, in a sense he is. My intuition has become sharpened and on occasions I sense there has been an alien presence. I notice that Folly is a little more nervous these days and I'm sure that, if she could talk, she would have much to tell me. Nothing of any consequence goes missing but sometimes things are moved, or they get lost and then reappear in a place where I would not have put them. Everyone in the village knows that I am chaotically untidy, but what they don't realise is that there is an illogical but very real order in my untidiness. Whoever is making entry into my house has underestimated my ability to notice where things are kept and where they ought not to be. I even found a large dusty footprint one day. So I'm not imagining things and nor is there a ghostly visitation. I do have faith in God but do not believe in poltergeist, which are spirits that supposedly make loud noises and throw objects around, neither of which is happening in my house.

As I am merely the tenant of this cottage, my landlord James undoubtedly has a key. I have checked with him and he said he would never enter my house for any reason without informing me in advance. My next-door neighbour, Bill, who has lived in the area all his life, is a good friend and he also has a key. This is in case I should ever mislay my own key, which I have been known to do! On rare occasions I have asked him to keep an eye on the house whilst I've been away, and his wife, Lou, looks after my cat in my absence. I now lock the door every time I leave the house.

There are two things that puzzle me: who is this person and why is he doing it? I have nothing of any value, I indulge in no illegal activities and have few secrets. I need to know how I can stop it happening. Any suggestions?

With love from an anxious,

GMJ xxx

"I was under the impression you were from Dorset," Harry says to Josie. They are sitting on a bench just outside his house enjoying some warm spring sunshine. Josie was walking past when Harry called her over, so she has stopped for a chat.

"My father was from here but I was born in Paris and so was my brother Henri. Our French mother insisted on returning to France for our births. Where were you born?"

"Born and bred in Dorset, from Shaftesbury. I'm still fond of the sturdy little town sitting on its hill."

"My father was born in Weymouth. He was an only child, like my mother." Josie is looking down Long Lane and can see a small figure trudging upwards.

"I was in Weymouth a couple of weeks ago," Harry says. "I happened to walk past a bookmaker and to my surprise I saw Matt Tapper come out of the door. He said 'hello' and mumbled something about being in Weymouth on business before quickly walking off. He's an awkward sort of chap."

"He was probably embarrassed about being seen emerging from a betting shop. He's difficult to get to know but I wouldn't have thought him a gambling man. I'm sorry for him – he's on his own. It's tough losing your wife when you're young." She can see that it's Alice who is approaching, carrying some tulips. She is probably on her way to the church to do the flowers.

As she draws level with Harry's house, Alice calls out, "Good morning, Harry. Hello, Josie," and gives them a knowing smile as she continues on her way.

Harry groans. "She's bound to misinterpret our friendly conversation."

"I shouldn't worry. Nobody takes Alice's comments too seriously." Josie smiles. "Did you know her husband? She never talks about him."

"That's because he left her. He was a quiet bloke and a good craftsman. But he couldn't stand the constant nagging."

Josie is surprised. "I thought he'd died."

"He did, but after they parted. She'd drive any man to an early grave! There's a proverb which says it's better to live alone than with a complaining wife."

"What was your wife like, Harry?" Josie knows that he has been divorced for many years.

Harry smiles and, looking across at the church, says, "What a lovely day!"

Josie feels a prickle of irritation. Harry is a man who is happy to comment on other people's lives but is reticent about his own.

19th June 2014

Dear Magpies,

I am now getting towards the end of the story of your father's life. You and your parents, Tom, were living in Western Australia where your father continued with his veterinary science course and your mother worked in various schools. They decided to have no more children until he was qualified and able to get a well-paid job as a vet.

I had always hoped to be able to get back to Australia for another visit but my finances were at this stage in poor shape, having spent all my savings on air flights. To supplement my small income, I had managed to get a job working in a bookshop which was poorly paid and gloriously peaceful, but after a few months it closed down. Such a disappointment! I had been renting a one-bedroomed flat in Bridport, an attractive Dorset town not far from the sea, but I found another job near Wimborne, further east in the county. So I moved to live there.

Then my mother had another bout of illness, and I had to go to France to look after her again. This resulted in losing my job and my accommodation. After I returned I looked for work in residential care homes and managed to get a job in a town not far from where I'd been at school, and moved to share a small flat near work with another care worker. I began to think I might be able to start saving for the airfare to Australia but my hopes were dashed.

For some reason the modest widow's pension I received from the Colombian shipping company suddenly ceased in 1999. When I wrote to ask why this had happened, I was told that it was their policy not to pay pensions to people who were of other nationalities and non-resident, that I was British and hadn't returned to Colombia for three years. I asked Natalia to intervene on my behalf but neither she nor I had any luck in reinstating the payments. This was a setback but I decided not to mope about it and got on with working towards my goal of having a real home. I'd discovered I liked Dorset and my aim was to live in a rural area. If you have to live on your own on a slender income, a village is a much better place to be than a big city.

Around this time, I received the wonderful news that Julian and Melissa were going to have another child, due the following January, just into the new millennium. I began to save for the airfare to enable me to visit them after the birth. Julian finished his long training in late 1999 and managed to get a job in a good veterinary practice, which specialised in larger animals rather than domestic pets. He would start in January 2000 and could support the family, giving Melissa a much-needed break from work, enabling her to spend more time with Tom and the new baby. Everything was going well for them.

Lottie, you were born in mid-January and within a month

I took two weeks' leave from my work and flew out to meet my granddaughter. Julian had just started work and Melissa was at home with the children and during my visit I helped look after Tom whilst she was nursing Lottie. I remember this holiday as a blissfully happy interlude. Before I left Julian and I had a serious discussion about my living so far away. We both agreed that during the year I should pack up my life in England and move out to live near them. He would persuade Melissa, who was doubtful about this plan, and I would have to think about care for my mother who would obviously remain in France. But nevertheless, the future looked full of promise.

But then it all imploded. In December that year when Tom was four and Lottie less than a year old, Julian died whilst on a visit to Colombia. I don't know whether you want to know more and, if you do, I need to think carefully before I tell you.

It is midsummer here and midwinter with you. On Saturday – which is 21st June – we have our usual Midsummer village fete. I must now go and meet the woman who is running the tombola. She wants some help collecting and ticketing donated items such as bottles of cheap plonk, jars of homemade jam and unwanted tins of food such as baked beans!

With love from a summery village,

GMJ xxx

23rd July 2014

Dear Lottie,

It was good to get your email and hear about the week you spent with your cousins near Christchurch. Pity the weather wasn't so good. You obviously get on well with Robert's sister Nicole, who likes to take you all off on adventures. You write that her husband Mark, who is an airline pilot, is 'ugly but funny'. I wonder why we always imagine pilots to be dashing and debonair. They are just ordinary working men and women who transport people by flying aeroplanes rather than driving trains or buses. Anyhow, having a sense of humour is better than having a handsome face.

Thank you for sending me a photograph of you and Bex. How pretty she is with her dark hair! She doesn't seem to be much like Melissa, so I guess she must be rather like her father. Do you have a family photograph of all five of you? I should love to see it.

So you are back at school now that your two-week holiday is over. I'm glad you enjoy English and history. They were my favourite subjects at school as well. I had a wonderful English teacher called Mrs Beckett who inspired me to read widely and taught me how to appreciate poetry. It sounds as if your history teacher, Mrs Price, is an enthusiast who can generate in her pupils a curiosity about history. Do ask her questions – and listen to the answers. Teachers appreciate students who want to learn.

It's a shame you don't like Tom's girlfriend. Just because you think that her lipstick is too red doesn't mean she's not the right kind of girl for him. He's the best judge of that.

All is well here – though I've got a stiff back from gardening. Flowers look beautiful but you can't eat them, so I spend a lot of time growing vegetables. The weeds grow well too and I find weeding very tiresome. Folly enjoys the kitchen garden too and loves to lie down in my herb patch – the smell of thyme sends her ecstatic!

I have a secret to tell you. Yesterday I received a phone call from Maggie Damon, who is about to be divorced from John Damon. She is planning to come down and remove some items from his house whilst he is at work. She wants to come and see me whilst she's here, but I don't want to be complicit in her underhand way of repossessing what she considers to be hers. Even though she used to be a good friend, I ought to tell her I'd rather not see her, because I don't want to wreck my cordial relationship with John. What a problem. I'll let you know what happens.

With love and indecision,

GMJ xxx

13th September 2014

Dear Tom,

It was good to hear from you. I know you are immersed in revising for exams, so you don't need to apologise for not writing before. I'm glad your plans for your gap year are progressing and that you think you've found a summer job in Dunedin to start in December. Will you be spending Christmas there or with your family in Canterbury?

How kind of you to be worried on my behalf and to ask me whether I have yet had the locks changed on my house. I took your advice and told my landlord about my suspicions that someone else might have access to the cottage. I admitted that now and then I had left my keys lying around in the kitchen or sitting room and I had currently mislaid my spare set. It was possible somebody had taken them. I couldn't imagine why anyone should want to rob me – it's not as if I have jewels and money lying around! And I often leave my door open so a key wouldn't be necessary. Anyhow, it's taken a few weeks but James finally got a locksmith in and now it's done. I had to pay for it but at least I know that the only people who have the new keys are me and him.

Tom, you say you want to hear the account of how your father died. As you may have guessed, it was appalling. He met a violent death. Unlike you, Lottie does not remember her father at all, so I don't want to shock her with the details. But since you have made this request yet again, I reluctantly promise to write it all down soon and send it just to you. I'll have to walk down the corridor in my mind to the dark door where I keep nightmares locked up and drag this one out into the open. As Julian's son, you have a right to know the truth and only I can tell you, as I was in Colombia at the time.

With love and cold feet,

GMJ xxx

It is past 11 pm and the village is dark, its occupants already asleep.

He leans back in his chair. He has just sent an email to the Colombian to say that that he no longer has access to the woman's house because the locks have been changed. He can still access her emails and these have warned him that she is now very much aware that somebody has been looking around her house and personal effects. It will not now be possible to try and enter the place again as she will be on her guard. In any case he has not found anything of significance which would help the search.

His investigation, which began from a chance encounter on the internet, is therefore over. What he has not mentioned is that he is angry. Very angry. The thrill he gets from spying has been curtailed. He will find some way to punish her for locking him out. He knows where she is vulnerable.

PART III

IN THE OPEN

27th September 2014

Dear Magpies,

I'm seething. Alice has just departed. She dropped in to feed me a tasty morsel of gossip, which has left me with a bad taste in the mouth. I shall of course repeat it to no one in the village but, as Alice will undoubtedly share it with everyone, I don't see that it matters telling you since you are thousands of miles away.

Folly and I were having a quiet Saturday afternoon. She was on my lap whilst I was reading a book. A familiar voice outside my kitchen door called, "Anyone in?" Unfortunately, I was at home. I sighed and put down my book.

"Come on in, Alice," I called and got to my feet. Without waiting she trotted through to the sitting room. She accepted my offer of a cup of tea and I suggested she sit down whilst I made it. Alice looked doubtfully at my sagging sofa but gave a small smile and perched on the edge of it. I went into the kitchen to make the tea and give her an opportunity to have a good look around. When I returned with two mugs she was sitting with her hands clasped innocently in her lap. She began to search in her bag to find her excuse for calling and triumphantly produced a book on butterflies, which I had lent her about nine months before and completely forgotten about it. She apologised for not returning it sooner. I sipped my tea and waited for the real reason for her visit.

Alice mentioned she had been having a coffee with Flora and had discovered that George had joined AA (Alcoholics Anonymous). Then she told me that the pub waitress, "a flirty Polish girl", had been doing cleaning work in James's holiday cottage and, since he has had success with this new venture, he told Lena he was looking around to find another place to renovate and rent in the same way. At this point Alice lowered her voice conspiratorially. "Yesterday,

I saw Lena with James in his car again. I think she's got plans to catch herself a wealthy husband. Then she can stay in England and lord it over us as his wife," Alice paused but I was so irritated I made no answer. "It's a bit delicate but I'm wondering whether I should warn James about her, because last week I was in Dorchester doing some shopping and, by complete coincidence, I spotted Lena having a meal in a café with a tall man who looked familiar. I could only see his back but when he turned his head, I was amazed to see Matt Tapper. They were too busy talking and didn't notice me. Since he's your next-door neighbour, Josie," Alice said leaning forward, "I wanted to ask if you've seen Lena visit Matt in his house and whether I should warn James that the young woman is not to be trusted."

At this point I could take it no longer and responded by saying I liked Lena and respected her. I added that her friendships were nobody's business except her own. Alice shrugged and examined a small chip in her mug before drinking her tea and murmuring, "Poor Matt, he's only thirty-seven and must be so lonely." Picking up her handbag, she stood up and looked around the room. "This would make a nice holiday cottage," she said casually as she left.

Now I've let off steam by writing this to you, I confess I'm not too bothered by what Alice said. Lena has been the subject of lots of speculation and she sensibly ignores it. As for the other matter, I know all about James's holiday cottage. I have a lease for 'The Haven' to the end of next year and I'm hopeful that James will renew it. I've lived in rented accommodation most my life and will no doubt continue to do so. Finding the monthly rent is sometimes a little difficult but God is good and somehow, I manage. There are millions of people who live on very slender incomes and millions more who have no home at all, so I have nothing to complain about.

By the way, Tom, I was horrified to hear from you about the terrible event in your part of South Island, when a man shot dead two women in an office because he was disgruntled with how he had been treated. It's the sort of atrocity that you don't associate with a peaceful place like New Zealand. These things happen all the time in war zones in the Middle East and in big cities in America where gun laws are very lax and also in South America. It's sad to say that even in England we have knife crime and in cities many schoolchildren carry knives to protect themselves. However, when people tell me that we live in a violent world, I say that we live in a world where the vast majority of people want to live in peace and to love their families. I want you both to grow up with hope in your hearts, enthusiasm for life and the ability to accept that difficult things happen – because they do – and learn to cope when tough times come along.

Lottie, thank you for telling me about the general election on 20th September. I'm so glad your school is farsighted enough to give you information about the various issues and the electoral process. You will be much better informed when you are able to vote at eighteen, as your brother can now. Getting young people to vote has always been difficult. But on the day before your general election in New Zealand, there was a referendum held in Scotland as to whether or not it should be a separate country from the rest of the UK, and a huge number of young people voted. By a narrow majority, Scotland decided to stay as a part of the UK, but it's not impossible that there won't be another referendum in the future when this might change. It would seem strange to have to cross a border to get to Scotland, which is where my stepdaughter lives, although on a personal level she and I have always had boundaries between us. This used to sadden Oliver.

I am reminded that I haven't yet told you about my second marriage – and I will soon.

With love and resilience,

GMJ xxx

Josie is driving Doris back to Winterborne Slepe after going shopping together. Doris has her own car but Josie offered to drive. She can hear a slight knocking noise and hopes one of the shock absorbers has not gone. Servicing the car is something she does rarely because of low mileage and low resources.

They are talking about Josie's dilemma. The Damons' divorce is almost finalised after acrimonious protracted wrangling and negotiations through their solicitors. Maggie postponed her proposed visit to the village when Josie contacted her to say that she did not want to be a party to Maggie's raid on John's house. Maggie had retorted that she was part-owner of the house and had a right of access, but as it happened, she was now unable to come on the day she planned.

It is Sunday but John is absent – he has gone to play golf with friends. Somehow Maggie, who works during the week, has found out about this and driven down to the village from London. As Josie went to church this morning, she caught sight of Maggie's red car outside the Damons' house opposite.

"She's bound to come over and say hello," Josie tells Doris. "How do I confront her? I thoroughly disapprove of what she's doing because it's underhand. But John is being very stuffy about letting her have anything. Surely she has the right to collect some of her possessions?"

"She only has the right to whatever has been agreed in the divorce settlement," says Doris. "If she helps herself to something that John is meant to keep, then she will have to return it. Don't get involved. I'd give her a cup of tea and send her on her way before John gets back."

"So long as he doesn't think I approve of her foray. I've been so careful not to let Maggie know that John has a girlfriend nor to let John know that Maggie is living with another man. Divorces are so fractious!" Josie brakes as she enters the village.

"You like helping people and try not to say a bad word about anybody. We shouldn't judge others but we can voice disapproval. Though I tend to keep my thoughts to myself." They stop outside Doris's house. "I have to hold my tongue about the way I feel towards my neighbour's relatives."

The other part of Doris's semi-detached house is owned by a frail elderly woman, whose adult children take little interest in her welfare. Doris is a good neighbour and friend to Lily and feels outraged at the way she is neglected. "I'm going to cook Lily lunch today," she says as she gets out the car. "She's been ill again, but she never complains. Thanks for the lift. See you soon."

Josie drives up the lane and parks her car. She sees Maggie carrying a pottery table lamp out of John's house to put into her open boot. Alice is taking her Sunday morning walk through the village and there is a car coming down Long Lane and braking. John has returned early. Hurrying inside her cottage, she hears a car door slam, a roar from John and a squawk from Maggie, who has been caught red-handed. A stand-up row ensues, which Josie does not want to witness. After twenty minutes, as she skulks in her kitchen waiting for soup to heat, she hears a door bang and the sound of a car departing in a hurry. No doubt in a day or two she will have to listen to the gory details from Alice who has witnessed it all.

7th October, 2014

Dear Tom,

This will be your last term at school and I know you're studying hard for your exams. Lottie emailed me and said you have a two-week autumn break before the final term of the year which starts in mid-October. I think I should now write and tell you what you so much want to know – about how your father died. There was never going to be a good time to do this and it isn't easy for me. Anyhow, here goes.

Towards the end of the year 2000, when you were four and Lottie only nine months old, Julian flew back for a visit to Colombia. He was now earning a proper salary as a vet and he saved up some holiday to take towards the end of the year, when the hot weather arrives in Australia. In Colombia, his grandfather, Juan Carlos, was becoming old and frail. His aunt, Natalia, had been living at home for five years, working in the city and looking after her widowed father, who had lost his zest for life since his wife's death. During the summer she was contacted again by her friend in the Tolima district who offered her the position of head teacher at the orphanage school. This was a project dear to

Natalia's heart, so she discussed the exciting opportunity with her father who insisted that she should return and take up the post. Natalia found a housekeeper to move in and look after her father.

In the autumn Natalia wrote to me in England saying that the old man had no wish to live much longer as he rarely saw his only grandson, who had been unable to return to Colombia for three years. I wrote to Julian, suggesting that, since he was qualified and with a good job, he might be able to take his family there for a holiday. He thought this a wonderful idea and was keen to revisit the country where he had grown up and to see his grandfather again – perhaps for the last time.

In February when I had been staying in Perth after Lottie's birth, Julian and I had discussed my moving to Australia within a year. Julian decided that if he was going to go back with his family to Colombia for a holiday and to see his grandfather, then I should be there too. He generously said he would buy me a ticket to fly to Colombia for Christmas and he hoped I would travel back with him to Australia afterwards. However, Melissa decided that it would be tiring to travel with two small children all the way to Colombia to see a sick old man, whom she had never met. She wanted to spend Christmas at home in Australia and was not to be persuaded otherwise, so Julian amended his plan, deciding to go on his own to Colombia in late November, stay for two weeks and return before Christmas. Melissa and the children would stay with her parents. Julian bought himself a return ticket to Bogota and arranged to meet me there. Natalia was so happy that we were coming to Colombia and invited us to come and spend three days with her. The rest of the time we would stay with Juan Carlos in his house. The old man was looking forward to our visit.

For me a new life was opening up. I handed in my notice at my job and arranged to leave my rented accommodation.

I disposed of the few possessions that I had, keeping only my clothes and some personal effects. There would be no going back – or so I thought. I arrived in Bogota a few hours after Julian had arrived from Perth and he met me at the airport. It was wonderful to see him and we drove to Chapinero to stay with Juan Carlos. The old man was so overjoyed to see his grandson again and for three or four days we had a great time together.

Juan Carlos wanted to give Julian a treat and he had obtained tickets for a Paso Fino championship to be held a few hours to the west of Bogota, not far from where Natalia's school was situated. This beautiful region, with green hills, coffee plantations and quiet villages is situated on the western slopes of the Andes. Julian and his grandfather were extremely fond of horses and in particular a breed called the Colombian Paso Fino. These horses are prized for their fluid natural pace and willing disposition, and are often used for trail riding. They are unusual because they have a strange way of walking where the hoof beats are evenly spaced creating a rapid unbroken rhythm which is very smooth and comfortable for the rider. The name Paso Fino means 'fine step', and these top-quality horses are highly prized and expensive, with many championships and competitions held at 'fiestas', where the animals compete doing a dressage walk or rapid trot. When Julian was a boy, his grandfather had taken him to some of these events and they both adored watching the superb Paso Finos compete.

Unfortunately, Juan Carlos was not well enough to make the journey, his doctor advising him against it. He was disappointed but insisted that Julian take advantage of the tickets and I should accompany him. We decided to go to the event and then stay with Natalia for a night or two before we returned to Bogota. We borrowed the Moreno car, which was seldom used, and drove to the equestrian stadium in the town where the fiesta was to be held. With a few thousand other spectators, we watched the championship and Julian was enthralled. I was intrigued to discover that high bets were placed on the outcome of the competitions with huge sums changing hands and it was fascinating to see these transactions going on whilst watching the horses perform. Men swaggered around with their colourful *carriels*, which are leather satchels or bags that Colombians wear over their shoulders. It was obvious that there were thousands of Colombian pesos and US dollars in these *carriels*, as some of the owners were accompanied by big silent men who were their bodyguards.

It was during an interval between competitions that Julian met up with an old school friend, whose name was Mateo. I remembered Mateo because he had been a boy who had got into lots of trouble in his teens and had been a bad influence on Julian. Our time in Texas had separated the two friends who had not seen each other for years. So I was not best pleased to see them slapping each other on the back and chatting together. Mateo was carrying a flamboyant orange and brown leather *carriel* with several compartments and a black shoulder strap. He had been betting and drinking heavily with other men. Later we caught sight of him carousing with friends after having won a large sum of money, but an hour later Mateo lurched up to Julian in an alcohol-induced rage, saying he had lost it all and been swindled out of a fortune. He staggered off swearing revenge whilst we made our escape and set off for Tolima, where we arrived in time for a late meal with Natalia, who was overjoyed to see Julian and me once again.

Julian had unwisely mentioned to Mateo the name of the town where we were to stay and that his aunt ran the school and orphanage attached to the main Catholic church. Later that night, when we were all asleep in Natalia's house nearby, we heard a loud banging on her front door. It turned out to be the local priest, who was extremely upset because a young man had arrived at his house next to the church, seeking sanctuary. The man was very drunk and it appeared that he was quite badly wounded. He was asking for Julian Moreno but desperately insistent that the police were not involved. The priest had opened the church to let the injured man in and had come straight round to Natalia's house, assuming that Julian was a relative of hers.

The priest set off to get a doctor, whilst we dressed rapidly and went straight to the church, where Mateo was lying on the steps near the altar. His face was ghost white and contorted in pain. He had crawled along the aisle and there were blood smears on the stone slabs of the church floor. Natalia knelt down and spoke to him in a low voice, but he began to babble that he was dying and had led a wicked life and wanted to pray to St Jude, the patron saint of lost causes. Natalia began to pray for the man and, whilst Julian tried to calm him down, Mateo told him what had happened.

He had been so enraged by his loss at the Paso Fino event that he picked a fight with the man who had cheated him. He knocked his opponent to the ground and grabbed his *carriel* containing the money. After the commotion he had run to his car but, as he climbed into it, he had been shot by pursuers who were friends of the man he had robbed. He flung the stolen *carriel* into the car, managed to start the engine and escape, knowing that he would be killed if they caught him. He was injured and bleeding but had managed to drive to the town where he knew Julian was staying. At this point, Mateo began coughing, crying and praying to God to forgive him before he died.

A few minutes later the doctor arrived and, seeing how serious the injuries were, he tried to persuade the injured man that an ambulance should be called, but Mateo said it was too late, he was in too much pain and he wanted to see the priest before he died. He grabbed Natalia's arm and in great distress whispered that there was a huge sum of money in a *carriel* – many millions of pesos. It was gambling proceeds and drugs money and he wanted to give it to her for the orphanage to help children. Then he became incoherent and the priest gave him Absolution, soon after which he lost consciousness. By the time the ambulance arrived he was dead.

Inevitably the police were involved and Julian had to explain the situation and tell them the identity of the dead man. Mateo's car was outside the church and in it they found his *carriel* which contained personal documents but very little money. It was concluded that he must have dropped the stolen bag whilst he was trying to escape, and it might have been found by someone else. They made enquiries at the stadium, but inevitably no one knew anything about the fight or the stolen *carriel* with its missing millions of Colombian pesos. The sum may not have been so large because 3000 pesos are only worth one US dollar. Natalia and I were interviewed only once by the police, because it was Julian who knew Mateo and had seen him at the Paso Fino event.

The police contacted Mateo's family and, after a couple of days, they concluded that Julian could be of no further help to them, so we were allowed to leave. We had recovered sufficiently from the shock to be able to say goodbye to Natalia and drive back to the capital. Julian and I decided not to distress his grandfather by telling him what had happened. We had only a few more days before our departure for Australia, which would sadden the old man. Natalia rang to say that the dramatic incident had been reported in the local papers, but everything was quiet and neither she nor the priest had been bothered by further enquiries. Shootings were common in Colombia.

Two days before we were to fly out, I decided to go shopping in the afternoon to buy presents for Melissa, you and Lottie. Julian and Juan Carlos had always enjoyed a game of chess, and although the old man was quite slow, Julian decided to sit down and have a game with his grandfather, so I left the two of them together in the house. I was mercifully not present at the horror that followed.

The story was told to me by my broken-hearted father-in-law. About an hour after I left, the front doorbell rang and Julian went to answer it. Two strangers standing on the doorstep barged their way in and one of them had a gun. They pushed Julian along the corridor into the room where his grandfather sat, looking startled. The men were demanding that Julian hand over the money, which had been stolen from one of their friends at the Paso Fino Championships. Julian said quietly that he had no idea about the money and asked why they thought he might know. They had heard about Mateo's death in a Catholic church, had visited the town and found out the name of the friend who had been present when he died and who had gone off to Bogota shortly afterwards. Nothing had been found at the scene and they assumed that Julian had absconded with the huge sum of money. Julian tried to calm them down and denied any knowledge of its whereabouts. The men became very angry and one of them pointed his gun at Julian, accusing him of lying. At this point Juan Carlos got to his feet and protested, whereupon the man without the gun punched the old man, who staggered back and fell to the ground. Julian was outraged at this attack on his defenceless grandfather and lunged at the man. The other one holding the gun lost his temper and Juan Carlos saw him aim and shoot Julian in the head. Though my son was dead before he hit the ground, the man fired a second shot to make sure.

The murderers knew they would not find out anything further from the stunned old man and decided to leave before anyone who heard the shots raised the alarm. After they had gone, it was some minutes before Juan Carlos, shuddering with shock and grief, managed to stagger to the front door, open it and cry for help. The police were called, Julian pronounced dead, and the old man, who had collapsed from traumatic shock, was taken to hospital. At this moment, I arrived back laden with gifts which would never be given and hopes that would never be realised.

Your father was killed trying to protect his grandfather. He was only twenty-seven, an innocent victim of violence and greed. The police searched the house but found no money or motive for the attack. The murderer was never caught, but later his accomplice was identified and arrested. At the trial he was convicted and sentenced to ten years in prison. Although Juan Carlos survived, he never fully recovered and rarely spoke again. Natalia and I were utterly desolate about Julian's loss and your mother was devastated by grief when she got the terrible news that she would never see her husband or the father of her children again.

Melissa made her first and only trip to Colombia as a young widow. Leaving you and Lottie in the care of her parents, she flew to Bogota for the funeral. It was unbearably sad. She was in a state of total shock the whole time and stayed for only five days before flying back to Australia. All the members of the Moreno family were in anguished mourning and full of sympathy for Melissa. I was very worried about her returning on her own, so I offered to fly with her. I already had a ticket (given to me by my son) and changed my flight to accompany her back to Australia.

Melissa and I had always had an uneasy relationship, but I did try very hard to be supportive and caring, even though I too was aching with grief. Whilst in Australia I saw you both and I tried to help console you, Tom, because you were aware that your daddy was not coming back, though Lottie was too small to realise what had happened. I saw your Australian grandparents, who were kind and sympathetic. But Melissa seemed frozen inside and did not want to talk to me. One evening she became quite hysterical and accused me of causing Julian's death because I had urged him to visit Colombia to see his grandfather. If I had not persuaded him to go, she raged, he would still be alive and her life would not be in ruins. It was unjust, I pointed out gently, to be blamed for the death of my own son.

Tom, I'm sorry to tell you that she shouted at me to go away. She never wanted to see me again. Bereavement had made her unbalanced so I forgave her outburst and decided that the best thing would be for me to leave, even though I had been in Australia for only nine days. I fully expected that in time, when the intensity of her grief lessened, she and I would re-establish a friendly relationship. But where was I to go? I had cut my ties with England and had no job and no home to return to. I felt that I might be of some help in Colombia in the aftermath of the family tragedy, and so on Christmas Eve I flew back to Bogota. Subsequently I was glad I did, because my poor father-in-law did not last longer than two months. With Natalia and me by his side, he slipped away from us. The death of his beloved grandson gave him nothing to live for. We buried him next to Julian.

Natalia and I consoled each other, trying to keep busy sorting out all the matters which had to be dealt with following her father's death. His will was very simple – he left half of his estate to his daughter and the other half to his grandson. Natalia was worried about me, for she knew I had very little money, but I said I would manage and was glad that Melissa and the children would be well provided for. We arranged for the house in Chapinero to be sold, and after a few weeks, in late March 2001, she returned to her post in Tolima and I went with her. She found me some work as an assistant teacher in the school, as my Spanish was excellent. I stayed in her house until the summer and gradually the aching loss lessened and we both learned to accept what had happened. I would probably have stayed longer but death was not quite finished with me and had somebody else to claim – my mother. I received a summons from my uncle Rémy in France, who said that my mother was ill yet again and this time it was serious. So I said goodbye to dearest Natalia and returned to Europe.

This is a rather bleak communication, Tom, but you did beg me to tell you how your father met his death. It was horrific at the time but now, after fourteen years and with God's help, I have come to terms with it. I can honour his memory and feel blessed by his life. I find I can feel joy again. You and I have every reason to be proud of your father – he was a compassionate man and a brave one. From the photographs you sent me, I see you look quite like him. I do hope and pray that one day you and I will meet up. Meanwhile, stay in touch and I'll keep writing to you.

Best of luck in the exams.

With love and optimism,

GMJ xxx

He slams the door shut. Tripping over some shoes in the hall, he kicks them out of his way, before going into his sitting room and throwing himself into a chair. His financial situation is deteriorating. He has made a few bad decisions and things are not in such good shape as he had hoped. He is aware of the tension in his shoulders and tries to relax them as he walks over to his computer. He reads a few emails and remembers he has not been into Josie's emails for a while. He rarely bothers with them these days, since he has given up on his investigation, but he casually glances through the one she has sent to her grandson on 7th October, and then reads it intently. When he gets to the end he is fuming.

He now knows that the large sum of money which went missing is completely irrecoverable and this makes him very angry. He will tell the guy in Colombia who, since his release after nine years in prison, has been trying to trace the money he considers his, and which he believes was spirited away overseas by the dead man's family. The Colombian had promised him a large percentage if he recovered it. But now that won't happen.

Josie's email to her grandson has revealed that neither she nor her son ever had or hid the money. She is in fact as poor as everyone in the village believes. He can never understand why she is so incurably cheerful and optimistic when there have been so many family deaths in her life. He almost envies her ability to keep going in spite of past misfortunes and current poverty. How does she do it?

19th October 2014

Dear Tom,

I don't mind short emails at all. I realise you are under pressure of work. But I was glad that you received my last about your father's death. Don't be worried – I never intend to let your sister have the details I gave you. It was so traumatic that I'm not surprised your mother doesn't want to talk about it. It's good to know you still have a hazy memory of your father from when you were about four. He was indeed a real hero trying to defend his grandfather and it's such a tragedy he died so young and will never see his children grow up.

Sometimes good things can come out of really bad events and one day I'll tell you about an unexpected benefit which came about subsequently.

I'm sorry to hear your school friend drank so much at a party that he got really ill. There is a lot of teenage drunkenness at weekends in this country but I was surprised to hear that you have problems in New Zealand. You remember I told you about our landlord, George Elford, who was addicted to drinking cider and had a nasty accident earlier this year when drunk. He was eventually persuaded to seek help to stop drinking, and afterwards he joined an organisation which is made up of people who have had problems with alcoholism. They share their experiences, try to stay sober and help others to recover as well. They have quite a good success rate and George admits this support has helped him. Being landlord of the local pub has not made things easy for him, as there is plenty of alcohol within reach. But he's making progress and with support he might manage to kick the habit. I hope your friend is not going to become a regular drinker as it can destroy lives. And I trust this is not the young man who is going to travel with you when you go on your gap year to Asia!

Obviously, you're fed up with mountains of revision work – but don't slack off now! Keep it up and in a couple of months the exams will be over and you will have left school. I never thought school days were the happiest days of my life. Too competitive and too much pressure. People often look back at their time at school with a warm glow of retrospective inaccuracy. They forget what it was really like – days full of tension and arguments and with lots of homework! But keep on slaving away and afterwards you'll be glad you made the effort. Then relax and go travelling before you start thinking about the future and the rest of your life.

With love and encouragement,

GMJ xxx

"We've won!" Josie can hear the smug satisfaction in Harry's voice on the telephone. "Winterborne Slepe won't be subjected to an unsightly, noisy wind turbine."

"I'm glad you're pleased, Harry," Josie says, frowning at an electricity bill which has arrived that morning.

"I'm more than pleased. I'm jubilant! The planning authorities have turned it down and the idea has been scrapped."

"Just remember that there's at least one person in this village who is very disappointed by this news." She puts the bill on the table and shoves it out of sight under a garden catalogue.

"James will get over it. He's got lots of other little plans afoot to make some extra cash. I don't know why he doesn't go out and get a job."

"I'm pleased too – if only because it will end all the discord in the village between the protesters against the project and its defenders. Everybody has heard about the spat between Lou and Alice during a coffee morning at the village hall. Like me, I don't think Lou feels too strongly about the matter either way, but she was trying to defend her husband who works for James. Alice takes everything personally and, as a strident member of the protest group, she's verbally assaulted anybody who didn't agree that the project was an evil plan to despoil the village. I've been on the receiving end too. I'm so glad the whole issue will now be dropped."

"Alice will stop being militant now she's victorious. Especially since she has another reason to be happy. Are you aware that Alice has hundreds of premium bonds? She regularly wins small sums, but last week she won £5000 and of course couldn't resist letting everyone know."

"Of course," repeats Josie drily. "Lucky woman. She can pay her bills without anxiety and we can all relax until she finds another crusade!"

Henry has picked up on the brittle note in Josie's voice and changes tack. "I've been doing a little investigation on your behalf, and perhaps we can meet up soon and I can put you in the picture," he says soothingly.

"I really don't need any help, Harry. It's very kind of you but I can manage on my own." Josie tries to suppress her irritation. Her independence is something she values highly.

"How about a drink in the pub next week?" Harry will not be deflected.

"I'm quite busy next week, but perhaps the week afterwards."

"I'll give you a ring then," says Harry and they end the call.

Josie is annoyed with herself. Harry is a kind man, but sometimes she thinks he likes gossip almost as much as Alice. She leans forward and switches on the computer and settles down to answer Lottie's email from Australia.

23rd November 2014

Dear Lottie,

I was sorry to hear that you fell off your bike and got a nasty graze on your leg. I hope you recover in time for your netball match. Your father regularly fell off his roller skates, but he wore pads for protection. If this is the third time it's happened, I'm not surprised your mother has pleaded with you to be more careful. I don't agree that her concern is an overreaction. Remember that when she offers you advice it's because she loves you and doesn't want you to get bruised. You mentioned you were rather late home from a friend's party at the weekend and that Mum was angry about it. Teenagers often find their parents a bit overprotective but you should try to understand their point of view – they get worried and wonder where you are and if you're safe.

Glad to hear your favourite subjects are arts, media, drama and English. Pity you don't like science and maths, which your brother prefers, because it reinforces the stereotype that girls like arts subjects and boys like science. It's interesting that your school makes it compulsory for students to learn either Maori or German up till the age of twelve and that you chose Maori. I admire your decision to learn an indigenous language.

I also approve of the fact that primary schools teach religious instruction, but in secondary education you learn about world religions. You asked me if I was a Christian. I am. I haven't always been – even though I was brought up with a Christian ethos by my parents and my father was nominally an Anglican. Because my mother was a Catholic, I was considered to be one, which made it acceptable in Colombia to marry my first husband who was a Catholic. But at that time, I didn't have any deep beliefs. (This came later, when I met and later married my second husband,

Oliver Cuff.) The Moreno family were Catholics and went regularly to Mass. Your great-aunt Natalia is a woman of strong religious conviction and so was my son. I remember Julian was angry and upset after the death of his father and as a teenager distanced himself from God, but he told me that he later regained his faith and was sad that Melissa did not share his conviction.

You have asked me to tell you more about our family. You were born in January 2000, a wonderful gift for your parents in the new millennium. In November that year your father went to Colombia to visit his old and sick grandfather, and tragically died in Bogota. A few months later your broken-hearted great-grandfather, Juan Carlos Moreno, passed away.

Then I heard that my mother, your great-grandmother, was in very poor health, so I went to France to nurse her. She lived in a small house in Normandy on land owned by her brother Rémy, who was very supportive and in whose house I had stayed on earlier occasions. This time my mother allowed me to stay in her home, and for the first time in many years we talked to each other about my father, my marriage, her emotions when Daddy died, and most of all about our difficult relationship. I always felt guilty that I'd loved my father more than my mother, whose aloof disposition meant she held at arm's length those closest to her. As she grew weaker, we tried to come to terms with the misunderstandings and the physical and emotional distance we had both imposed between us. When she died in October we were at last at peace with each other. Having mourned together our lifetime estrangement, I think it was a comfort for her, as it was for me, that we were close at the end of her life.

Just remember that however much you do or don't get on with your mother, the bond between a woman and her child is unique and special.

After my mother's death, I stayed in France for a while to sort out her things and to try and contact my brother, Henri. (He was your great-uncle.) But although I searched through her papers, I could find no address for him – he had always been a reclusive man. The family was never able to contact him and had given up hope of his being alive. I had now lost every member of my family, except for my grandchildren, but with Julian's death, my plan of coming to live near you in Australia had died also.

But life goes on. I returned to England once more and went back to my roots, to Dorset where my father had originally come from. I moved to west Dorset, where I had spent happy times in my childhood. This was fortunate because I ran into one or two families I had once known. People have time for one another in the country and I was shown much kindness. I managed to get caring work with an agency and found somewhere affordable to live.

Perhaps the most significant thing that happened was meeting up with someone with whom I'd been at school. I had taken a bus into Dorchester and after doing some shopping I went into the library. I was leaving the library in a hurry to catch my bus when I collided with a man in the doorway. I dropped my books and we banged our heads together when we bent down to pick them up. We both apologised and then began to laugh. As he handed me one of the books he had picked up, he said he had read it and I would enjoy it. Then he offered me a cup of coffee and, as I had probably missed the bus, I thought, "Why not?"

There was a small café nearby and we ordered our coffee and got talking. When he told me his name was Oliver Cuff, a very small bell rang in the recesses of my mind. I told him my father was Miles Hansford who was originally from Dorset. After a few minutes conversation we realised that he and I had been at primary school together and our parents had known each other.

Coincidences are always entertaining and after a pleasant chat, he offered to drive me the few miles to where I was living. After that we became friends and met up from time to time, sometimes going to a concert or film together. He had been married and had a daughter called Emily. Sadly, his wife had left him a few years before to live with a man she had known since childhood who now worked in the oil business in Aberdeen. After her divorce from Oliver they got married, and Emily at the age of thirteen went to live with her mother in Scotland.

While on the subject of divorce, I have some news to report from my village. The Damon divorce has finally come through just after John broke up with his new girlfriend, so he is now on his own again. He is a little bitter about the cost of the divorce and is continually moaning about how little money he has left after the pay-out to his ex-wife. Another couple have separated: Polish Lena has broken up with my landlord, James. She doesn't seem too bothered by this, though James is wandering around with a rather glum face like a chipped pottery mug.

Yesterday I took a train to London. I wonder whether you have heard in New Zealand about a memorial art installation at the Tower of London, where a ceramic red poppy has been laid for each British military death in the First World War. The last poppy was laid on 11th November and now there are 888,246 flowers to commemorate the war a hundred years ago. I went to see the display, which was extraordinarily moving and beautiful. I felt quite emotional standing there with all the red porcelain poppies carpeting the ground and flowing down from one of the windows in the ancient stone walls. You will know there were many New Zealand troops and nurses who served overseas in the First World War – over a hundred thousand, which I consider amazing from a population of just over a million in New Zealand at that time.

Apparently, when Great Britain declared war on Germany in 1914, the New Zealand government followed without hesitation despite its huge distance from the action. Large numbers were killed fighting in the Gallipoli campaign and on the Western Front where over 16,000 New Zealanders were killed and many more wounded – a huge casualty rate. There were also Maori soldiers serving with the New Zealand army and many of them died. The horrific loss of life from 1914–1918 affected the entire world. We should not forget.

In the final two lines of a poem by First World War poet Siegfried Sassoon, he laments:

> The unreturning army that was youth;
> The legions who have suffered and are dust.

With love and poetry,
GMJ xxx

"I saw you with Harry in the pub last weekend having a serious conversation," Flora says, with a question in her smile. They are in the kitchen at the pub, preparing for a Christmas event in the village hall, the food for which the Elfords have been asked to supply.

"You can't do anything in this village or talk to anybody without people jumping to the wrong conclusions," Josie complains as she prepares a pasta salad. "Harry has decided to investigate the disappearance and death some years back of my only brother, Henri Hansford. They were friends a long time ago and Harry has been trying to find out more details. He's discovered that Henri had a two-bedroom flat in the north of England. The other people in the block of flats knew him as a mad archaeologist who came and went, often absent for months at a time on archaeological projects overseas. It seems that he went away in the year 2000 and no one has seen him since."

"What a mystery. Very upsetting for the family." Flora wrinkles her nose as she chops onions.

"Not really. We were never close. He wasn't married and he took little interest in his sister. We hardly saw each other for many years. Our mother died in 2001 and I was unable to trace him."

"So why is Harry investigating his disappearance?"

"He thinks that I may be entitled to Henri's assets because I'm his only living relative. I was unaware he had any property so I've never given it a thought. Harry found out from the local police that my brother was missing for a long time, although they only discovered it after a few years. There was no evidence within the flat of his whereabouts or any indication that he was still alive. His passport was missing so it was assumed he had died abroad. Somebody called the Treasury Solicitor has undertaken searches to try and find any surviving relatives. Harry isn't sure if any relatives were found and doesn't yet know what's happened to his assets."

"What an extraordinary story. You might be an heiress."

Josie, who has placed the salad into two large bowls, keeps the exasperation from her voice as she says, "I was surprised to hear that my scatty brother owned anything very much, so I can't imagine that it's really worth pursuing the matter. I told Harry that, but he seems determined to ferret it all out."

"It's nice of him to try and help you." Flora is putting all the prepared food into the refrigerator.

"It is kind of him." Josie sighs as she wipes her hands. "He says he'll find out the legal position and 'inform the Treasury Solicitor that Henri Hansford, deceased, has a sister still living'." Josie mimics Harry's voice, and then reverts to her own. "He tells me that I may have to come up with various documents, such as birth certificates and information about our parents. I'm not sure it's worth all the hassle to plough through old boxes of damp family papers, now wedged into the cupboard under the stairs." She has more urgent concerns to occupy her and picks up her bag. "I must go."

George enters the kitchen and Flora looks at her watch. "Opening time soon. I'm glad you're back in the kitchen, George. Tonight we'll be a bit short-handed in the bar. Lena says she can't manage more hours and I'm beginning to think she may have other work elsewhere. I hope that she doesn't leave me in the lurch over Christmas."

"I'm sure she won't," Josie reassures her friend as they go through to the bar. "She's a responsible and loyal young woman. But if by any chance you need extra help, I'd be happy to come along on the evenings when I've not been on my feet all day. I rather enjoyed working in the pub when George was laid up." She does not mention that it might help to distract her from anxiety about the possibility there is somebody still slinking around her house in her absence.

"That's so kind of you, Josie." Flora looks relieved. "You're a natural behind the bar. I'll let you know."

4th December 2014

Dear Magpies,

What a lovely suggestion that you might ring me over Christmas. It would be simply wonderful to HEAR your voices and actually TALK! I realise that you cannot use your parents' telephone and I am concerned that the call from your mobile might cost you rather a lot. I would be happy to telephone you but you may think that will be too risky if either of your parents are around at the time. Don't forget that New Zealand is 12 hours ahead of UK time, so you will have to call me in the evening to speak to me here in the morning. How exciting! Are you sure it won't cause difficulty at your end? It doesn't have to be actually on Christmas Day – it could be the day before or afterwards, if it's easier for you. What excitement! I have just realised you will probably both have New Zealand accents. How strange! But then I might sound quite different from what you expect. How sad you cannot tell your mother about this plan. Are you sure we ought to continue keeping our communication secret? Perhaps she wouldn't object, although I suspect she might be upset that it's been going on so long without her knowledge. I'm all for being open about it now. What do you think?

It occurs to me that the last time I saw and heard you was on Christmas Eve in the year 2000, the day I left Australia. Almost fourteen years ago! Melissa and I were both in a state of shock over your father's death and it was an emotional and difficult time. Your mother wanted to be alone and, though I had intended to stay to spend Christmas with my fatherless grandchildren, I had to leave. I believed that Melissa's grief would lessen in time and our relationship would be re-established. But it never happened. I wrote supportive letters hoping she was beginning to rebuild her life, but they were never answered. I telephoned but she would not talk to me. I was desperate to have news of you and wrote to Melissa's parents – your other grandparents – at their home, but they never responded.

This went on for a year and a half. Then my letters were returned as undeliverable, your telephone number was disconnected, and I knew you must have moved away. Frantic to keep in touch with my family, I travelled to Australia and spent a few weeks desperately trying to track you down. But when I discovered that Melissa's parents had also moved, I gave up and returned broken-hearted to England. I'd no idea you had gone to live in New Zealand and lost touch completely until Tom miraculously contacted me in the spring of last year.

I want to be fair to your mother – she was devastated by Julian's loss, but after a time I imagine that she wanted to dissociate herself from tragedy and misery – and I was a part of it. She needed to move on and I can't blame her. A new life in New Zealand, away from painful memories, was a wonderful idea, and, as you have told me, there she met Robert Brown and managed to find happiness in a second marriage.

I too needed to turn my back on grieving. I decided to rebuild my life in England and returned to Dorset, where, with my earlier contacts, I could find work as a carer. I managed to find a job in Bridport and decided to resume my friendship with Oliver Cuff. A Dorset man, he lived in a small village and had been a history teacher but taken early retirement following a bout of illness. Having led a gregarious and active life in a school community, Oliver now spent most of his time on his own at his home. I too was feeling lonely and dispirited from losing contact with my grandchildren on the other side of the world. We both needed companionship and naturally saw quite a lot of each other.

Oliver was very knowledgeable about the history of Dorset and was happy to share this with me. When I wasn't at work, we drove around the county and visited his favourite places, which rapidly became mine too. He took me to the old port of Lyme Regis on the coast for a Dorset cream tea. Afterwards I slipped on some steep cobblestones and twisted my ankle badly. Oliver was very efficient getting me to a doctor and then back home. There, in spite of being the world's worst cook, he managed to make us a meal that was just edible, whilst I sat with my bandaged foot resting on a cushion, giving him instructions. It was hilarious. I think I fell in love with him over this disastrous meal, prepared with little skill and much kindness.

Oliver was good company and had a lively, teasing sense of humour, something I'd missed since Raul died. He was gentle, truthful and kind and I soon realised these characteristics were the outward manifestation of a very strong inner Christian faith. My belief in a caring compassionate God had been seriously undermined by what I had gone through, but Oliver finally convinced me that God did love me and that although He never promises us a life without suffering, He will always be there to help me through it. In more ways than one, Oliver was a Godsend! I began to go to the church he attended, where I met other friendly believers. Gradually my faith grew and I experienced peace and a sense of coming home.

Oliver proposed to me one breezy Sunday afternoon whilst

we were walking on Eggardon Hill. This place is very special – it's an ancient hill fort about 800 feet above sea level. It was built in the Iron Age – about 2,300 years ago – and so steep sided that would have been daunting for the Romans attacking it. We stood near the top with a brisk sea breeze in our faces, gazing across the green undulating downland toward the English Channel. Walking back along the path, we met a solitary man with a long beard who told us that there were excellent edible mushrooms to be found in the vicinity. We spent a happy hour trying to find them without any luck, but we did find some pretty wild flowers. Oliver picked a few and then gave them to me along with a small ring and a proposal of marriage. I can truthfully say I was blown away!

In 2003, aged fifty-one and having been a widow for ten years, I married Oliver at a quiet ceremony in our church and changed my name again – from Moreno to Cuff. His daughter Emily made the effort to come south and attend the wedding, which pleased her father enormously. When she got married the following year to Angus Robertson, we both went to Scotland for her wedding day.

After a few days' honeymoon in Wales, I moved into Oliver's home and it was wonderful. We shared a curiosity about people and an optimism about life. The house was small and comfortingly chaotic – to my delight he was almost as untidy and unworldly as me. His home was crammed with books, pictures, and small 'treasures' of no great value that he had collected from junk shops and emporiums over the years. I had few possessions so it was delightful to be able to enjoy his and to share my life with someone again after so long on my own. He was now doing some private tutoring in Bridport and I got some part-time work at a residential home in Dorchester. We both became involved in voluntary work in the local community. After all my travels and trials, I hoped my life had settled down and we would spend many years together, but sadly our marriage lasted for only four years. I'll tell you what happened another time.

Are you going to be at home for Christmas or will you be going away? I'll be in Winterborne Slepe. Where else? It's my home. James will probably be going to Scotland to stay with his parents, but most villagers like to celebrate Christmas here. This year Harry has decided to host Christmas lunch for some of his friends. He's not bad at cooking – rather better than I am – and I expect I'll be invited. I feel a little sad for my solitary neighbour Matt and confess I have seen little of him recently. John seems to have perked up a bit and tells me he has got a new job with better prospects, though he doesn't say what these are. Most of the cottages are too small to host a big gathering so there will be a New Year's Eve supper party in the village hall which I shall help organise.

That's all the news from Dorset. I'm so looking forward to speaking to you over Christmas.

With love and anticipation,

GMJ xxx

It is 2.33 am. All is dark and still outside the closed curtains. The man lounges in his ergonomic desk chair, watching the monitor screen flicker in front of him, his right hand like an eagle's claw gripping the black mouse beneath it, his left hand clenched as it lies on the desktop within inches of a cold mug of black coffee. These days he derives most of his entertainment and vicarious pleasure from his forays online. He watches a lot of films, visits a lot of websites and has become immersed in virtual reality video games, which he often plays late into the night, wearing a VR headset. He chooses to deny himself sleep with the result that tiredness makes his days seem blurred around the edges, whereas in sharp contrast the nights glitter with promise and excitement. He has recently become involved in online chatrooms and forums, using icons and calling himself by a number of screen names: Hipgloss, MIFT (an acronym for 'masked infiltrator'), fRiend, and Prowler, which is his favourite. Prowler finds it easier to communicate with people he has never seen than with those he encounters in his work or in the village. It is the anonymity of these virtual identities that allows fRiend to create other personas and enable him to become the man he yearns to be in real life. Hipgloss is a super intelligent secret operator, whose ruthlessness and charm is irresistible to women. MIFT longs for power over other people and has become adept at spying on their conversations and lives. Prowler's nights and dreams are invading his days and give colour and meaning to the pallid life that he shares with no one. Yet.

30th December 2014

Dear Magpies,

What a wonderful moment it was to hear both your voices on Christmas Eve! I was in such a whirlwind of emotions that I can hardly remember what we spoke about. I had stupidly forgotten that Tom's voice would be a man's, whereas I was still imagining him with the childish treble he had the last time I heard it. You sounded so like your father – it was quite uncanny. And of course, I had never heard Lottie speak – only the crying and burbling of a baby. You now have a high-pitched girl's voice and a delightful giggle. It was altogether a magic few minutes. Folly was here with me to share the emotional few minutes. You told me you were making the call from your bedroom whilst your parents were downstairs. My only regret is that I still have no reconciliation with your mother. It would have been great to speak to her too. I hope you all had a wonderful Christmas Day together and that Bex was pleased with her bicycle.

I've just returned from work where I had some sad news. David and Jean, the elderly couple I care for, have been in poor health for some while. The husband is now quite sick and needs to go into a nursing home and his poor wife is very distressed by this. Their family have been visiting over Christmas and made a unilateral decision that the couple must move from their home into residential care. I'm sorry about this because I'm fond of them and know they would far prefer to stay in their own home with carers such as myself coming in to help them. I expect to get further news about their plans in the new year and will continue working there for the moment.

Old age brings its difficulties; when a person lives alone and isn't well enough to go out, they can feel isolated. Doris's neighbour, Lily, who's in her nineties, is gossamer frail and almost incapable of looking after herself. She does not want to move from the house where she has lived for many years and we hope she won't have to leave. Lily has lived here for years and used to be an active member of the local community, so now it's our turn to help her, though it is mainly Doris who gives time and support. That's what I like about village life here.

I'm sorry to say that not all villages have a community spirit.

I discovered this when Oliver became ill less than a year after our marriage. Because he had already had a run-in with cancer, doctors referred him to hospital to have various checks. After a few anxious weeks, we were told that the cancer had come back and he would need treatment. He was stoical and practical when he heard, and initially we were both optimistic he would beat it once again. But as the months and years propelled him through operations and further treatment, we began to accept that he might not get better. I had plenty of experience looking after sick and incapacitated people, whether members of my family or the people I worked for, so I gave up work to look after him. I nursed him for three years through various bouts of chemotherapy, and we still had good times during periods of remission, when we were able to go out and do things together. What surprised me was that neighbours living close to us were not that supportive. They seemed embarrassed by our predicament and, although sympathetic, they didn't find the time to help or even to visit and be with Oliver when I had to go shopping. We hid our disappointment but were grateful that members of our church were kind and thoughtful. I know they prayed for Oliver.

When he became seriously ill, we decided that we would cheer ourselves up by looking at old films on DVDs which I bought or borrowed. We used to sit together on the sofa in gales of laughter over Charlie Chaplin's *Modern Times* and other hilarious classics with Buster Keaton, Laurel and Hardy, and the Keystone Cops. I don't expect you have ever heard of any of these – as they were old classics even when Oliver and I were young. Laughter is good medicine and for a while Oliver felt better and we began to make plans for the future. But another relapse meant that time ran out for Oliver. He did not wish to end his days in hospital and died peacefully at home on a bleak November day in 2007, with me beside him and his hand in mine. I was devastated to lose my lovely, funny, eccentric husband, but do still feel blessed that I had the pleasure of his companionship for five years.

I knew that Oliver in his will had left the house to his daughter, Emily, but I had imagined I would be allowed to stay there for a while. Soon after the funeral, Emily turned up with her mother, Oliver's first wife, whom I had never met. They informed me that they were putting the house on the market and would be selling all the contents without delay. This was cruel – they must have known this would make me homeless. Within two months I was out – and on my own once again. Widowed for a second time and still grieving, I had to come to terms with my radically altered situation: no secure future. I was offered a room temporarily in the home of a kind friend from church and moved in with my few meagre possessions. But I am adaptable and decided I should stop feeling sorry for myself and find a job and somewhere permanent to live. I was fifty-five and still had energy and zest for life, though I was unsure what to do or where to go.

In early 2008, I received a letter from Natalia, to whom I had written with the news of Oliver's death and the change in my circumstances. I had not seen her for five years, and she wrote saying she was buying me an air ticket to come and visit her in Colombia. I had grown to love Dorset and knew that this was where I wanted to live in the long term, but suddenly a change of scene and a temporary respite from sickness and sadness seemed attractive. And so I went back to Colombia, expecting to stay for only a month but I did not return to England for a long time. The reason for this was connected to a strange and unforeseen consequence of your father's death.

I hope you find this intriguing and I will satisfy your curiosity in my next email. But now I must go and help prepare the village hall for the New Year's Eve party – we have lots of tables and chairs to arrange. We have a sound system and music so there's going to be a bit of dancing. Alice Diffey has decided that we should wear exotic masks and I shall have to fabricate something quickly or drive into town and buy one from a joke shop. It should be fun and I must admit that Alice comes up with a good idea – occasionally.

My dearest grandchildren, I send you much love and wish you a happy New Year,

GMJ xxx

Josie presses the 'send' button and leans back in her chair. She wonders what the new year will bring. She's unhappy about evidence that there's a weirdo who still finds his way into her house and moves things around. He does not steal anything so it must be because he wants to frighten her. Who is he and why is he doing it? She is indeed afraid - but determined to catch him. And identify him.

5th January 2015

Dear Lottie,

Your friend's New Year's Eve party sounds as if it was riotous. A chocolate fountain sounds exotic and extravagant. Just as well you were sleeping over at Sarah's house, so at least your parents don't know how late you went to bed! You say you like Sarah's older brother, Gary, and enjoyed dancing with him.

Our New Year's Eve party was an all-age event in the village hall – almost everybody turned up in hilarious masks. One or two of the men came in full head masks – John turned up with a great big shaggy wolf's head which rather suited him, and Harry came as Darth Vader – which was very out of character. There was a man I didn't recognise who was wearing a balaclava covering the whole of his head and face with round circles cut out for his eyes – he looked like a terrorist – and unlike the rest of us, he didn't take it off all evening, nor did he let on who he was. No one danced with him because he looked so sinister. I managed to make a mask out of some black card and I stuck on glitter round the apertures for eyes. The glue I used wasn't very efficient and I shed my sparkle all evening and ended up looking like a cat burglar – all I needed was a bag marked 'swag' to complete the transformation. It was a good party. Although much wine and beer had been consumed, quite a few of us turned up the next day to clear up – that's village life!

I don't think you should feel pleased that your brother has broken up with his girlfriend. I realise you didn't like her very much, but he's probably quite upset. Just as well he's now down in Dunedin for his holiday job and where he'll be until he's got enough money saved to set off on his travels to Asia in March. I know that you fall out with him from time to time, but you'll miss him when he's gone away for six months.

Good news that you'll be given a laptop for your fifteenth birthday later this month! Then you won't need to use your friends' computers to get your emails. Every family is different – although some of your school friends have had their laptops for a year or two, there may be good reasons why Melissa thought you should wait.

Why don't you want your mother to throw you a birthday party? I'm sure she won't stalk round and keep watch on everybody.

Usually parents steer clear of their children's parties but want to keep a presence in case there are any problems that need a parental hand. You might try to have a sensible discussion with her – I suspect you may have lost your temper and that doesn't solve anything. I used to throw tantrums when I was a teenager, so I know what I'm talking about.

By the way, I wasn't preaching about faith in God. You asked me genuine questions and I gave you my answers. You are now at an age when you enquire about many things and test the answers, and it's up to you to make up your own mind. Yes, I do still get angry about what happens in the world. All the violence and suffering. Like millions of others, I've had a hard life – some might call it tragic as you do – but I'm not melancholy. Surely you can see that from my emails. I'm the sort of person who bounces back and this is because God is always there for me, helping me through bad times. Amazingly, life is still worth living without Raul and Julian and Oliver. I can survive their loss – but I cannot live without God. He gives meaning to everything and I'd be lost without Him. We all need love and God is love.

I was interested to hear that Robert is a churchgoer, which I hope means that he's a believer. Do you ever discuss faith with him or accompany him to church? It might be stimulating.

You say you love nature in all its variety and colours. Here's a few lines of poetry for you, which seem appropriate. The poet is Gerard Manley Hopkins and the poem is called: *Pied Beauty*. 'Pied' is an old-fashioned word, but since you know about horses you'll know what a piebald is.

> Glory be to God for dappled things –
> For skies of couple-colour as a brinded cow;
> For rose-moles all in stipple upon trout that swim;

Fresh-firecoal chestnut-falls; finches' wings;

Landscape plotted and pieced – fold, fallow, and plough;

And all trades, their gear and tackle and trim.

All things counter, original, spare, strange;

Whatever is fickle, freckled (who knows how?)

With swift, slow; sweet, sour; adazzle, dim;

He fathers-forth whose beauty is past change:

Praise him.

Which poets do you like best? Give me the names of some of your favourite poems and I'll read them. You say that many of your friends at school dislike poetry because they don't understand it. Teenagers often jeer at things they find uncomfortable or unsettling. I'm all for making fun of pomposity and stamping on hypocrisy, but there are some things you should take seriously. You can be irreverent about everything except God and perhaps poetry.

With love for your honesty and respect for your opinions,

GMJ xxx

Bill Stickley comes into Josie's kitchen, removes his muddy boots and leaves them by the door while Josie puts on the kettle to boil.

"That load should keep you goin'," he says as he removes his thick jacket.

"I'm so grateful. I'd almost run out of wood." Bill has brought round a pile of logs and stored them in her shed. It is understood that these are from a surplus on James Trevett's land. Each year trees come down and are cut up by Bill and stored. James gives his worker as much wood as he wants for his house and Bill kindly passes on some to his neighbour.

Josie makes them both a mug of tea and they sit at the table in companionable silence and drink it. Her neighbour is a man of few words and much work. James is away in Scotland, and leaves Bill to get on with everything that needs to be done around the estate.

"How's Lou?" Josie asks. "I haven't seen her for a week. Has she got over her dreadful cold?"

"She's fine now. Busy gettin' the house ready for our grandchildren who'll be comin' over half term."

"I forget how old they are."

"Two girls of eight and six, and the boy is a little'un of three. He's a sturdy lad and he don't cry much." Bill adores his grandson. His daughter and her husband live about three hours away and it is usually Bill and Lou who drive to see them. "It's the first time we'll 'ave the three of 'em 'ere on their own. It'll be hard work keepin' them occupied, but Lou loves 'em and I can grin and bear it."

"I hope they'll come and visit me during their stay – I've got some games which might amuse them. With no school in the village there aren't as many children around during the day as I'd like. Where I'm at work, there's a first school down the road and with the windows open I can hear the children at break time and my heart sings."

"You said you 'ave two grandchildren in New Zealand. What 'appened to your boy?"

Josie is touched that Bill, who is a reticent man, has

asked her about her son. "Julian married an Australian girl and died aged twenty-seven in a tragic accident while on a trip to Colombia."

Bill nods in sympathy. "Too young! Harry told me the other day that he has a son and a grandchild livin' in Australia," he says, getting to his feet. "Thanks for the tea."

Josie blinks in surprise, because Harry has never mentioned having children. "Thanks for the logs," she says as Bill leaves.

Harry is a strange man, sometimes very friendly and at other times rather distant. He telephoned her recently and told her that his efforts to get her declared as a relative and heir of Henri Hansford have been stalled and he is not now hopeful of achieving this. Josie is quite relieved as she is not sure that she wants Harry beavering away on her behalf, trying to obtain a small sum that she never expected and doesn't deserve. She thanked him for his efforts and said she wanted him to let the whole matter drop. He sounded disappointed.

She goes outside to pick up a few logs that Tom has left on the doorstep, and carries them through to the sitting room to light the fire. She looks around - none of her things seem to have disappeared or reappeared. She and Folly will have a warm evening, purring together on the sofa.

19th February 2015

Dear Tom,

Well done in the exams! You must be pleased with the results, and your mother and Robert too. So you have not yet decided about further education – I can understand that, having just concluded thirteen long years of school. I'm sure your stepfather doesn't mean to pressurise you into making decisions but he probably wants to get things set up before you go off on your gap year. There is some sense in that but in the end, you are the one who has to choose what you want to study at college or university. My only advice is that you do something that you enjoy; don't plod into a subject because it might lead to a job and a career. You must burn with enthusiasm to learn about it.

I'm glad you like the slow pace of life in Dunedin. Not all teenagers like quiet places, although the place where you work sounds quite lively. Tell me a little bit more about your school-friend, Liam, who will be travelling with you on your gap year. It's best to travel with a friend you can rely on when you hit problems. It's also a good idea to have someone you can laugh with. You say you'll leave in early April shortly after Easter – how exciting!

You mentioned you plan to go to Brisbane in Australia first, travel up the east coast to Cairns and go out to the Great Barrier Reef – sounds wonderful! Bali in Indonesia always attracts travellers but I hear there are amazing things to see in Java as well. You have Vietnam, Cambodia and Thailand on your itinerary, but how about Malaysia? I spent three years there in my childhood, when my father was posted to the British Embassy in Kuala Lumpur, though I don't remember a lot except the startling greenness of the vegetation – trees, grass, paddy fields, tea plantations against a backdrop of misty green hills. Thailand is the most popular Asian destination for European gap year students and many of them aim to get to Australia and New Zealand. I've always wanted to go to Sri Lanka, which sounds fascinating, but you probably won't get as far as the Indian subcontinent.

I've just read in the newspaper that New Zealand has won against Sri Lanka in the Cricket World Cup held in Christchurch. I know you're mad about rugger but do you like cricket? Oliver was an enthusiast and even though he tried to explain the subtler aspects of test cricket, I always preferred watching the one-day matches with him which are far more exciting. Cricket wasn't fashionable for women when I was at school, otherwise I might have got involved. It is hardly played at all in Colombia, although I recollect the British Embassy did have a few games with other foreign embassy staff. But in England right now, few people are thinking about cricket. We find it hard to envisage warm summers when there's frost on the ground and it's hard to keep our homes warm.

Winterborne Slepe seems to have become like its name – wintry and sleepy. Villagers are hibernating in their cottages, eating comfort food and watching TV. A few hardy walkers, including me, emerge from our burrows to put our noses outside and sniff the air to see if spring is coming. This was enjoyable earlier this month, when we had a lot of frosty nights and clear sunlit days. But now we have rain, dreary rain so Folly and I cower indoors. Roll on spring with birdsong, pale blue skies and frothy hedgerows.

I'm glad Lottie is sending you emails, using her new laptop. She probably misses you, though she won't admit it. She seems to have forgotten about me recently but I expect she'll send me an email soon. It's incredible to think she's now fifteen and even more strange that I haven't seen either of you for most of your lives.

I shall end now, before I start to get gloomy about the winter, the cold and the long distance between you and me.

    With love and longing,

    GMJ xxx

28th February 2015

Dear Lottie,

    Thanks so much for your long chatty email – good to hear that all is well with you, even though you are now getting lots of schoolwork. It sounds as if your social life is taking off too. Though it's much easier to access your Facebook page on your new laptop, I'm glad to see that you don't do all your socialising on the media and that you still go to good old-fashioned parties where friends talk face to face with each other. And who is Hunter? A boyfriend? Do tell me – I'm the soul of discretion – especially as I'm 12,000 miles away and in touch with no one else in New Zealand apart from your brother. I won't breathe a word to him. Anyhow, he's off in six weeks on his travels. I expect you'll do the same in three years' time.

    A few of my friends in the village have been on holiday. Flora and George employed a temporary manager to run the pub with some local help, and went for a fortnight to Tenerife in the Canary Islands, off the coast of Africa – the first holiday they've had for ages, bless them. John has been away and returned with a suntanned face, but is very mysterious about where he went. I can't think why. Perhaps he was skiing. James went up to Scotland to see his parents and cousins and stayed longer than usual, because he met a woman called Harriet, whom he describes as 'absolutely perfect'. It seems she's coming down to stay with him in the spring and no doubt we shall all meet her. Poor thing! She has to live up to his glowing description or we'll be disappointed!

I'm so sorry to hear about Robert's accident on the farm – cracked ribs can be very painful. Just as well he has Mason to help him with the sheep. I'm glad Melissa has found work she can do from home, mainly on her computer. I know you feel outraged that she's banned you from using online chat rooms to socialise, but you are only fifteen and do need to be careful. We hear so much about older men 'grooming' young girls online, and she's only trying to protect you. Of course, you believe you can look after yourself and wouldn't be taken in, but mothers everywhere are always worried that harm might befall their children. Try to see things from her angle – it helps reduce confrontation.

On the subject of confrontation, there has been a big falling out here between Harry and James. Harry, on the crest of a wave from his success in defeating James's project, has written an article in the local newspaper on the subject of: 'Wind Turbines – the Bane of Country Life'. On his return from Scotland, James decided to stoke things up by announcing that he hadn't given up and would re-submit another application to the planning authorities. Harry is furious and has bragged about his intention of punching James on the nose. In the pub James has been heard to say, "Let him try!" Harry is in his sixties and is not the fittest man. Though James could never be described as athletic, he is much younger. I can't believe these two grown men are seriously considering fisticuffs! I'll keep you informed about who gets the black eye! Even if I don't witness the contest, I know that Alice will let us all know what happens.

With love and mirth,
GMJ xxx

Josie is puzzled. A week ago, in spite of the fact she has been much more careful since the locks were changed in September, she mislaid her keys to the house. After a desultory search, thinking they would turn up eventually, she has been using her spare set. This morning, whilst searching for a rubber band in her kitchen drawer, crammed with clutter that she doesn't know where to put anywhere else, she found the keys. She is almost certain that this is a place where she would not have put them, but she can't be sure. Anyhow she is relieved that she now has both sets and knows that the only other set is in the possession of her landlord, James. She walks through to the sitting room and decides to write an email to her grandchildren.

It is nearly two years since Tom began emailing her and, in that time, she feels she has come to know him and Lottie as well as anyone can through letters alone. Though she experiences occasional moments of panic that she might lose touch with them again, most of the time she believes that one day they will meet up and she will be able to wrap her arms about her grandchildren and hug them. She dreams of this moment. She aches for it. Perhaps it will happen when 'her ship comes in' (though there are no ships on the horizon), or when she wins the lottery (though she never buys a ticket). Her best hope is that God may answer her prayers. She throws the keys onto the sofa and sits down at her computer. For the present, letters are a blessing.

8th March 2015

Dear Magpies,

It's Sunday today. I've been to church, had a walk and visited Doris's neighbour Lily, who is still unwell and pecks at food like a bird. I'm now back home and have fed Folly who seems ravenous. I'm not that hungry so I think I'll sit down and write to you.

It will be Easter in four weeks and it was two years ago that you got in touch with me and we began emailing each other. I'm so happy about this. I know that one of the reasons you tried to re-establish contact, was that you wanted to find out about your father and his life in Colombia. This has inevitably involved telling you a lot about my life as well and I hope you found that interesting too. In just over a month you, Tom, will be off on your travels, so now is the time to tell you the final chapter about the unexpected legacy of your father's death.

In the last episode, we were in the year 2008 and I had lost my husband Oliver. My first husband's sister Natalia invited me to visit her in Colombia and generously sent me a ticket. I went for a holiday and stayed for two years.

As you know your great-aunt was the headmistress of a school in Colombia, and she was also in charge of the orphanage attached to the church in the town. The school had been set up with modest funding some years before, and Natalia had worked and been involved with the project over a number of years. Money was always short and there were many improvements that were delayed or set aside because of lack of funds. But the school and the orphanage struggled on with help from local people and the church. There were always more families who wanted their children to attend than the school could accommodate. The teachers were dedicated and caring, and the children received as good an education as was possible in that community, even though the buildings were modest, the facilities stretched to their limits and the classrooms overcrowded. I had worked there in 2001 for some months and knew it well.

Imagine my surprise when I travelled down from Bogota to find that the school had undergone major improvements. A plot of land had been acquired adjacent to the school and there were two new classrooms and a well-equipped playground. The orphanage had also been upgraded with a new dormitory and dayroom. Natalia had mentioned in her infrequent letters that there had been various works undertaken at the school, but I was unprepared for the extent of them. After she had shown me round the new facilities, we went back to her office and, over a cup of Colombian coffee, she told me the story of how this transformation had been possible.

Your father had been at school with a boy called Mateo, who was a dubious character. In late 2000 whilst we were visiting Colombia, Julian and I were staying the night with his sister, Natalia. Mateo arrived in the town unexpectedly that evening, knocking on the priest's door and seeking refuge in the church. He was badly wounded and told us he had a large sum of money in his *carriel* – a traditional leather bag. Knowing he was dying, he prayed and became convinced that he should give this money to the orphanage and school. He told Natalia and Julian that the money came from gambling and drugs, and he wanted it to be spent on helping children, who are often the ones most abused by drugs. After he died, his old *carriel* was found and there was little in it, so it was assumed that the dying man had become confused and the money did not exist.

Tragically, your father was murdered because those pursuing Mateo thought that he had absconded with the money. After your father's funeral, when I had gone to Australia with Melissa, the priest contacted Natalia and asked her to meet him at the church. He went up to the chancel, lifted the altar cloth, and pulled out a colourful leather *carriel*. She was astonished and they assumed that the dying man must have pushed it beneath the altar to try and hide it. This *carriel* was undoubtedly the one which Mateo had talked about. When the priest and Natalia opened it, there were many millions of pesos inside it and many US dollars. A peso is worth very little (3000 pesos were then worth about one US dollar). After they counted it, they realised that the total value was in the region of US$ 430,000. They debated and prayed about what they should do with the money, and they decided eventually to respect the dying man's wishes and donate it to the orphanage and school.

Natalia said that they decided to wait a couple of years before spending the money, in case there were any repercussions or claims. But nothing happened and nobody ever questioned where the money had come from. Eventually they drew up plans for the work that had long been necessary and used the 'gift' for building new classrooms and other much-needed facilities. The work was undertaken during 2004 and 2005 and all the new improvements were funded by the 'donation' from the *carriel*.

At the end of this story Natalia told me that, if he had not met up with Mateo, Julian might still be alive. Mateo escaped from his attackers, fled to a place where he knew Julian was staying, and endangered his friend. Mateo had died leaving the money in Natalia's care and she regarded the benefit to many children from the upgrading of the school as the abiding legacy of her much-loved nephew. God had made good things happen out of evil and tragedy.

She ended and we sat in silence finishing our coffee, gazing out over the playground where carefree children were running around. We had known each other for thirty-five years and she was like a sister to me. I had little to draw me back to England, having lost husband and home, so Natalia persuaded me to stay. My Spanish was a bit rusty but it came flooding back and I decided to help in the orphanage. I loved working with the children, which was a change from looking after the elderly. Months passed and I stayed on, finding once again a reason for living. However, in 2010 Natalia reached retirement age and decided to stand down as head teacher, work fewer hours and spend more time in her beloved garden. It was then that I became convinced I might have more chance of finding my grandchildren one day if I returned to live in England. Natalia urged me to stay, but I was as fond of Dorset as she was of Tolima, and so I came home.

I have never had qualifications but always managed to get work as a care assistant. Caring work is lowly paid, involves unsocial hours, and is often tiring – but I've always found it hugely rewarding. If you look after your patients with a real zest for doing it well, you can make such a difference to people and improve their quality of life. I rented a room in a friend's house, bought an inexpensive fourth-hand car and signed on with an agency that supplied care workers. After a couple of weeks, I was sent to work for a gentleman in his early seventies, who had been an accountant. He was undergoing chemotherapy for a cancer condition and had declined going into a nursing home for recuperation. As he was divorced without children, he needed help to enable him to live in his own home. A kind and courteous man, he loved his farm and was passionate about nature but also liked poetry and listening to music.

The gentleman's name was Charles Trevett and he farmed a small estate on the edge of a Dorset village called Winterborne Slepe. After I had spent six weeks working there, he asked me if

I liked the place. I replied that I had walked around, met a few people and I liked it very much. Knowing that I was renting a room some miles away, he asked if I would like to rent a cottage of his that had recently become vacant. I was astonished at this suggestion because he did not know that I was looking for somewhere permanent where I could put down roots. He offered me a lease for five years and I gratefully accepted. I moved in on 1st December 2010 and continued to work for him part-time for a few months, during which my agency found other work for me in the surrounding area. In the following spring, Mr Charles, as everyone in the village called him, became seriously ill and his condition deteriorated when his cancer returned aggressively. Eventually he had to go into hospital where he died. I was sad because I had come to respect him and enjoy his company – he had lots of good stories about the village and the local area. As you know, I continue to live in 'The Haven', as a tenant of his nephew, James, who inherited the estate.

I first met James Trevett when he came to see the woman who was occupying one of his cottages. When I asked him whether he was happy to have me as a tenant, he hesitated at first and then grinned and said, "Absolutely." Later I discovered this is an expression he uses often, though I don't know why he just can't say 'yes'.

My lease still has nine months to run and I am hoping I can stay on. I love living in glorious Dorset and have found friends and a satisfying life in this village. But I am a bit worried because I've heard rumours that James now wants to develop a holiday cottage business. Alice says he has his eye on my cottage. I am now nearly sixty-three and I hope I can continue working for a few years yet so I can pay a proper rent. But things are tight – they always have been.

I shall leave it all in God's hands. Meanwhile the daffodils are out, Folly keeps me company, and soon spring will come dancing into my life again.

With love and optimism,

GMJ xxx

Rain streams down the windowpanes and spatters on the windowsill. Beyond all is dark, apart from a solitary light in one of the houses in the vicinity. The fact there is at least one other person awake in the village is no comfort. Prowler gives the curtain a savage jerk to pull it closed and shut out the rest of the world. One of the hooks pulls out of the ring on the pole and he stares at the sagging curtain in resentment before turning his back on it and walking back to his computer. The screen is on but the icons do not beckon him as they once might have done. The pleasure he used to get from his computer games has waned and he's sick of watching films and other stuff – on his own. He throws himself into his office chair and stares at the screen without enthusiasm. His mind is focusing elsewhere.

Apart from his work, little else is happening in his life. The woman he is pursuing does not seem to take much notice of him anymore. She appears to have other things on her mind. How can he reawaken her interest? His fingers start restlessly moving over the keys – he will check his emails. When he has done this, he takes a look at what Josie has been writing to her grandkids in New Zealand, something he hasn't done for a couple of weeks. In her sent emails, he finds the most recent sent on 8th March. He starts to read. Suddenly he sits up and leans forward, his attention now fully on the words that tell him that the money he had tried in vain to trace never left Colombia! The Moreno family did have it after all and it is clear that Josie has known for some years where it went and how it was spent. A red anger floods his head. She has cheated him.

After a few minutes he picks up a small box in which he keeps paper clips and rummages around in it until he comes across a key - the key to Josie's back door. He copied it when he 'borrowed' the keys which she carelessly left lying around and which he later returned. With access to her cottage he is still able to invade her life, sabotage her sense of security and destroy her peace of mind. He can intimidate her. He's in control.

21st March 2015

Dear Tom,

I was horrified to read your email this morning which you began: 'Our secret has been blown wide open'. So your mother has found out about our emails and accused you and Lottie of deceiving her. In one way I'm glad she knows because I've thought for some time that Melissa should be told we are in touch. It wasn't right to keep her in the dark. She is now fully in the picture – and you say she is furious.

I find it hard to believe that your mother has been surreptitiously checking Lottie's new computer to make sure that her daughter is not being groomed online by anybody unpleasant. Inevitably, she stumbled across my last couple of emails and Lottie's replies. You sounded annoyed that Lottie doesn't always switch off her laptop or use a password to protect her files, but you have been using computers far longer than her. She has a trusting nature and didn't expect her mother to snoop.

I'm sorry this discovery resulted in a big row when your mother demanded that you both stop communicating with me. Thank you for digging your heels in and saying that, since you are now eighteen and an adult, you would communicate with whoever you chose and that you had no intention of cutting off contact with your own grandmother. I'm so grateful you think our relationship worth preserving and I do hope that in time your sister and I will re-establish contact. Lottie will obey the ban because otherwise her laptop will be taken away from her. I realise she thinks her mother has been totally unreasonable and it must be awkward that they won't speak to each other at the moment. How fortunate you returned from Dunedin a few days before this happened, so you could stand up for your sister, share some of the guilt and deflect some of Melissa's anger! I am truly sorry that our secret correspondence has upset her so much. I wonder what Robert thinks about it all. Perhaps he might persuade your mother to reconsider.

Today is the first day of spring – and there's often unsettled weather with storms at the equinoxes. At the end of your letter you mentioned that a few days ago the tail end of Cyclone Pam had moved down the east coast of New Zealand causing heavy flooding, power failures and evacuations from near the coast. When you said that Cyclone Pam had nothing on your mother, I had to smile in spite of my distress at her outburst and her obvious dislike of me. I don't know what I've done to warrant such antipathy. Please tell Lottie that I'm sorry she's in trouble over a normal exchange of letters with her grandmother. Melissa is making a storm in a teacup. Let's hope it all blows over.

Tom, I know you are off to Australia after Easter and I do hope that you'll make things up with your mother and leave on good terms with her and Robert. Keep in touch from time to time as I should love to hear about your travels and the people you meet. Take care of yourself and have fun. There's an Irish blessing which begins:

'May the road rise up to meet you.

May the wind be always at your back.

May the sun shine warm upon your face.'

And it ends:

'May God hold you in the palm of His hand.'

With love and prayers,

GMJ xxx

Easter has come and gone. The sheep are back in the field below her house and there is blossom on the trees. Josie has been out walking and is now heading home. She is thinking of her grandchildren and how much she misses hearing from Lottie. She realises that Tom and his friend Liam set off for Australia two days ago, and even though he has taken his small laptop with him, she must learn to accept that his communications from now on will be infrequent and brief. She arrives at her cottage where she is slightly surprised to find the back door locked. She thought she'd left it open - as she does when she goes on a brief walk. Thinking she must be mistaken, she fishes for the key in her pocket and lets herself in.

When she has made a cup of tea, she goes through to the sitting room, failing to see that the framed photograph of her and Oliver on their wedding day has been turned upside down and that the picture to the right of her fireplace has been swapped with the one on the left. It will be three days before she notices. Sitting down, she hears the comforting clatter of the cat flap and seconds later Folly joins her on the sofa. After half an hour with a book, she puts it down and goes over to her computer. Perhaps, after all, there is an email from one of her grandchildren. She's disappointed but unsurprised when there is not, but sees that she has incoming mail from an 'mmbrown' and opens it. It takes only a few seconds to realise that this is the first communication she has had from her daughter-in-law for fifteen years. Melissa has found out her email address from Lottie's laptop and has sent a curt message, demanding that Josie immediately cease all communication with Tom and Lottie. This is so totally unreasonable that Josie is outraged. She will not be bullied by Melissa Brown who lives on the other side of world. She clicks on the reply button.

11th April 2015

Dear Melissa,

I have just read your email to me. The content of it has destroyed any pleasure I might have had in receiving a communication from my daughter-in-law after so many years of silence.

Years ago, following an emotional misunderstanding, you

decided to deny your children the right to know their paternal grandmother. When you moved house, you made sure that I could not trace you. I wonder if you have any idea how much that hurt me. Lottie and Tom are my only living blood relatives.

Why do you have such a problem with me? Julian loved you passionately as his wife and he loved me differently, the way sons love their mothers. You lived with him every day and I saw him very rarely. You had no reason to be jealous of me.

Julian went to Colombia of his own free will to see his sick grandfather and tragically died. I will not be held responsible for his death because I happened to be in Colombia at the time. You have no reason to be angry with me.

With regard to my emails to your children, I would like to point out that it was Tom who finally traced me. Many young children who lose a parent are later curious as to what they were like. Apparently, you were unwilling to talk about Julian, so he decided to find me and ask me to tell him about his father. Nothing could be more natural. Later on, Lottie joined in the email correspondence and I can truthfully say that I think all three of us have enjoyed hearing about each other's lives. These are my grandchildren. I am their grandmother and I love them.

The only thing I apologise for is the secrecy. I pleaded with your children to let you know that we were in communication, but it was their decision not to do this, because they feared it would upset you. And they were right. But your absurd knee-jerk reaction is completely irrational and unjust. Tom is now an adult and will make his own decision about the matter, but I do ask you to reconsider and allow Lottie to continue to stay in touch with me if she wishes to do so. It is not kind to pressurise her. It is not fair to deny me access to her.

May I suggest that you discuss this with your husband

Robert? From what I have read about him in emails from my grandchildren, he sounds a reasonable and caring man. You are a fortunate woman, who has had two loving marriages and three lovely children. I live alone and have no relatives except for Tom and Lottie who are far away. Melissa, you have so much and I have so little.

Let me be quite plain. Unless I hear from Tom and Lottie themselves that they no longer want to have anything to do with their grandmother, I shall continue to write them emails and to receive any they may send to me. I would rather do this with your assent. I entreat you to give it.

Yours in hope,

Josie

18th April 2015

Melissa,

Three days ago, I received your unreasonable response to my measured email to you. I will repeat what I said before: I categorically refuse to stop communicating with my grandson and my granddaughter whilst they wish to keep in contact with me. I am sorry to say that I do not want to hear from you again unless you would like to re-establish a sensible relationship between us.

Josie Cuff

1st May 2015

Dear Tom,

You have now been in Australia for three weeks and I'm hoping all is going well and that you are enjoying the carefree freedom of travelling with a backpack and without time constraints. I know you have an outline itinerary, but it's good to be flexible and able to decide from day-to-day where you'll go next.

Village life trundles on into spring. The little battles and tittle tattles have subsided somewhat – which is a relief. Lou Stickley has stopped looking pinched with cold and the Elfords have started to smile now that business is picking up at the pub. Harry has emerged from his study and John is spending less time on his computer and more time in his garden. Alice has been away staying with cousins and Doris is as kind as ever and looking after her neighbour, Lily. Everyone seems alright. Except for me – I have been a bit unwell and have been unable to work, which is unusual. But I'm sure I'll bounce back into good health very soon.

I'm also having a few problems in the cottage. One night during last week the electricity cut out and, because my small torch wasn't in its usual place, I had to search around in the dark to throw the trip switch. I wasn't sure which appliance or light had fused. Yesterday, I had a problem with my computer. I telephoned Harry, who is quite knowledgeable about them, and he dropped round in the afternoon and managed to eradicate the glitch. The washer seems to have gone in my kitchen tap and it spouts water through the joint, so I'm going to ask Bill if he will call in after work and help me replace it. A damp patch has reappeared on an upstairs ceiling and I think there might be a leak in the roof – so I shall have to get in touch with my landlord. Oh dear!

James has been looking glum recently, because his girlfriend

Harriet, who works in London, has had to cancel her visit again. We have all been looking forward to meeting her and I think James is hugely disappointed.

I have, as expected, not heard a word from Lottie and realise this is because she is obeying her mother by not emailing me in order to be allowed to use her laptop. I have to confess that I do miss her emails and I hope in time that your mother will relent and allow Lottie to write to me again. When you next contact your sister, please give her my love and say that I'm hoping so much that we can be back in touch sometime soon. Meanwhile take care on your travels and if you have time send me the occasional update.

With love and expectation,

GMJ xxx

Doris's garden is as neat as her house. Josie is sitting in a chair with a mug of tea in her hand watching her friend sowing seeds. Normally Josie would be helping her or working in her own garden, but she doesn't seem to have much energy after a bout of infection. Doris straightens up, walks along the path and sits down in the other chair.

She looks across at her friend – Josie can see the concern in her face – and says, "You still don't look very well."

"I'm alright – much better than I was." Josie does not want to discuss her illness.

"You've lost weight. Are you eating properly?"

"I'm just fine. I'm always thin."

"You don't eat enough to put on weight!" Doris

says in her disapproving nurse's voice.

"I'm not hungry and I don't feel like cooking." Josie closes her eyes and turns her face towards the spring sun.

Doris looks at her friend's face. "Josie, what's the matter? Is something troubling you?"

With her eyes shut Josie says, "I'm not sleeping well and wake up a lot during the night. I have curious dreams in which I embark on tasks I can never seem to complete." She pauses, remembering last night's scenario when she was moving house and packing endless suitcases with an ever-increasing pile of stuff. It was confusing and demoralising because the harder she tried the slower she worked.

She opens her eyes and looks straight at Doris. "I'm tired so I lack energy. My cottage is in a mess – nothing new there. Tidying up has never been high on my list of priorities and normally it doesn't bother me if the place is in a bit of a muddle. But now I can't seem to find anything." She forces a smile. "There seems to be a gremlin in my cottage – lots of things are breaking or going wrong."

"Can't you get them fixed?" Doris is always practical.

"Yes. But in addition, I have this irrational conviction that someone is coming into my house."

"That's very unlikely."

"I know. I try to keep calm, read a book or write an email." Josie does not mention that reading is often an antidote to loneliness or that writing letters and choosing words can be a way of trying to create order out of chaos.

"Have a rest in the afternoon."

"I've never been able to do that. It's like wiping

out part of a day - and life's too short. Thanks for tea and sympathy - I appreciate it." Josie gets to her feet. "The real problem is that I feel I'm losing touch with my grandchildren again and I don't think I can cope with that."

9th May 2015

Dear Tom,

It was great to hear from you yesterday. And you remembered my birthday! Though you admitted it was your sister who reminded you. Thanks for letting me know that Lottie is fine and that she sends her love. I'm not sure about her plan of setting up another email address which she can use to read my letters on a friend's computer rather than her own. It's bending the rules but that's up to her.

I expect Lottie already knows that the Duke and Duchess of Cambridge have decided to call their baby daughter, born a few days ago, Charlotte – after her!

The Great Barrier Reef sounds amazing, though I am sorry that Liam got so badly sunburned. It's a combination of sunlight and water that makes snorkelling without a T-shirt such a bad idea. So you are now back in Cairns and are off to visit Daintree National Park in the rainforest. Your month in Australia must be nearly over and soon you will be winging your way to Bali in Indonesia and then onto Vietnam. I can't work out why you decided to drop the plan of going to the Philippines. Is it because you and Liam are keen to meet up with friends in Vietnam?

In the UK we had a general election a couple of days ago and the Conservative party won. I've just realised how little I know about

New Zealand politics – and I suspect that's true of many people in England, which all goes to show how insular most of us are, particularly in countries situated on small islands near bigger neighbours, like Great Britain and New Zealand. The new government here has promised to hold a referendum soon on whether the UK remains as a member of the European Union. There is a growing section of the population who are unhappy with Europe and unwisely want to go it alone. I wonder what will happen.

Winterborne Slepe is in mourning! Lena, the pretty Polish waitress at our pub, has left and all the young men are distraught! It seems she has gone to work for a restaurant in the local town. Flora tells me she needed a change of scene, but Alice says it is because she failed to nab our Mr James as a husband and has gone to new pastures to find another rich man. Who knows? Anyhow, Flora has found someone else to help in the bar and village life continues. I'll miss Lena – she was a smiling face and always friendly to everyone.

My little car has developed a problem – it won't go! Flat battery! Bill says he'll try to get it started with some jump leads. I hope I won't have to buy a new battery. Anyhow I don't want the car until Tuesday when I need it to drive to work.

What are the roads like in Vietnam? Do you travel by bus?

With love from your,

GMJ xxx

4th June 2015

Dear Magpies,

We are reliably informed that it's summer in England – but we've clearly been misled. It ought to be sunny and warm in

June but the month has begun with low pressure, rain and strong winds. I expect it is wintry and cold in South Island, New Zealand where Lottie is, and probably hot and humid in Vietnam, if that is where you still are, Tom.

I had two depressing items of news this morning. Firstly, my agency phoned me to say that the couple for whom I have worked for two years are to be moved into a residential care home, and that I will not be required to work there after the end of the month. This is very upsetting for them as they valued their independence so much, and sad for me as I shall miss them. I hope my agency can find me other work locally.

The other was related to me by Harry who dropped by this morning. You may recall that I had a brother called Henri who had disappeared. Harry used to know him and has been trying to find out what happened. He has now discovered that Henri owned a flat in Durham, which had been abandoned for a long time. His council tax, utility and flat service charges were paid by direct debit, but when his bank account ran out of money and the debt started increasing, the various creditors were pressing for repayment. They applied to the court for an order that he should be presumed dead. Thorough checks were carried out and it now seems almost certain that he died in South America. After he had been absent for more than seven years, a Certificate of Presumed Death was issued and his flat was sold to repay the outstanding debts. Before the contents were disposed of, the police had made a thorough search and found no will. Searches were made some while back to find out if he had any relatives alive, but Harry seems to think that Henri's property, whatever it is, may have already passed to the Crown. I don't this will make much difference to the Queen, as she's one of the world wealthiest women. He told me that he's sent my details and copies of my birth certificate to some authority in the hope that I might be recognised as Henri's only surviving family member, but there's been no response. Poor Harry! He is disappointed – and upset that I don't seem too bothered about it. Though I wouldn't say no if some family photographs or letters were to eventually find their way to me, I have learnt that 'windfalls' and unexpected blessings are rarely bestowed on me by anyone other than God.

I will email this to both my Magpies, in the hope that both of you will read it, Tom when he finds somewhere on his travels where he can connect to the internet, and Lottie when she logs on to her new email address on a friend's computer.

With armfuls of love from your,

GMJ xxx

19th June 2015

Dear Lottie,

I was overjoyed to get an email from you. I'm so glad everything is alright. I understand you don't use your own laptop to email me, which was what you promised to your mother. However, I am a little concerned that she may find out that you are writing to me once again. I'd like you to be truthful if she asks, so do please be careful. I wouldn't want you to get into deep trouble nor do I want to be the recipient of another angry email from her – and if that happens, I too will change my email address.

So after the final weeks of the winter term, you'll have two weeks' holiday in the first part of July. How very exciting that you are to go on a school trip to Auckland. It's kind of Robert to say that he will pay for it. I'm sure you don't really mean that you'll be pleased to get away from Bex. She cannot be a 'pain' all the time.

Remember she's growing up too and pushing out the bounds!

I said that you'd miss your brother. By the way I haven't heard from him since early May and I've forgotten where he said he was going next. Do you have any news?

So how are things here in Dorset? This week I have been helping David and Jean to pack up as they are to leave their home in ten days. They cannot take too much with them to the residential home, where they are to have one double room with a bathroom. They are quite distressed at having to make decisions about what they can take and what must be sold or thrown away. I'm surprised their family are not assisting them with these difficult choices. Anyway, I'm glad to help them through the move and I'm really going to miss them. They are such gentle people.

My neighbours on both sides seem well. I was very surprised that Matt Tapper came and spoke to me over the garden hedge yesterday evening whilst I was weeding one of my unruly flower beds. He's not usually one to initiate conversation, but he was almost chatty. He says he is going away on holiday with a 'friend'. He didn't say who this person is and I didn't ask. I'm not aware he has a girlfriend and I don't intrude on his privacy. I was pleased because he works hard but rarely goes away. He told me he needed a break because in his job he has a female line manager, who is difficult to work with. I asked him in for a cup of tea but he shook his head and actually smiled. He's not a bad looking man and still quite young.

The Stickleys on the other side are also in a good mood. Shortly after Matt had gone back indoors, Bill leaned over the fence to tell me that their grandchildren are coming to visit again during the summer holidays. I enjoyed taking the little ones on a scavenger hunt the last time they came and offered to take them this time to the beach. He says that Lou has already started making cakes and meals to freeze down, ready for their arrival. I went to bed last night sandwiched between two sets of contented neighbours. And I felt cheerful too – because I'd heard from you.

With love and joy,

GMJ xxx

28th June 2015

Dear Magpies,

What a good weekend! Yesterday I heard from you both – a postcard from Phuket in Thailand from Tom, and another 'forbidden' email from Lottie, sent from Sarah's house. Who is Sarah? I hope she's discreet. The weather has turned very warm and summer is magnificent here.

Tom, did you get to Cambodia? I'm wondering if you made it to the Angkor Wat temples – somewhere I should love to see. Oliver once went there and used to tell me about them, and Harry too has been there and bought some charcoal temple rubbings of bas relief sculptures which he framed up and put on his walls. Nice to hear that you and Liam are travelling with a couple of girls you have met. Where are they from and are they also on their gap years?

Lottie, you are off to North Island on 4th July. I'm glad your new friend, Sarah, will be part of the school group. I'm so pleased that you and Mummy had a fun couple of days together in Christchurch. The whole world heard about the tragic destruction of the cathedral in the 2011 earthquake and I was sad to hear it has not yet been rebuilt. I was fascinated when you described a temporary Cardboard Cathedral which seats around 700 where people have been worshipping for nearly two years.

I must tell you something slightly curious. My cottage has been invaded by spiders, even though there aren't that many webs. Folly has been a little off-colour recently, which may account for why she has not been more active in evicting them. As it happens spiders don't bother me that much. It's always seemed idiotic to be so frightened of such small creatures, and I began to feel rather affectionate for the leggy little beasties after reading years ago a wonderful children's book called *Charlotte's Web*. Have you read it? It changes your perspective on pigs as well. I began to admire them after reading a book by George Orwell entitled *Animal Farm*. You've probably come across this book at school – it's well known. The other day I was driving on a road alongside a large field containing lots of pig shelters and huge sows rooting around happily with their piglets, blissfully unaware of a large and ominous sign erected in the field which says: 'Put British Pork on your Fork'. I felt really sorry for these pigs – their destiny is to be eaten. Roald Dahl, the amazing children's writer, has a hilarious poem about a 'wonderfully clever pig' who eats the farmer!

Doris has driven up and is sounding her horn. Must dash or we'll be late for church. My car's still a bit dodgy, so she's giving me a lift. Do keep writing. A few words from you cheer me up so much.

With love and in haste,

GMJ xxx

Josie has finished sweeping the stone flags and she hums 'All Things Bright and Beautiful' as she polishes the lectern. This month she is on the rota to clean the church in Winterborne Slepe and is dusting the pews when she hears footsteps. Peering around a pillar she sees Alice Diffey, who has arrived with flowers and greenery to arrange them for Sunday.

"Hi, Alice. How's everything with you?" she calls.

Alice walks down the aisle, plonks the flowers down on one of the pews and sniffs. "I seem to have caught a summer cold."

"Perhaps it's just the pollen," Josie suggests, moving on to the pulpit with her duster.

"No, it's a cold. I caught it from Louise who sneezed over me at the coffee morning last week."

"Fortunately, I'm in good health," Josie says. "Though my poor cat has been vomiting and I'm going to take her to the vet." She is reminded of the need to find the money for the vet's bill. As she doesn't have any work at the moment, she might have to delay paying the rent.

Alice goes into the vestry to get a couple of vases and then starts to cut the ends of the flower stalks and strip off some leaves, before arranging them on the altar.

Josie has paused by the lectern and is looking at the open page in the Bible. She silently reads a few lines from Proverbs 13: "Hope deferred makes the heart sick, but a longing fulfilled is a tree of life." It always amazes her how apt some proverbs are.

"We might have a church wedding here one of these days," Alice says with an air of mystery.

Josie knows that Alice wants to strike up a conversation but stays silent.

But Alice is not to be put off. "Mr James seems to be very happy since his lady friend Harriet arrived to stay a few days ago. I had a friendly chat with her when I called in on Mr James to see if he wanted to buy some tickets for the raffle at the summer fete. She's a nice lady - very pretty. They both seem devoted to each other. Let's be honest, he's quite a good catch - a single gentleman and a landowner."

"So she's finally decided to come down from London," Josie says as she brushes up the flower detritus, thinking about the last time she ran into James. He had been lamenting the fact that his girlfriend was too busy at work to find time to visit him in Dorset, but he was 'absolutely' certain she would come soon. "Harriet obviously works hard."

"She told me she runs a successful interior decorating business and works 24/7." Alice is clearly delighted she is the only one in the village to have met James's girlfriend. "And she generously bought five raffle tickets."

"Well, I'm done now," says Josie, going into the vestry to put away her cleaning kit.

When she emerges, she sees Alice has made an attractive display. Josie is no good at flower arranging and everyone knows it. "That looks lovely, Alice," she says and means it.

"Thank you, Josie. Can I persuade you to buy some raffle tickets?"

17th July 2015

Dear Tom,

Thanks for your update. I'm not surprised you're still on the islands off the west coast of Thailand – they sound marvellous. I see that Sam (I assume this is short for Samantha) and Megan are still travelling with you and Liam, until he returns to New Zealand in early August. How very generous of your stepfather Robert to send you some money to help you to stay overseas for longer, and go on to India with the girls. I didn't realise they were English and that Sam's family live in Wiltshire. This county is adjacent to the north-eastern part of Dorset and it's where Stonehenge is situated. Where is Megan from?

I have stopped working for David and Jean, who now live in a care home. I will visit them occasionally but the place is some distance away and, although my little car is now running better, it's a long way for her to trundle. My agency has found me work but for fewer hours, and I have to drive from one place and one client to another. I am looking around for something else to do and I may be able to find some cleaning jobs. Flora has now taken to paying me when I help out at the Anchor. The rent has to be paid somehow and I'm sure I'll manage.

It's your birthday in three days so, wherever you are, have a happy one. This reminds me that it's Harry's birthday next week and he's invited me for a supper party, which is kind of him. His house is surrounded by an attractive garden and it's comfortable inside – unfussy and uncluttered as suits a bachelor. Harry is kind but can be controlling and sometimes he's almost secretive. I discovered recently to my surprise that his ex-wife had a child from a earlier relationship. They were divorced years ago but he still keeps in touch with his stepdaughter. I told him I'd like to meet her one day.

You're probably aware that Lottie is now emailing me from her friend Sarah's house. I'm delighted to be back in regular touch, but I'm troubled by the possibility of upsetting your mother again. I trust you are keeping in good contact with her and Robert and of course with Lottie who misses you. Take care.

With love and birthday wishes,

GMJ xxx

Josie opens her kitchen door and immediately sees the small sparrow, mangled and bloody on the floor inside, just below the cat flap. A surge of pity gives way to surprise. Folly catches the odd bird occasionally but she always leaves the remains outside near the back door and never brings them in. As she bends down to scoop up the dead bird in some kitchen paper, Josie experiences a momentary stab of terror, sharp as a shard of broken glass. She straightens up and turns to look out of the window. No one is there. Is the premonition of danger inside her head or outside her house?

30th July 2015

Dear Lottie,

Thank you so much for the photograph of you and school friends during your trip in Auckland. It sounds as though you crammed lots in and I'm glad it was fun. I was touched you told me about your friend Leo. He may not look like Brad Pitt and he may have a few spots, but what matters is that he's kind to girls and has a sense of humour. How sad that he lost his father last year. I can see why you're pleased to be back at school – because he's in your class and you'll see more of him than you do during the holidays. Don't forget to tell your mother if he asks you to go to a party with him, and work out before you go how you're going to get home and when. You are after all only fifteen. I expect your mother is saying the same.

I must tell you about an extraordinary thing that happened to me last week. Harry had invited me round for his birthday supper. I fully expected there would be other friends coming, but when I arrived – a little late as I often am – there was no one there but Harry. There were only two places laid up at the table, with two wine glasses and a single candle already burning, even though it was still light outside. I was a little discomfited to be the only guest but decided to enjoy the meal he had prepared, thank him profusely and leave as early as I could afterwards.

Harry had made a big effort although cooking is not his thing. But I was hungry, the meal was edible and I was grateful. He is not the most gregarious man and that evening he was more reticent than usual and, because I felt awkward, I chatted about trivial things – as one does! We were each munching our way through a solid slice of (shop bought) cheesecake when he suddenly put down his spoon and leant forward, his eyes fixed on me.

"Josie, my dear," he began. "You must by now have realised how fond of you I am."

I began to feel really uncomfortable so I picked up my half full glass of wine and took a sip to give me time to brace myself.

He reached out and placed his hand possessively on my arm.

"I've been so concerned for you, because you have so little money and find it hard to pay the rent or buy decent food. You need a real home. You need security."

Horrified, I stared at him, slowly putting my glass back on the table. Was he going to offer to lend me money...or something else?

But he seemed completely unaware of my negative reaction and went on, "I own this nice house and there's plenty of room. I get a little lonely sometimes and could do with company. We like the same things; we both enjoy books. So, it occurred to me that you could live here. I'll probably get used to your untidiness and I think we would rub along well together." Then he patted my hand and withdrew his.

Lottie, I tell you, by this time I was squirming with embarrassment and pleading to be out of there: 'Beam me up, Scotty'!

But living in sin was not what he was proposing. "I hope so much, Josie, that you'll do me the honour of becoming my wife."

I was stunned. I stared at the candle, unable to look at him. I knew without a shadow of doubt that he didn't love me and I didn't love him. With marriage there must be love on both sides.

Somehow, I managed to tell him gently that I couldn't possibly become his wife, that I was very touched by his kind offer, but reassured him that I could manage very well on my own and that he would be much better off without a chaotic wife. I hoped that we would remain good friends and neighbours.

He stared at his plate to avoid looking at me, but he did not try to persuade me to change my mind and I detected a hint of relief in his face as I left.

I must say that although this was a most unwelcome proposal of marriage, I was grateful for Harry's concern about me. But I do not want to be housed or caged – and when he put his hand on my arm, my skin crawled. It was Harry's birthday – poor man – and the evening was a disaster! I just hope that we can be unembarrassed and natural with each other when we next meet. I doubt it.

Well, Lottie, it's not every day a woman of my age gets a proposal of marriage but I've no inclination to tell anybody about it, apart from you, and I can't believe that Harry will. It's good to have you as my 'confidante' – a trusted female friend. And it's mutual – you've shared your secrets with me. I must confess that I confide in someone else as well – Folly. But she is always discreet and never purrs a word to anyone.

With love and trust,
GMJ xxx

He is driving too fast. He is angry with all women. He misses one woman - she was different - she was perfect.

The other 'she' torments him: she is not amenable. She just wants to be friends. She is independent. She pities him. She does not notice his interference in her life. She continues to be positive in spite of all he does. She walks around the village with a smile on her face. She infuriates him.

She can go to hell!

He swerves to avoid an oncoming car. Concentrate. She is unguarded. Retaliate.

11th August 2015

Dear Lottie,

At last our correspondence is permitted – what good news! It was the right thing to talk to Robert about it. No doubt your mother has withdrawn her opposition because he persuaded her that grandmothers who live 12,000 miles away are not that threatening! Or maybe she's missing Tom and is beginning to understand how I might feel. However, in order to keep things private, why don't you continue to use your new email address? And then Mummy won't be able to read our emails if you happen to leave your laptop on. I'd be so grateful if you would thank Robert for his kind intervention. He's obviously a compassionate man.

Yesterday I was pulling up some stubborn weeds in the front garden and John walked over to say hello. He told me he's got to sell the house, because Maggie owns a share of it and it's the only way to raise the money. He didn't look too downcast so I imagine the decision was made some time ago. He then told me that on his skiing holiday he met a lovely person called Nina who lives and works in Hampshire and that he might move to be nearer her. I said we'd all be sorry to see him go. I didn't mention that Maggie had telephoned me a couple of weeks earlier to say that she was getting remarried and that, at the age of thirty-nine, she was pregnant. She and John never did have children. I told Maggie I was happy for her and she invited me to come to the wedding, which she wants to have soon so that her bump doesn't show! John is clearly in blissful ignorance of this event and I shall keep it secret. It does seem a little unjust that he has to leave his home, when she is already installed in another, engaged to be married to her new man and with a child on the way.

John stood looking wistfully across at his house with a slight frown on his face, and said, "Perhaps Nina and I will get together and who knows – maybe we'll have a family. It's not too late."

It was as if he was reading my thoughts. "Living alone isn't for everybody. It suits me, but perhaps not you," I said. "You'll be happier with another woman. You should go for it."

"Maggie was a nightmare," he said. "Such a selfish cow. Anyhow it's the end of an era. To hell with her!" He wandered back across the road, kicking a stone out of his way.

John's got a bit of a temper, but Maggie was a difficult lady and I hope Nina suits him better.

I forgot to mention that caring work seems to have dried up or perhaps my agency doesn't think I'm competent any more. But I've managed to get work in a local shop for three afternoons a week. The woman who owns the shop knows one of my friends from church. It's in a pleasant village a few miles away but nothing like as amusing as Winterborne Slepe.

By the way, how are you and Leo getting on? You didn't mention him in your email. I haven't heard from Tom for a while and it seems that you haven't either. I wonder where he is and hope he's safe. The last time he was in touch, he said he was off to India in the company of two English girls. He's a tall, strong nineteen-year-old, so I expect he's fine.

Did I mention that Folly had been ill? She is much better, I'm glad to say. She loves the summer and spends hours lying in the sun in my vegetable patch and herb garden. In the evenings she condescends to sit on my lap. I read poetry aloud and her ears twitch. Someone, whose name I cannot recall, once said that dogs are prose but a cat is a poem.

That's all for now.

With love from summery Dorset and

GMJ xxx

17th August 2015

Dear Tom,

I've not heard from you for over a month and do hope all is well. Lottie emailed me a few days ago and wrote that you had telephoned the family to say that your laptop had been stolen. How very unfortunate! I expect you will now have to rely on internet cafés in order to keep in touch as you travel around. I assume they have such things in India. I should love to hear your impressions of the country. Are you still backpacking with the English girls? I forget when you are due back in New Zealand. If at all possible send me a few words, letting me know where you are and reassuring me all is well.

We are having a warm and sleepy August in Winterborne Slepe. I think many of the residents are away on holiday as everything is quiet, apart from the birds and the distant sound of farm tractors working in the surrounding fields. I haven't seen much of my neighbour Matt, who travels around in his job and seems to get home late and leave early. Bill and Lou are here – they rarely go away, and at this time of year he's very busy working on James's land. The other day I returned from the shop where I work until 6 pm. When I'd parked and got out of my car, Bill ambled over and asked if I had a guest staying, because an hour before he thought he'd caught a glimpse through the window of a person inside my house. We both went into the house together and it was empty. Very unsettling. I'd locked the door when I went out, so Bill was reassured. After he'd gone, I was uneasy because for a long while I've known that some nasty individual has been sneaking around inside my house. I will try not to feel too threatened by whoever is intruding on my privacy.

With love and apprehension,
GMJ xxx

Josie is trying to do a quick clean of her sitting room. James has telephoned her to ask if he may call round at midday. She is wearing her only tidy skirt and a white shirt, in an endeavour to look reliable, but she fears her appearance will have little chance of deflecting James from what he is about to do. She sees him as a 'prophet of doom' and plumps up the dented cushions with an extra thump to work off her irritation.

The doorbell jangles and Josie hastily crams a pile of papers into a drawer before going through to the hall to open the door.

She sees her landlord standing on the doorstep with his usual awkward posture. Behind him she notices John's house across the lane with the prominent 'For Sale' board outside it. "Come in, James. Good to see you." It is not good to see him at all!

"Ah, hello, Josie." James is clearly embarrassed by what he has come to say. "Lovely weather."

"So warm too," says Josie pleasantly as they enter the room. "Do sit down."

James sits in the low armchair that she is indicating, whilst she seats herself on the office chair which puts her slightly higher than him. Elevation may give her an edge.

As he clears his throat, Josie launches in, "I realise I haven't paid the rent this month but I should be able to soon, if you'll give me a couple of weeks leeway."

"Of course. Absolutely no problem there. You've always managed to come up with it in the end. But there's something else."

The axe is about to fall. Will she lose her home? She smiles but says nothing. Why should she make it easy for him? It isn't going to be easy for her.

With an apologetic sigh James begins, "I'm sorry to say I've come as the bearer of bad tidings. You are, of course, aware that your lease ends on 30th November this year. I had hoped I was going to be able to accommodate you by extending the lease, but I now find that I must maximise my assets. I have plans to convert this dwelling into a luxury holiday cottage for discerning holidaymakers to rent." He pauses, a little confused by the fact that Josie is staring bleakly out of window. "I'm awfully sorry that I'm obliged to give you notice to leave."

Josie turns to look at him. "I am of course disappointed that I can't stay in the cottage which I've grown to love. I don't expect there's any point asking you to reconsider?"

James shakes his head, saying, "It's been difficult to do this as you are something of a friend, but I hope you see it from my point of view. The rent you pay isn't much and you are often in arrears. I want to upgrade the cottage and increase the income from it." He fumbles in his tweed jacket pocket and pulls out an envelope which he hands silently to Josie.

She takes it from him without opening it and says, "So I can stay here until the end of November but have to be out then. Is that right?"

"Absolutely. I'm sure you'll find it easy to rent somewhere else locally."

I'm sure I won't, thinks Josie. She has only just over two months to find a place to live. This time she will have to find a deposit and things are very tight. "Any chance that you can let me stay until the end of the year or at least over Christmas?"

James winces. "I'm afraid not, Josie. I don't think you've met Harriet yet but she's an interior designer and has arranged the renovations to start in early December. She hopes to get access before then to look around the property and make further decisions about the redecoration. I trust that will be alright."

"Of course," says Josie wearily, sadly discarding her plan to have a last Christmas with her friends in the village. She gets to her feet.

James struggles to get out of the sagging armchair as quickly as possible. He's almost cringing with embarrassment. He holds out his hand. "No hard feelings, Josie. I do hope we can still be friends."

After he has gone Josie returns to the sitting room and slumps on the sofa. She is going to be homeless again. With an effort she squares her shoulders. She will manage - she always has in the past. She looks up as she hears the clunk of the cat flap and sees Folly trotting towards her, tail erect. She scoops up the cat into her arms, saying, "You and I are going to move. Together!"

15th September 2015

Oh dear Magpies,

I'm completely devastated. My beloved Folly is dead. She was run over in the lane by a passing car and the monster driving it didn't even bother to stop. I'm so angry. And heartbroken – because I loved the little cat and she was such merry company. I can't stop crying.

It's all bad news at the moment. In the past I've tried not to be gloomy and negative in my emails to you, but today I need to share my anguish.

I have recently heard from my landlord that he will not extend my lease, which means I have to be out of this house by the end of November latest. I have no idea where I can go, as affordable properties to rent are few and far between. I have a part-time job but no savings and only my state pension. I'm really upset that I must leave this friendly little village and the home I have here.

Another item of sad news is that Doris's neighbour Lily, who recently went into a hospice, has just died. She was such a gentle soul and I didn't have a chance to say goodbye because she slipped away so quickly.

Finally, I haven't heard anything from you, Tom, for two months, and I'm really worried. I do hope that you are safe. Your family are anxious about you too.

Lottie, thank you for your last email – I'm so grateful that we are still in touch and I feel close to you, even though you live far away. I ache with longing to see you both and I must hold on to the hope that, one day in the future, this will happen. I'm going to pray about that. We are not promised an easy ride in this life, but God does promise that He will comfort us when times are hard.

With love and tears,
GMJ xxx

Josie is lying down on her sofa, her head resting on an old velvet cushion at the end nearest the fireplace. She is looking out of the window as the light drains from the sky and darkness rolls in. The door to the passage is behind the sofa and she has left it open by habit for a Folly who no longer inhabits the house. She has been lying there for nearly an hour, thinking, praying. Life is full of uncertainty at the moment and she is weary of the constant battle to subdue her fears and to keep cheerful and optimistic. She is lonely.

She hears a car going by, and glances at her watch – it is 7.35 pm. At this time on a Friday, she would normally be working at the Anchor. She had driven to work because she was tired but Flora said it would be a quiet evening and made Josie go home. She went outside but her unreliable car would not start. She decided not to bother the Elfords but to walk home, leaving the car outside the pub. She should have bought a new battery and will ask Bill to help her start it tomorrow. She let herself in by the front door as she cannot yet cope with the absence of Folly who always darted in from the garden to greet her at the kitchen door.

It is almost dark. She cannot be bothered to get up, draw the curtains or turn on the light. The ebony shadows reflect her sombre mood. Once more she is in a state of transition, from light to dark. She senses something is about to unfold and her instinct is to avoid action and wait for it to happen. She closes her eyes and lies back, hoping to let go of cares and worries. She drifts off.

Josie is suddenly wide awake. Alert. She has heard a click in the kitchen and it takes a few more seconds to realise that it cannot be Folly. She listens and then hears the faint sound of the kitchen door closing. There is someone else in the house.

She remains still, eyes wide open, unmoving – this time she will find out who it is. She has known for a long while that a prowler regularly roams around her house, but she needs to know who the person is and why they do it. There are sounds of stealthy footfalls in the adjacent room – she tenses and keeps silent. This time she is the one who is watching. The tingling she feels is not fear but excitement. Her fingers creep silently to the light switch for the lamp, which is in the flex which hangs from the table next to her.

Lying prone on the sofa, she cannot see the door that she left ajar but she senses it opening wider. The person now coming will not see her behind the back of the sofa. She hears the soft padding of feet on carpet and sees the figure of a man, outlined against the dark grey sky, standing in front of her desk, his back to her. She inhales softly through her nose and she can smell him – and knows instantly who it is. With one fluid motion she switches on the lamp and sits up, swinging her legs to the floor. There is a gasp from the intruder as he spins round to face her.

"Good evening, Matt," Josie says. "I'm not aware I'd invited you in." Her icy sarcasm is accompanied by heart-thumping fear. She stays seated, not wanting him to feel threatened. He is, after all, a strong man in his forties and they are alone in her house. And he has just been caught trespassing.

Matt Tapper is standing motionless, staring down at her as if she were a ghost. Josie finally confronts the apparition from hell, who has been disturbing her life and tormenting her peace of mind for a year or more. She shudders with anger but must keep control.

"The house was dark. No car outside." He speaks gruffly. There is no attempt to excuse his behaviour. "I thought you were out."

"Evidently." Josie pauses to choose her words carefully. "And you've been in here dozens of times whilst I've been out. Over the past year. Snooping. Moving things around. Borrowing items and replacing them later in different places." She sees Matt has recovered from his shock. He folds his arms as he stands with his back to the desk looking at her. She tries to subdue inner trembling and appear calm.

"I thought you'd never notice," he sneers. "You must need your eyes tested."

"Do you have any idea how much anxiety your persecution has caused me?"

"I do. That's the intention," Matt snaps backs. "And to see if I could get away with it."

"But why? What have I done to you to make you so vindictive?"

Matt says nothing but his eyes glitter in the lamplight. His silence worries her.

Josie stands up slowly. Matt does not move but he

is watching her. As he has done for months. She takes a deep breath. "Matt, because you lost Ann and because we are neighbours, I'll consider not going to the police. But if you threaten me or set foot in this house again or in my garden, I shall call the police immediately and have you arrested for harassment. I've no wish to speak to you ever again – so keep out of my way from now on."

Matt shrugs his big shoulders. "That shouldn't be too hard. I'm leaving this crappy village. I'm going away to Spain." He suddenly grins. "With Lena."

Josie flinches. "Polish Lena. From the pub?" Matt inclines his head. "Well, I feel sorry for her. She's a nice girl and can't know what you're really like and how malignant you are." This erases the smug look from Matt's face. "You're a sick weirdo. You have a real problem and need help."

"Not as much as you," Matt snarls, taking a menacing step forward.

Josie realises she has made a bad mistake and begins to pray silently. As she backs away the front doorbell rings.

They both freeze. The bell shrills again. Matt leans forward, arm outstretched, his large hand in front of her face, his fingers splayed as a threat to prevent her moving. She prays on, trying to control the pounding throb of panic in her head. She has left the front door unlocked and hopes desperately that the person will try the handle and not give up and go away. She glances wildly at the window and sees a face outside the glass illuminated by the lamp light from the room. She is hallucinating – it is her son's face. Her expression makes Matt swing round but he sees nothing.

The face has disappeared. The doorbell rings again and again. Then someone starts pounding on the door.

Matt's aggressive stance starts to crumble and, when Josie suddenly shouts: "Help me", he savagely pushes her out of his way and bolts out from the room, through the kitchen and out of the rear door. As he slams it shut with terrifying ferocity, Josie's balance deserts her and she sinks to her knees. She feels the cool rush of air from the front door as it opens and then a tall young man appears in the doorway holding a rucksack. He sees her and darts forward.

"Are you hurt? What happened?" He crouches down and puts his arm round her trembling shoulders. "Don't worry. He's gone now." In shock, she stares wildly at him.

"I'm Tom. Your grandson from New Zealand. Are you alright, Grandma?"

Josie clings onto him and looks up into hauntingly familiar eyes and says, "I am now."

27th November 2015

Dearest Magpies,

Tom, it was good to hear that you arrived safely after your long journey back to New Zealand. It must have been wonderful to see your family after seven months away. You don't need to repay me for the airfare – I am a grandmother who has not had the opportunity to give you presents before. And your unexpected visit to me was the best gift I could ever have had. Now you are home – and you need to make some big decisions about what you are going to study at university and where you are going to apply to start early next year.

Lottie, I was very touched by an email I received from your mother a couple of weeks ago. I was surprised but pleased by her sudden change of heart. It seems that now she doesn't merely tolerate our correspondence but encourages it. Reading between the lines, I think she was asking for my forgiveness. Or perhaps Robert pointed out to her that you are both growing up and ought to be allowed to make up your own minds about people you want to know. I too have been guilty of negative and critical thoughts about your mother. I responded to her, of course, and hope that we have now dispelled any ill-feeling between us. She even hinted that a visit to New Zealand to stay with you all might be possible in the future. I'm almost dancing with joy.

Here's some amazing news: Harry Scaddon told me in late October that the Treasury Solicitor had accepted that I was the only living relative of my brother, Henri Hansford, and that I would be receiving the remainder of his 'estate'. I assumed this might be a few personal effects so I was completely astounded to hear that I had inherited £187,943. My brother's flat in Durham was obviously larger and more valuable than Harry or I realised, and it seems he had some valuable artefacts which were sold. I'm immensely grateful to Harry for persevering on my behalf.

I was stunned to realise that I could now buy a modest place of my own and have somewhere permanent to live. I have mentioned that Doris's neighbour Lily sadly died in September. Her small semi-detached cottage, adjacent to Doris, was eventually put on the market by her relatives at the end of October, about a week after I'd heard about my unexpected windfall. God has been good to me. I promptly made an offer of the asking price, £149,500, which was accepted. I asked for an early completion at the end of November and this was agreed so I shall be moving in on Monday, 30th November, the day when I must be out of 'The Haven'. The place needs some decorating but that can be done whilst I'm living there. James has kindly told Bill that he can borrow the tractor and trailer to move my furniture and clobber down the road. I hope it doesn't rain!

I can hardly believe that a home has been provided for me at a time when I most need one. And in the village that I love. I am utterly blessed. There will even be some money left over! I'm not good at saving, so I shall probably throw a house-warming party, buy a case of wine for Harry and give Natalia in Colombia an air ticket to visit me here in England, where she has never been. I shall definitely put some aside for a trip to New Zealand next year to see you all.

Tom, I had such a wonderful three weeks with you. Lottie, in case he hasn't told you, we visited Stonehenge in Wiltshire (not far from where Sam lives) and Portsmouth Harbour where we saw HMS *Victory*, Nelson's flagship. We went to an international rugger match and a pop concert. It was so lovely to meet Sam when she came for a weekend during her university term at Exeter, whilst Tom was staying here. He spent a few days in London and came back here before he left to fly home. I was able to give him his airfare as a present – I can afford such things these days! When I get the landline in my new home reconnected we can speak on the telephone from time to time. What fun! Which reminds me – Tom, I had a phone call from Sam a few days ago wishing me luck with the move.

I want so much to see you and spend time with you, Lottie. When I come to New Zealand next year, I hope you will show me around and I want to meet your friends. In your last email, you asked me to give you an update on my village friends that you have both read so much about in my letters.

You may be interested to hear that John Damon sold his house in October and a delightful family with three young children have moved in. John now lives with Nina about two hours to the east near Alton in Hampshire, where he has found a new job. I wish them well. Sadly Harriet, the smart interior designer, decided that James isn't the man for her and jilted him. He has been drooping around the village like a wounded puppy, but I expect he will soon get involved in his next scheme and forget about her in time. There must be someone out there who will marry him! He's enlisted a building firm to 'upgrade' my cottage, starting next week, after I've gone. I think he plans to buy Matt Tapper's house, which is on the market, and convert it into a holiday cottage too. Luckily for Harry's peace of mind, it seems that James is not going to revive his wind turbine project or submit any further planning applications for it. Harry is inordinately pleased at what he has managed to achieve for me and delighted I am to stay in the village. I'm happy to say that he has put aside all romantic notions and marriage plans and we are just good friends.

Tom, I'm glad you persuaded me to go to the police and report the dreadful incident with Matt on the night of 9th October. I remember how relieved we both felt when he moved out of his house a few days afterwards, obviously worried that I would press charges. Though the police told me I would have a case, I decided not to go down that route and in the end he was given a formal warning. I've heard he is renting somewhere in a village about thirty miles away. Only last week, I discovered – from Alice of course – that Lena has split up with him. I'm glad. He's a strange tormented person and Lena deserves better. I still don't understand why the horrible man harassed me for so long, and I trust I'll never set eyes on him again.

I am in the sitting room, surrounded by various boxes and black plastic bags. It's chaos but I know that somehow, if I make a real effort over the weekend, all will be ready for my move. I should tell you my new address: Blithe Cottage (I love the name!), Long Lane, Winterborne Slepe, Dorset, England. I'll let you have the telephone number when they allocate me one. Lottie, I'd love to talk to you over Christmas on my new phone.

I'll never forget the night you arrived, Tom, as long as I live. I was so distraught that when I saw your face in the window, I had the illusion it was Julian. You look so like your father! I'm so glad you finally tried the door handle and came to my rescue. You were immensely gentle and supportive – I felt safe for the first time in ages. My heart skips a beat when I think of it.

My name, Josephine, means: 'God will add or increase'. He has added you, my grandchildren, to my life – and increased my joy. The promise implicit in my name has come true at last.

With love to my Magpies – as always,

from their Grandma Josie XXX

Discussion Questions:

1. Why might someone write long letters or emails to a person despite knowing there is no possibility of sending them?

2. What are the causes of the main character's vulnerable situation?

3. At what point does Josie finally become convinced that someone is prowling around her cottage when she is not there? What triggers this certainty?

4. How well does Josie cope with insecurity and threat? What defining quality does she possess that enables her to be resilient?

5. Did you find that the South American parts of the book helped contribute to your understanding of Josie's character?

6. Do you think Josie is wise to tell her young grandchildren so much detail about their Colombian father's life and death?

7. Teenagers are not generally inclined to write long letters, but do you think they would have enjoyed reading Josie's lengthy emails?

8. Is it significant that the village community of Winterborne Slepe are supportive of each other? Do you think this typical of village life?

9. Josie values her friends and her home. How close does she get to losing them and is this her fault?

10. Do you think it is possible to forge a loving relationship through correspondence alone?

11. What did you think might have been the reason for Tom's lack of communication during the latter part of his travels in his gap year?

12. Which inhabitant of the village did you think was the intruder and why? Were you right in your guess?

13. What aspects of the story, if any, are reflected in the cover design?

14. How does this book demonstrate that it is possible to suffer tragic loss and poverty and to remain hopeful and positive?